Praise for
DEBORAH RANEY
and her novels

"A story that will touch readers from many different stages of life. There will be times of tears, times of laughter, and times you'll question your own reactions to situations. *Within This Circle* is sure to touch a nerve."
—*Romance Readers Connection*

"Raney has fashioned a startlingly honest portrayal of love, commitment, and redemption in the midst of tragedy that will appeal strongly to fans of Janette Oke and Neva Coyle."
—*Library Journal* on *A Vow to Cherish*

"Raney immediately draws the reader into the story. Well-defined, empathetic characters have true-to-life motivations, and the strife-filled country of Haiti is depicted so that readers will feel compassion rather than despair."
—*Romantic Times BOOKreviews* on *Over the Waters*

"*Over the Waters* is a poignant and memorable look at love and sacrifice."
—Karen Kingsbury, bestselling author of *Someday* and *Sunrise*

Also by
DEBORAH RANEY

Above All Things

DEBORAH RANEY

Steeple
Hill®

Published by Steeple Hill Books™

STEEPLE HILL BOOKS

Steeple
Hill®

Recycling programs
for this product may
not exist in your area.

ISBN-13: 978-0-373-78655-8
ISBN-10: 0-373-78655-7

ABOVE ALL THINGS

Copyright © 2009 by Deborah Raney

www.SteepleHill.com

Printed in U.S.A.

To my sister-in-love, Krista,
who has taught me so much
about courage and about steadfast faith

The heart is deceitful above all things and beyond cure.
Who can understand it?
—*Jeremiah* 17: 9

Chapter One

Lifting the lid from the slow cooker, Evette McGlin caught a fragrant whiff of the stew that had been simmering all day. That first savory note lasted all of two seconds before her stomach began its tap dance of betrayal. She gave the mixture of beef and vegetables a quick stir and clamped the lid back in place. She'd be glad when this morning sickness finally passed.

After all the years they'd been trying, she couldn't complain about being pregnant. But she was fifteen weeks along now, and the morning sickness didn't seem much better than it had been in the beginning. According to what she'd read in the towering stack of books on her nightstand, it wasn't all that unusual to feel a little queasy throughout pregnancy, but she wasn't looking forward to almost six more months of this roller coaster.

The oven timer sounded and she stooped to take the brown-and-serve rolls from the rack. All these maternal hormones were turning her into a regular Rachael Ray. Not that Judd minded. She smiled to herself, imagining his reaction when he walked through the door to find a home-cooked meal on the table for the second night in a row. She might be sorry she'd gotten into this routine if Judd came to expect home cooking every night, but it was healthier to make things from scratch—and cheaper.

Now that she'd quit her job as manager of Furniture Gallery, every penny counted. There'd be no more eating out three times a week once the baby arrived and she was a stay-at-home mom.

She checked the clock on the microwave, then glanced out the open kitchen window overlooking the driveway. Judd would be home any minute. The days had been growing longer, but now the sky was dark, even for a late February evening. It smelled like rain. She hoped he didn't get caught in a storm on the highway. Funny. She'd never worried about him like this before she'd found out she was carrying their child.

She went to the pantry for candlesticks and matches. She couldn't keep up the Rachael Ray routine indefi-nitely, but they might as well enjoy it while it lasted.

The clouds broke as she closed the pantry door. Plump drops of rain hit the metal awning over the back door and she headed to close the window, but before she was halfway across the room the phone rang. That would be Judd.

He'd always been thoughtful, but since the day she'd told him about the baby, he'd become a big goofy sap, doting on her and rushing to meet her every need prac-tically before she knew she had one. Okay, so the steak-and-potato dinners might have had something to do with his recent attentiveness, but he gave himself away cooing baby talk to her belly. He might not admit it to the guys at work, but he was as head over heels for this baby as she was.

She checked the caller ID. *W. Greene.* Hmmm…not Judd. Who did they know named Greene? It was probably another annoying telemarketer.

She lifted the phone from its cradle. "Hello?"

"Is Judd McGlin there?" The woman's voice quavered, whether with age or emotion, Evette couldn't tell.

"No, I'm sorry, he's not home right now. Could I take a message?"

There was a long pause. Evette thought for a minute they'd been cut off, but the tremulous voice came back on the line. "Have him call Carla Greene…Carla Jackson Greene, please."

"Just a minute." She jotted the name down. "May I ask what this is concerning?"

Again, an overlong hesitation. "Just tell him it's about Tabrina."

Evette's pulse stuttered. "Tabrina?"

"Tabrina Jackson. He'll know who I'm talking about."

Evette knew who she was talking about. But why, after all these years, would Tabrina Jackson want anything to do with Judd? "Does he have the number?"

She scribbled the phone number the woman gave her on the corner of an envelope from yesterday's junk mail. She started to read it back to the woman, but the line had gone dead.

Carla Jackson Greene…a relative of Tabrina's, maybe? But why would someone be calling Judd about his old college girlfriend? A woman he'd been engaged to for a short time. That was, what…almost seven years ago now? An image of the stunningly beautiful woman played in her memory—Tabrina's smooth dark skin and the full features of her African-American heritage. Evette hadn't thought of her in ages, although early in their marriage, she'd wasted plenty of time wondering if Judd still thought about the woman he'd almost married.

She went to the kitchen window and peered out. Sharp spears of rain now pelted the driveway, bouncing back in buoyant splatters. Where was Judd? He should be home by now. As she backed away from the window, she caught her reflection in the darkened glass. Her hair had gone limp from the kitchen's humidity, and she suddenly felt middle-aged and frowzy.

Mired in old, uneasy memories, she turned and picked up the box of matches and went to the breakfast nook where she'd set the table for two. She slid open the cover and struck a match on the rough edge of the box, touching it to each blackened wick. The acrid odor of sulfur made her eyes burn, but the candles bloomed into flame. She shook out the match and moved to the stove to stir the stew again.

After a moment, she put down the spoon and placed a hand lightly over her belly. Her stomach was acting up again. This time Evette wasn't sure she could blame her pregnancy or the aroma of beef stew.

Chapter Two

Judd McGlin leaned over the steering wheel and peered through the windshield at the thunderheads boiling overhead. He'd be lucky to get home before the clouds let loose their contents. It looked like he might be driving right into the storm.

Work was crazy with tax season upon them. And his part-time coaching job wasn't much better. Whatever had made him think he could combine a CPA's job with coaching the local high-school basketball team? They were headed into tournament season, and practice tonight had not gone well.

He blew out a stream of air. His recliner and the evening paper were calling his name big-time. Dinner was in the Taco Bell bag on the passenger seat beside him…emitting a delicious smell. Evette had been craving a certain burrito she kept seeing in the TV commercials, and he couldn't wait to see her face when he presented her with the bag.

He should have called her during the day to see how she was feeling, but time had gotten away from him.

Something in his chest stirred at the thought of his wife. In spite of how miserable she was feeling, Evette had that proverbial maternal glow about her. He loved the way she savored each day of her pregnancy.

She'd longed for a baby practically since the day they married. It had been all he could do to convince her he needed to finish school before they started a family.

Their excitement had dimmed as month after month rolled by with no baby in sight. After four years of trying, with two early miscarriages and two surgeries for Evette, they'd finally reached the end of their possibilities.

And, of course, that's when God stepped in.

A baby. The thought alternately thrilled him and scared his socks off.

It still amazed him to remember the day Evette made the happy announcement. They'd been overly cautious at first, terrified of losing the baby, but she was almost four months along now and the obstetrician assured them everything was going exactly as it should. They'd told only a few of their closest family and friends, but if everything was still good at Evette's next doctor's appointment, they planned to throw a big party to make the announcement official.

The rain started, hitting the pavement like needles, but his exit was just ahead. With any luck he'd beat the downpour.

Ten minutes later, he clicked the remote and watched the garage door roll up. He still didn't take an automatic garage door for granted. This new house in Hanover Falls wasn't a mansion by any stretch of the imagination, but it was a big step up from the string of apartment complexes they'd lived in for the first four years of their marriage. The mortgage still made him nervous. He'd wanted something a little more modest, but Evette had talked him into this Tudor-style house in the oldest neighborhood of their little town. He'd acquiesced since Evette had already made a sacrifice moving two hours from St. Louis and her family.

He punched the remote again and watched the door close on the rain before he snagged the Taco Bell bag and went in through the laundry room. "Hey, I'm home."

Uh-oh. He smelled dinner cooking. And if his nose was any judge, it trumped the meager offering in his take-out bag.

The table in the breakfast nook was set and Evette was at the kitchen sink, filling a water pitcher. "Hey, babe," she called over her shoulder. "Did you get wet?"

He dropped his briefcase by the back door. Evette turned to look at him, and he held up the bag, trying to look appropriately sheepish. "Burritos. A midnight snack, maybe?"

She gave him a look. "Oh, Judd…"

"Sorry. I didn't know you'd made dinner. You were craving these last night, and I just…"

She made that cute pouty face he loved. "You're so sweet. I'll…I'll save them for lunch tomorrow. Or—" she rolled her eyes "—I'll eat them tonight and gain ten pounds. And it's your fault if I do, buddy."

He laughed. "I'm not too worried."

She lifted the lid on the slow cooker and he went to stand behind her, pushing her silky dark hair off her neck and nuzzling her nape while she stirred. "Mmm. Smells good."

Laughing, she replaced the lid and leaned back into his embrace. "Are you talking about me or the stew?"

He gave her a peck on the cheek and reached around her to lift the lid off the pot again. "Both."

She laughed. "Good answer."

"Any mail?"

"No, but you had a phone call."

He stopped short at the table. "Whoa… Candles? What's the occasion? Last time there were candles on that table it was about the baby. Wait a minute…we're not having twins or something, are we? Please tell me we're not having twins."

She laughed her musical laugh again. "No, silly." She waited a beat. "Triplets."

He studied her, making sure she was joking.

"Relax." She patted her belly. "Little Bambino is just fine. And all alone in there."

He pretended to mop his brow in relief.

"Twins do run in the Bryant family, though…" She patted his cheek. "Just so you know."

"You never told me that."

"Didn't want to scare you off."

"As if." He drew her into his arms and kissed her. "So really…why the fancy dinner? I could get used to this, you know."

"I just thought candlelight would be nice with the rain."

"So who called?"

"Huh?" She brought the pitcher to the table and poured water over the ice in a tall tumbler.

Something in her voice set off a silent alarm. He eyed her, but nothing in her posture validated his concern. She poured water into a second tumbler.

"You said I had a phone call…?"

"Oh, yes. It was kind of weird." She looked up at him, wrinkling her nose. "Some woman. Said she was calling about Tabrina Jackson."

Judd's heart lunged in the direction of his throat. He swallowed hard and tried to make his voice sound normal. "It wasn't Tabrina?"

"No. It sounded like an older woman. She just said she was calling *about* Tabrina. I forget her name. The caller ID just said *Greene,* I think, with an *e,* but there wasn't a name. Maybe an initial? I don't remember."

Judd was aware of his wife's studied gaze. "Did she say what she wanted?"

"No. Just that you should call."

"I wonder what that's about?" He glanced at the clock. "Do I have time to call before dinner?"

She shrugged. "Sure. I won't dish up the stew yet."

He grabbed his water glass off the table and resisted the temptation to hold it against his temple. Evette handed him an envelope with the phone number printed on it in her curvy, precise handwriting. But he walked past the phone on the kitchen desk. "I'll take it back here," he said, hooking a thumb in the direction of the family room.

Her eyebrows lifted almost imperceptibly, but she didn't voice the question her blue eyes posed.

He moved through the house and took sanctuary at his desk in the small bedroom they'd turned into a den. Tabrina Jackson. *Man.* He hadn't heard one word from her since college. Since he broke off their engagement. They'd lost touch after that long-ago day in Simmons Park. He shook off the images. No use going there.

There'd been a time, after he married Evette, when Tabrina popped into his thoughts with frustrating regularity. But as the years passed and his love for his wife deepened, Tabrina had become a buried page in the scrapbook of his youth.

Unbidden, a vision formed in his mind. Smooth, soft café-au-lait skin. Thick ink-black hair. The mental image of Tabrina's full, pouty lips brought a rush of surprisingly familiar—and decidedly uncomfortable—feelings.

Tabrina's almond-shaped, espresso-bean eyes weren't hard to conjure, either, but he couldn't bring the sound of her voice or the shape of her face into focus. Tabrina Jackson. What in the world could this be about after all this time?

Holding the slip of paper in one hand, he dialed the number. A woman's voice answered, almost a whisper. "Yes?"

"Judd?" Evette's voice carried from the kitchen.

For some strange reason, he felt as if she'd caught him sneaking a peek at the *Sports Illustrated* Swimsuit Issue.

He pushed the mute button and worked to keep his tone casual. "Just a sec, babe. I'm on the phone."

He depressed the button again. "Um, yes…this is Judd McGlin. I had a message…to call here?" The silence lengthened. "Hello?"

A sigh filled his ear. "It's Carla, Judd. Tabrina's mother. Carla Greene now."

Tabrina's mother. "Carla? Wow…I haven't… How are you? Are you still in St. Louis?" Why was she calling him?

She ignored his volley of questions. "It's Tabrina, Judd. It's bad, real bad." Her voice broke into shards of emotion.

"Carla?" He paced around the desk. "What happened?"

"They think she's had a stroke. She's been unresponsive for two weeks now. They don't know now if she'll… ever come out of it."

"What? I don't understand. What happened?" He could hardly imagine the vivacious Tabrina of his memory being comatose in a hospital bed. He reached behind him and pulled the desk chair closer, resting one knee on the seat for support.

"They're not sure." A heavy sigh filtered through the miles of phone line. "They think maybe a blood clot…or something. We don't know for sure. Every doctor I talk to says something different, but they seem to agree she had a stroke…the kind that affects the brain. She wasn't taking care of her diabetes. You know how she was. I guess it finally caught up with her."

He remembered. Tabrina had been diagnosed with diabetes as a teenager, but she'd never taken it seriously. He'd had to rush her to the emergency room once when her blood sugar spiked and she started acting weird. "I'm sorry to hear it, Carla…so sorry."

He searched his brain for what to say next. Why on earth had Carla thought to call him after all these years? Surely Tabrina had someone else in her life now. "I…we'll be praying for her. Thanks. Thanks for letting me know."

The woman harrumphed and instantly Judd recalled a clear picture of Tabrina's mother, a striking black woman. Tabrina told him once that her mother had done some modeling in New York in her teens, but she'd apparently reserved her glamour for the runway. Judd had never known her as anything other than a hard-nosed, no-nonsense woman who seemed more suited for wrestling than mothering. Truth was, he'd been a little scared of her back then.

The same hard-boiled tone he remembered edged her voice now. "This isn't exactly a courtesy call." She cleared her throat loudly. "I need you to come and get your girl."

What was she talking about? He held the phone away from his ear and gave it the same look he would have given Carla had she been standing there. "I'm sorry? I don't understand."

"I know Tabrina didn't want your help, but I can't take care of her and her girl, too. Tabrina's daddy died a few years back and Walt—that's my husband—he's not crazy about kids, and especially not kids like her."

Judd remembered Tabrina's father. Harrison Jackson. A big man. Three hundred pounds, at least, but carried it well. Always laughing, showing even, white teeth that almost glowed against his gleaming ebony skin. Harry had been Tabrina's champion when she and her mother got into it—which was most of the time. Tabrina had inherited her father's musical talent and his love for history and art. She'd never said it in so many words, but Judd thought Carla had been an embarrassment to her.

But what did *any* of this have to do with him? "Carla, I don't understand what you want from me."

"You have a child, Judd. You need to come and get her. I've had her since Tabrina went in the hospital, but I can't take off any more work and—"

"Wait a minute, wait a minute." Judd's mind whirled like a dust devil. "What are you talking about? Tabrina has a child?"

"Tabrina and *you* have a child. And you need to come and get her!" Her shout pierced his eardrum, and he jerked the phone away. When he brought it back to his ear, he thought he heard a strangled sob.

"If you don't take her, I'll have no choice but to call county services." Carla's voice wavered. "She's a good kid. She's no trouble. But I can't do this all over again. Walt's on disability and somebody's gotta put bread on the table. Besides, we both know I wasn't so great at it the first time around."

"Are you—" He reached for the glass of water, and knocked the tumbler on its side. Water and half-melted ice flooded the desk and cascaded onto the carpet.

He swore under his breath and yanked his shirttail out to sop up the mess. "Sorry…hang on." He put down the phone and righted the glass. His wet shirt touched his belly and he stifled a gasp. But the tremor inside him didn't come from the icy fabric.

A wave of nausea hit him. He and Tabrina had gone too far that night. Only that once, but… With a sinking awareness, he knew what Carla was accusing him of was possible.

He picked up the phone again, struggling to regain his equilibrium. "I'm sorry. Are you saying… Tabrina thinks her daughter is *mine?*" She'd never said anything to him. Not once. Had he missed hints? Had she tried to tell him?

"Oh, she's yours, all right." The bitterness in Carla's voice hit its mark. "Jolie was born October third, seven months after you dumped Tabrina. You do the math. Besides, you get one look at her, there'll be no quibblin' about who her father is."

Blood like ice sluiced through his veins. He started to speak, but a flicker of movement danced in the corner of his vision.

He turned and saw Evette framed in the doorway, her face drained of color.

Chapter Three

"I'll have to call you back, Carla. I—I can't talk about this right now." Judd hung up and dropped the phone on his desk. He forced his head up and made himself look at his wife.

"Judd?" Evette stood straight, her back against the doorjamb as if she couldn't support her own weight. "What was that about?" Her belly formed a rounded C beneath her loose shirt. He hadn't noticed before how much she'd started to show.

He hunched over the desk, scrambling for something to say. He caught his reflection in the glass of an antique barrister's bookcase behind the desk. Even distorted by the wavy glass, he saw the deer-in-the-headlights glaze his eyes held. He shook his head, refusing to meet Evette's stare. "I'm...not sure."

"I don't understand. Judd?" She gaped at him, waiting.

What could he possibly tell her? That he'd unknowingly gotten his girlfriend pregnant? Almost seven years ago now. The kid would be six years old. *Dear God.* The walls seemed to close in on him. He kept his hands flat on the desk and fought to fill his lungs. "Sit down, Evette."

She started shaking her head, rooted to the spot under the door frame where she stood. "I don't need to sit down. Tell me what that was about." Her voice was monotone.

"That was…Tabrina Jackson's mother. She… Tabrina's had a stroke."

She looked confused, as if she were trying to put together pieces of a puzzle that didn't fit. "A stroke? Why are they calling *you?*"

He shrugged and fought the temptation to lie. "I'm not sure what she wants…"

"Well, what did she say?" The confusion in her eyes turned to suspicion.

How much had Evette overheard? The numb expression on her face gave him his answer.

He came around from behind the desk, intending to take Evette in his arms, to reassure her. But she held up her hands, palms out, rebuffing him.

He took a step backward and slumped onto the edge of the leather wing chair in the corner—an early Father's Day gift from Evette. "Carla claims…Tabrina has a child." There was nothing to do but tell her the truth. He braced his hands on the smooth arms of the chair, feeling like he was drowning, knowing that his next words would change both of their lives forever. He took a deep breath and blew it out. "Tabrina claims…she claims her child—her daughter—is mine."

Evette stared at him. "Well, why didn't you tell her? Why didn't you deny it?" She jabbed a finger at the phone. "You're just going to let her get away with it?"

But Judd saw in her eyes that she knew the truth. Hers were words of denial, wanting to believe it wasn't true.

His tongue felt like sandpaper on the roof of his mouth. "I don't know. I…I need to think this through."

"Judd! What's to think about?" She looked at him like he'd lost his mind. "Judd? What is going on?" Her voice hiked up an octave, cracking at the top.

Without looking at it, he slid the paper with Carla's number into his palm, wadding it into a ball as he stuffed it in his pants pocket. He went to Evette, touched her rigid arm, trying to offer reassurance he didn't possess. "I'm sorry, I can't talk about this right now. Give me a little time…to sort things out. Then we'll talk. I promise."

Feeling like a trapped animal, he pushed past her and hurried from the room. He heard Evette behind him, but he took the length of the hallway in three strides and all but ran through the kitchen to the garage, stopping at the top of the steps long enough to hit the remote that opened his side of the double garage.

The Caliber was still warm. He revved the engine, threw the car in gear and backed down the driveway. He aimed the car west, knowing that if he turned to look back at the house, he'd see Evette standing at the window in the living room, watching him go.

He drove aimlessly, finally heading north out of town on Highway 63. After a few miles, he pulled off the road and fished his cell phone out of his pocket, along with the crumpled envelope with Carla's number on it.

He dialed the number, not having a clue what he would say when she answered.

"This is Carla."

"Hi. It's Judd. Sorry…I couldn't talk earlier." He stared through the windshield at a bug squashed against the glass…a pretty good metaphor for what had happened to his life tonight. "What do you want from me, Carla?" He hadn't meant to blurt the question quite so bluntly. Or maybe he had.

"Tabrina's got a long haul ahead of her."

"What happened? You said a stroke?"

"That's the doctors' best guess. I'm not sure I believe them." Carla repeated what she'd told him earlier. "It's been a nightmare. Two weeks and she still hasn't woke up. I have my hands full just trying to get her well. I can't deal with the girl, too. You're going to have to take her…at least till Tabrina's back on her feet."

Maybe Tabrina was mistaken about him being the father. Maybe Carla was trying to con him into taking the child off her hands. Maybe it was all some kind of a mix-up. "How old is she—Tabrina's daughter?"

"*Your* daughter, Judd. She's six."

"Tabrina said she was mine?"

"She didn't have to say. There hasn't been anyone else, Judd."

That took him aback. Tabrina was a beautiful woman. Talented, intelligent, outgoing. He'd always imagined that by now she was married with a family. He'd comforted himself by imagining that breaking up with her had been for her own good in the long run.

"You want me to send you a picture?" Carla's voice made him shelve the memories. "The girl has your eyes, your mouth, your long fingers. She even shoots a basketball like you."

He propped his forearms on the top of the steering wheel and hung his head between them, the phone just grazing his temple.

After a minute, he heard Carla again. "Are you there?"

"Why didn't she tell me?"

"Would it have made any difference, Judd?"

"Yes!" He sat up again. "Of course it would have made a difference. This is my child we're talking about."

"Then you won't mind coming and getting her. Come to the hospital. You can see Tabrina."

"No!"

Carla was silent on her end. He'd spoken too quickly, and he wasn't sure if he was protesting taking in the girl—his daughter—or seeing Tabrina again. Probably both. He still couldn't make this seem real.

He cleared his throat. "I'm sorry. Evette doesn't—I'm married, Carla."

"I know you are. I assume it was your wife I talked to this afternoon."

"You didn't tell her anything, did you?" Maybe Evette had known before he did. He tried to remember exactly what Evette had said.

"Don't worry, Juddy. I'm not that stupid."

He flinched at Carla's use of Tabrina's pet name for him. He'd been a first-class jerk walking out on Evette like he had just now. He'd call her. As soon as he got things straightened out with Carla Greene.

"What do you expect me to do?"

"I need you to take Jolie."

Jo Lee? "What did you call her?"

"It's Jolie." Carla spelled the name.

Suddenly, everything came into focus. He had a daughter. And her name was Jolie. He shook his head. All these years, he'd been a father and he hadn't even known. He couldn't take it all in.

"There has to be another way, Carla. Isn't there someone else who can take her? Someone she knows?"

"There's nobody, Judd. Unless you want your daughter put in foster care."

The statement hung like a threat on the line between them.

He stared at the clock, shocked that an hour had passed since he'd walked out on Evette. His brain raced to assemble everything he'd learned in the space of that sixty minutes. He could barely wrap his mind around the fact that he had a daughter, much less on how that might change everything about his life—and Evette's. "You're going to have to give me some time," he finally said. "Evette is pregnant. I can't just decide this for her."

"I understand. But I don't have much time. Something has to change—and soon. I can't keep going on like this."

"Where are you, Carla? Still in St. Louis?"

"No. Walt and I moved out to Charlack. But Tabrina took a teaching job in Springfield when Jolie was a baby. They live here. She's in the hospital here in Springfield. That's where I am now. St. John's. But her insurance is pushing us to get her into long-term care, and it's taking everything I've got just to jump through their hoops and take care of my baby."

"Okay…okay. I—I'll talk to Evette tonight. I'll try to let you know something by Monday."

Carla's breathy sigh evoked an image of her chiseled features. "Monday's a long way off, the way things are going with Tabrina."

"I'm sorry. I don't know what else to say. I need time to talk to Evette…to think things through."

"Yeah, well, it's too bad you weren't so rational seven years ago."

Judd opened his mouth to defend himself, but closed it just as quickly. There was nothing he could say. She was right. Carla Greene was dead-on right.

Chapter Four

Curled in a fetal position on the sofa in the living room, Evette stared into the flames of the gas fireplace. The room had grown warm, but she clung to the cusp of sleep, afraid to let herself fall over the edge into dreams, yet desiring the release at the same time. Her eyes fluttered closed. What nightmare could be any worse than the reality she was living?

A sound from somewhere in the house startled her into wakefulness and she tossed off the afghan and sat up, easing her feet to the cool hardwood floor. A desperate hope swelled in her chest. Maybe she *had* been dreaming. Maybe Judd was just down the hall in the den. He would come and put his head on her belly and coo to "Bambino," then coax her to bed like he did every night. And she would laugh and dare him to analyze the dream her crazy imagination had conjured.

He appeared in the doorway and she came fully awake, forcing a hopeful smile. Come on, babe. Tell me it was all a dream. Tell me. *Please.*

But his face wore the stark truth. And even if it hadn't,

she had her senses about her enough now to know that this was no dream. She remembered too clearly his hasty exit earlier this evening. She couldn't get the image out of her mind—of Judd's face after he'd hung up from talking to Tabrina's mother. He'd worn guilt and fear—and regret—like overwrought masks.

She huddled on the edge of the sofa. Studying her husband's face in the dim light of the fire, she saw reflected in his eyes the same tension and fear that must glaze her own. But she didn't know this man sitting across from her now.

"I'm sorry, Evette."

Anger flared inside of her. "What are you sorry for? Lying to me? Or getting caught?" She hadn't wanted to turn ugly. But how could she be anything else right now?

"I've never lied to you. I didn't know. I swear to you. I had no idea she—had a child."

"But are you…the father?"

He dropped his head. "I— Yes, I think I am."

"You *think?*"

"There was only one time. I swear, Evie. Just that once that we…went too far."

A wave of nausea took every ounce of strength from her. "You never told me. I thought—"

"I prayed you'd never ask."

He started across the room toward her, but she held up a hand. She couldn't touch him, didn't even want to look at him right now.

He halted in the middle of the room. "I'm sorry. I'm so sorry, Evie." He took another step toward her, but her expression must have told him she wasn't ready to forgive, because he stopped, then took two steps backward and stood there, staring at her with a look that tore her apart.

But what was there to say now? He'd lied to her about *that*. What else was there that she didn't know? "I need you to go," she whispered.

He closed his eyes, dropped his head. "Go where? We need to talk this out, Evie."

"I don't care where you go. Just please get out of here. I need some time." Her own reaction took her by surprise. It had seemed like an eternity waiting for him to come home, and now she was kicking him out? She got up, cradling her belly as she rose. She seized the arm of the sofa, steadying herself, then swept past him, feeling as if a thousand-pound boulder had attached itself to her shoulders.

"Okay…fine. I'm going to pack some things. I…I guess I'll get a room somewhere…probably that Holiday Inn on the south end of town. I'll call you when—"

"I don't care where you stay. I don't even want to know. Please…just go, Judd." She wanted to collapse in tears, but she wouldn't give him the satisfaction of seeing her fall apart.

"I…I've got practice in the morning. Early. Call my cell if you need me." His voice had turned raspy. "I love you, Evette." He made no move to leave.

She knew he expected her to change her mind, to insist he stay and talk things through. She'd always been the peacekeeper in their marriage. He was the one who usually fled when an argument heated up.

Well, let him flee this time. She had nothing to say to him right now. She curled into the corner of the sofa again and waited until she heard the kitchen door slam and the garage door grinding up, then down again.

She forced herself off the sofa and walked down the hall to their bedroom. The strength seeped from her body, and she crumpled to the floor at the foot of the bed. The bed where she and Judd made love, where their baby had been conceived. It made her sick to think of him with another woman. She thought of the soulful look Judd's hazel eyes always held when he looked at her after they'd made love. She'd treasured the thought that those smoldering gazes were for her alone. She'd once suspected that Judd still had a thing for the woman he'd been engaged to marry. But they'd gotten past that long ago, hadn't they?

Or had Judd never stopped loving Tabrina?

She buried her face in the carpet. It still had a chemical, new smell to it. The nausea rolled over her again.

"God…please. This can't be happening."

How had their perfect world fallen apart in the space of one phone call?

Judd slid the key card into the slot and pushed the door open. His mind felt as dark and stuffy as the room. He groped for the light switch and flipped it on. Would this cheerless hotel room be his home for longer than tonight?

He threw his bag on the end of the bed and went into the bathroom to splash cold water on his face. He met his own reflection in the mirror. Was it just the harsh lighting, or had he really developed dark circles under his eyes already?

He grabbed a towel from the shelf over the toilet and buried his face in it. It smelled antiseptic, like one of the many doctors' offices he and Evette had sat in over the past four years in their quest—Evette's quest—to get pregnant.

He wandered out of the bathroom and opened the

heavy drapes. His room looked over a mostly empty parking lot. The lights of Hanover Falls blinked to the east. This was ridiculous. Who checked into a hotel half a mile from home? But he couldn't really blame Evette. He should have told her. Surely the subject had come up when they were dating, though he honestly couldn't remember if he'd actually lied to her about the depth of his relationship with Tabrina, or if he'd merely omitted the whole truth.

Tabrina. It had taken him so long—years, really—to get her out of his system…out of his mind. To stop loving her, when it was his wife who needed his attention, his heart. His *whole* heart.

Now Tabrina lay unconscious in some hospital… dying, maybe. He thought about what Carla had told him. That Tabrina had a teaching job in Springfield. She'd taken her child—*their child*—and moved away from St. Louis. She'd always talked about getting out of the city. He closed his eyes, and her face—chiseled, cinnamon-colored cheeks dimpled in a smile—appeared behind his eyelids.

"Oh, dear God." He whispered a prayer he'd almost forgotten, yet one he'd prayed a thousand times in the first year of his marriage to Evette. "Help me let her go, Father. Help me move on."

But how could he let her go now? He had a child. He'd been trying to make that seem real from the moment he'd hung up the phone from talking to Carla, but now it hit him with a force that set him down hard on the edge of the mattress.

He braced himself, staring—unseeingly—out the window of his fourth-floor room. He was a father. He had a daughter. Tabrina's child. He pictured a miniature of

Tabrina…a little girl with cinnamon skin and jet-black hair, teeth as straight and white as chalk, and bright, dark eyes. No, Carla said she had his eyes. Hazel eyes? And she was six. He didn't even know what six meant. First grade? She could probably read and write, speak eloquently, if she was anything like her mother.

He realized he was smiling…remembering the way Tabrina Jackson had made him laugh with her impassioned arguments on every issue under the sun.

"You have an opinion on everything, don't you?" he'd tease.

She'd wriggle out of his reach, working to keep a serious face. "Cut that out, Judd," she'd say. "You never take me seriously."

"Oh, I'm serious, all right." He'd touch his nose to hers, try to convince her with his kisses…

He brought a hand to his mouth, trying in vain to shield his lips from the memory of those kisses.

Why, God? Why are You doing this to me? Instantly, Evette's hurt expression took the place of Tabrina's smile. *Why are You doing this to us, God? Why now?* Evette had been distraught when he left tonight. If anything happened to the baby, if she miscarried again, he would never forgive God. Never forgive himself.

He rested his elbows on his knees and buried his face in his hands, then lifted his head long enough to scrape his fingers through his hair before hiding his face again. *This isn't fair to Evette. She shouldn't have to deal with this.*

Did he really think he could convince God that it wasn't his own hide he was worried about? He gave a humorless laugh. He didn't want Evette to suffer for his sin. But he didn't want to suffer for it, either.

His mind galloped in forty different directions, grasping for a way to make this all go away. Maybe Carla would change her mind. It wasn't fair to the child that she couldn't stay with people she knew. People who loved her.

Maybe DNA testing would prove he wasn't the father of this child after all. But Carla had said the baby had been born in October. That meant Tabrina was pregnant when he'd broken off their engagement. He raked a hand through his hair again. Had she known?

He didn't doubt for a minute that Tabrina had been faithful to him while they were together. And remembering that night—remembering her heartbroken sobs after they'd put their clothes back on, crawled into the front seat of his Chevy Impala in silence—he knew she would never lie about something like this. It wasn't in her nature to lie.

So…he had a daughter. What was he going to do about it?

The clock on the nightstand behind him clicked and he turned to check the time. 11:14 p.m. He had early practice tomorrow. He couldn't be late because the girls' team had the gym reserved after his team was finished. He had to get some sleep.

A horrible thought gripped him. If this thing with Tabrina went anywhere, if he ended up having to…take responsibility, there were people he would have to face with his confession. His parents, of course. But also the principal and the other teachers and coaches he worked with at the high school. His boss, Karl Jantzi, and his colleagues at Jantzi and Associates.

Still, as much as it would pain him to talk to these people, it wouldn't come close to the dread he would feel at telling his boys—-the basketball players who looked up to him, thought he was a Christian man, an example to follow. He'd had some good conversations recently with a couple of his seniors about faith, about morals. How would he explain this to them without destroying everything he'd tried to instill in them?

A heavy weight settled in the pit of his belly and stayed there. He pried off his shoes, turned down the bedspread and crawled under the sheets fully clothed. Paralyzed, he watched the numbers on the clock turn to midnight, then 1:00 a.m., then 2:00 a.m. His last memory was a whimpered prayer as the digital numbers flipped to three o'clock.

Chapter Five

Evette staggered into the bathroom. The baby must have decided to sit on her bladder. She squinted at the clock on the bathroom wall. Almost six o'clock. Judd's alarm would be going off in a few minutes anyway. Might as well stay up now.

But a minute later, washing her hands at her side of the double sink, the fuzz cleared from her brain and it all came flooding back. Judd wasn't here. He'd left last night. No, she'd asked him to leave. Tears burned her eyes at the thought of him alone in some anonymous hotel room.

Maybe Judd had been as blindsided by that phone call last night as she had. For all she knew, the accusation wasn't even true. Maybe that woman's mother was just trying to get some money out of them. Maybe Judd's old girlfriend—fiancée—hadn't had a stroke at all. She was awfully young for something like that.

Maybe this was just a big hoax, something that would be cleared up before another night passed. Hope swelled inside her. Maybe there was some crazy mistake and one phone call could fix everything as quickly as that one phone call had brought this firestorm into their lives.

But it was a fragile hope she felt, and as she reviewed everything that had happened last night, her hope deflated. This wasn't going away. They *would* have to deal with this.

She felt bad about asking Judd to leave. He would never have put her out in the cold if the tables were turned. But then, things didn't work that way. The tables couldn't exactly be turned with something like this. And Judd had admitted that he *could* be the father of Tabrina Jackson's child.

It was too much to deal with right now. She showered and dressed, then made the bed—an easy task with Judd's side barely wrinkled.

She measured coffee into the filter and pushed the button. The coffeemaker was spitting the last of the water into the filter, filling the room with a tantalizing scent, when she realized she'd brewed it for nothing. She wasn't drinking the stuff because of the baby, and Judd wasn't here. She poured herself a cup anyway.

The house felt so empty without him. She hated what was happening. She slipped on a pair of flip-flops and walked out to retrieve the morning paper from the driveway, then tossed it beside the front door as she went back through to the kitchen. She didn't want it sitting on the table, reminding her that Judd was gone.

It was wrong to shut down with him like she had. Even when things were at their worst between them, they'd always been able to talk through their conflicts.

Disconnecting her cell phone from the charger on the bar counter, she checked the time. He was probably at practice already. The boys were on early practice this week, trading off with the girls' varsity. She pressed Judd's number on speed dial.

"Hello?"

"Oh. I…wasn't expecting you to answer."

Silence from his end.

"Judd…I'm sorry. Can we—can we just talk? Please."

She could imagine his jaw tense as he bit back a caustic reply. And she deserved it. He could have said, *Gee, why didn't I think of that?* or *Nice of you to hold your offer till after I spent a miserable night in a hotel.*

As the seconds ticked by, she held her breath.

"I'm ready whenever you are," he finally whispered.

She so desperately wanted things back the way they had been before. "I'm sorry, babe."

"You know I have practice, Evie. And I'm in meetings all morning. But…I think I can get away for a couple of hours around lunch. We'll talk then, okay?"

"Okay."

"See you later." The phone went dead.

"Judd?" Slowly, she slid the cover over the phone. She couldn't blame him for being a little cool toward her. She'd overreacted last night, hadn't given him a chance to explain before she kicked him out.

For the next four hours, her bare feet wore a path in the carpet in front of the arched window in the living room. Every time she heard a car drive by on their quiet street, she hoped it would be him. That he'd found a way to get home sooner.

But it was fifteen minutes after noon when he finally pulled in the driveway. He didn't bother parking the car in the garage, so she knew he had to go back to the school.

She hurried to the door, suddenly feeling as nervous as she had the first time he'd picked her up for a date.

Through the tiny window in the arched front door, she watched him climb the steps, his shoulders slumped and his hair in disarray, as if he'd been scraping his fingers through it—the way he did when his Hawks were down by three with ten seconds to play in the fourth quarter.

She opened the door and he ducked in, eyeing her, as if trying to determine what kind of mood she was in.

"I'm sorry," she said again.

"I understand. I do." He blew out a sigh. "Do you want to go somewhere? To talk?"

"No. Let's stay here." This was one conversation she did not want to risk being overheard. "Do you want some lunch?"

He shook his head. "I'm not hungry." His gaze fell to her midsection. "But you need to eat something. Do you feel okay? I can make you some soup."

"I'm fine. I had something earlier." She didn't tell him it was only a cup of coffee. She could feel her heartbeat racing already from the caffeine. "Let's go in the living room, okay?"

He nodded and followed her into the spacious room, her favorite part of the house. Judd had refused to let her parents help them with a down payment, so they'd had to settle for a smaller house than she'd hoped, but when she sat in this room she could pretend the house was as grand as the one she dreamed of. Sunlight spilled through the tall fanlight window, painting an arch of light across the rich taupe carpeting.

The light turned the room into a jewel box, playing off the red, gold and emerald upholstery and curtains. It had cost a small fortune to decorate this room. Even though she'd saved a bundle with her employee's discount at Furniture Gallery, Judd had balked at the four thousand dollars for the furniture—and she dared not tell him that her mother had paid for the draperies and the Oriental rugs. But she always felt like the queen of her castle when she sat in here. She felt safe here.

Judd took the leather chair in the corner. The fronds of the silk tree towering over him cast dappled shadows on his square jaw. Evette took the love seat adjacent to him, huddling in the corner, clutching a throw pillow to her chest.

He sat there, as if waiting for her to go first. She stared him down, challenging him to say something—anything—that would make things right again.

Judd put his elbows on his knees, steepled his fingers beneath his chin. "Evette, I—first I want to tell you how sorry I am that…I wasn't honest with you. About what happened between us—me and Tabrina, I mean."

The queasy feeling of the past night returned. "That's why I asked you to leave, Judd. It wasn't so much that you might have a child out there. I mean, that's bad enough. But mostly it's just knowing that you made love to another woman, and you didn't tell me."

"I didn't even know you then, Evie. And it was only once. I swear to you, we never meant for things to—"

"Judd." She held up a hand. "I don't need your excuses right now."

He bowed his head. "I know…I know. I'm sorry."

The strength went from her and she rested her head against the back of the love seat. How could she want to kill this man, and take him in her arms at the same time? "I waited, Judd. I saved myself for you." Her voice rose to a shrill pitch, and she forced it back down. She did not want to be the hysterical "other woman." She scratched the thought. What was wrong with her? She was Judd's wife. She was the one who'd been betrayed.

She pulled in a breath, scrambling to think straight. To be rational. What happened was years in the past, and Judd didn't have to say anything for her to see how terrible he felt. But that didn't change the way it felt. It still hurt like mad.

"I don't know what else to say, Evie. I'm sorry."

She made a decision. One that didn't feel genuine right now, but one she knew was right. She took a deep breath. "I forgive you. That's in the past. Let's leave it there. We have other things to worry about."

He nodded, but remained silent. It seemed as if the ball was still in her court.

"So, what do you want to do?"

He chewed the corner of his lip. "Let's…let's lay out our options." He leaned forward and swept aside a neatly arranged stack of magazines on the coffee table between them.

This was the Judd she knew. Take charge, get 'er done, make a list and check it twice. It drove her crazy sometimes, but right now, it was exactly what she needed. What *they* needed.

He formed his hands into two corners of a frame and laid the imaginary picture on the surface of the table. "I think the first thing we need to do is find out exactly what the situation with Tabrina is. Carla wants me to take her—my daughter. She said Tabrina is in a coma, but she may pull out of it. We might be worrying about nothing."

A bright spark rose in Evette's chest. She pulled in a breath, surprised at how much room was in her lungs. "She—Carla—may just be trying to get some money from you, too."

Judd shook his head. "I honestly don't think she'd do that. She's not like that."

Evette's defenses went back up. Was he going to defend Tabrina's whole family to her? She swallowed back a terse response and willed her voice to remain steady. "Okay… so you'll call Carla again and try to find out more?"

"I think I should go see her."

"At her house?"

"I mean Tabrina. In the hospital. Carla, too, of course. But I think I need to see what's going on. Maybe talk to her doctors and see what they can tell us."

"Us?"

"I'd like you to go with me, Evie."

Was he serious? One look at his face told her he was. "No, Judd. I don't think I can do that. Why can't you just call Carla back?"

He pushed himself up from the chair. "I think you're hoping this is just going to go away. And I'm afraid it's not."

"What do you mean?"

His eyes bored into her. "I have a daughter, Evette. A daughter who has no place to call home. I can't simply ignore that."

If Judd didn't have any doubts that the child was his, then it was true. The tightness in her chest returned. "What are you going to do?"

"I guess that depends on you."

"What's that supposed to mean?"

"I can't just make a decision that affects you, that affects our lives…"

She placed a protective hand over her belly. "And our baby's life. You have a child *here*, Judd. I don't know what you're thinking of doing, but what about this baby? What about our baby?"

"Do you think I haven't thought about that?"

"I don't know. What are you thinking? What exactly do you think our options are?"

He eased back into the leather chair, then sat forward, rubbing the bridge of his nose. Finally, he looked up and met her eyes. "Would you be willing to take her in? Bring her here? My daughter?"

So he *was* thinking what she feared most. The room tilted, but she forced herself to hold his gaze. "What if I'm not?"

He breathed out a deep sigh. "Then…I don't know. I can't force you to do that. It's asking a lot. I know that, Evie. But I don't know what else to do."

"You could pay child support. That's what fathers do in cases like this." Of course, she'd ranted plenty of times against fathers who did nothing more than pay child support. Her self-righteous attitude came back to haunt her now. "I don't know where the money will come from…especially after we have our own baby to think of."

She looked around the room, through the hallway into the house they'd saved so long to afford. "I do not want to lose everything we've worked for, Judd. And I am not going back to work." The steam of anger built inside her. "I *will* stay home with this baby. I don't care what else happens. That has always been our plan, and I won't let this ruin my life. *Our* lives." She'd been a little too late adding him into that statement.

His expression said he'd noticed her slip. He opened his mouth to speak, then closed it again. He swallowed, his Adam's apple bobbing. He couldn't seem to meet her gaze. "I'm sorry. I am so sorry."

"Stop. Please stop it, Judd." Her voice came out harsher than she intended, and she worked to soften her tone. "All the apologies in the world won't help. We have to figure out what to do."

A fire lit his eyes, turning their usual hazel to gold. It was the same fire she saw on the basketball court when one of his boys wasn't performing to the best of his ability, and Coach McGlin wasn't going to stand for it. "That's what I'm trying to do. And I am truly sorry. It tears me up that you have to be involved in this mess, but you *are,* Evette. You just are. I can't do anything about that."

"What do you want me to say? That I'm delighted you want to bring your illegitimate daughter into our home?" She winced. The words sounded harsh and thoughtless now that they'd escaped her lips.

"I'm not asking you to be 'delighted' about any of this. I'm asking what you're willing to do." His voice broke. "I don't want to lose *you* over this."

Everything in her wanted to close the distance between them, take him in her arms and tell him that would never happen. But it was too late for that. *Too late.*

Chapter Six

Evette sat across from him, her face a mask of ambiguity, and for the first time in their marriage, Judd could not tell from his wife's expression what she was thinking. He felt the clock ticking and knew that at the office they'd be wondering where he was. But this was more important. This couldn't wait.

Over the five and a half years they'd been married, he and Evette had dealt with some tough issues, most of them ultimately tracing back to his relationship with Tabrina. Still, they'd always been able to work things out. And he'd finally gotten his head on straight. But now it seemed his issues with Tabrina had come back in full force. And this was bigger than anything they'd ever dealt with. Again, he was to blame.

Worse, he still hadn't told Evette everything that was behind this, how he'd wrestled with letting Tabrina go, how he felt he'd made a mistake in marrying Evette. Why, just when he'd finally learned to put his loyalties with Evette, had Tabrina come back to haunt him? To haunt his marriage? He had to resolve things, fix this before it destroyed them.

He rose and leaned across the coffee table to touch her shoulder, afraid she would shake him off. But she let his hand rest there, though her own hands remained in her lap.

"I'll call Carla and set up a time to talk things out with her. I'd like you to go with me, but I understand if you won't…if you *can't*," he quickly corrected. "I truly do understand, Evette."

"Would you—" Her voice came out in a squeak. "Would you really bring her here? The…girl?"

"Not without your blessing. No. Of course not. But, Evette, now that I know, I can't let my daughter go to some stranger."

She narrowed her eyes at him. "And you're not a stranger?"

"You know what I mean."

"No, Judd, I don't. I don't see how it's any better for her to come here—where she's not expected, not wanted—than go to a loving foster home where they're going into this knowingly, where they've been trained to care for kids like her."

"What do you mean by that? Kids like her?" He hadn't meant for his words to come out sounding so defensive, but there they were.

"I just mean that she's dealing with having her mom in the hospital. She's probably got issues anyway, being raised by a single mom."

"Evette, you don't know anything about her or Tabrina. Why don't you just hold off on the judgment until we know more?"

"All I'm saying is that you talk like you're swooping in to rescue a darling little angel who will bring joy and laughter into our lives. If that's what you think, Judd, you're living in la-la land. This kid is six years old. She's lived who-knows-what kind of life, and now her mom is sick, and she has a grandmother who doesn't want her. Nobody wants her, apparently. This is not going to be a well-adjusted kid, Judd."

"Why can't you ever see the positive side of things? Why do you always have to expect the worst of every situation, every person? You don't know one thing about my daughter. Is it too—"

"*My* daughter?" Evette's laugh held no humor. "You make it sound like you already know her."

"No. Of course I don't know her. But is it too much to ask for you to just reserve judgment until we see for ourselves?"

"I'm not making a judgment about her personally. I'm just being realistic. And if it comes to the point where we have to meet her, I'll be fair." She cocked her head at him. "But you're talking like it's a done deal that we're going to take her in. Talk about expecting the worst…"

"I'm not talking about taking her in. I'm talking about getting to know my daughter. I'm talking about giving her a chance and not making snap judgments before we've even met her."

"You're assuming I *will* meet her."

That stopped him in his tracks. He hadn't told Evette, but he realized now that he'd already made up his mind: no matter what he found out about Tabrina's situation, he wanted to meet his daughter. Maybe even be a part of her life. Evette needed to know that.

He came around to sit on the edge of the coffee table, as close to her as he dared, their knees almost touching. It was all he could do not to reach for her hands. But they were clasped tightly in her lap, sending a clear message.

"I want to meet my daughter, Evette. You need to know that. No matter what else happens, now that I know I have a daughter, I want to meet her."

Silence.

He scooted closer, but she shrank back, and he gave her a little space. "Surely you can understand that…for her sake as well as mine. Think about her future. How would you feel if you found out your father knew you existed and didn't care enough even to get to know you, let alone provide for you?"

Her jaw tensed. "So we've gone from 'meeting her' to paying child support *and* getting to know her. I suppose you'll want her to know her half brother or half sister, too?"

He hadn't thought of that yet. The child Evette was carrying didn't seem real to him yet. Not really. But somehow he already had an image in his mind for Tabrina's little girl—Jolie, Carla had called her.

"We can just all be one big happy family? Is that it, Judd? Goodness, maybe Tabrina and her mother can move in with us, too." Evette's words dripped resentment.

He gritted his teeth. "Now you're being ridiculous. That's not fair, Evette."

She shot off the couch, as if to put as much space between them as possible. "Life's not fair, Judd. Don't you think I know that?"

He watched as she trudged up the stairs looking like she could barely shoulder the weight of their trials. Seconds later, he heard their bedroom door slam.

He was going to have to do this solo. At least for now, he was in this alone.

The stretch of Interstate 44 east of Springfield was almost deserted at six-thirty on a Friday morning. Judd had reluctantly turned this morning's pregame walk-through over to his assistant coach. Not that he didn't trust Randall Hazen, but with district play-offs next week, every practice counted. Not to mention it killed him to miss a game day practice. Could he tell Carla that whatever arrangements they might make would have to wait until after the state basketball tournament? Until after April fifteenth, tax day, because of the huge work-load at the firm?

Just when would be a good time to meet the six-year-old daughter you hadn't known you fathered?

He pressed the accelerator, wanting to get to the hospital, get this over with. When he'd talked to Carla last night, nothing had changed with Tabrina's condition. She was still unconscious, and there was still no long-term prognosis. But Carla was insistent that arrangements be made for Jolie. "I can't do this anymore," Carla had said, exhaustion evident in her voice.

Evette was still acting cool toward him. He'd told her that he'd talked to Carla and that he'd agreed to go to Springfield where Tabrina was in the hospital. He hadn't asked Evette again to go with him, and she hadn't offered. "I promise I won't make any commitments without talking to you first," he promised. But Evette seemed unmoved.

He didn't expect to meet his little girl today, but he would see Tabrina, and thinking of that moment shook him to his core. A few years after he'd broken up with her, an alumni newsletter reported that she had received her master's degree and accepted a teaching position. He didn't remember where, and that was the last he'd heard of her. He hadn't laid eyes on her since the day he'd told her goodbye almost seven years ago. He'd tried to block that afternoon—the hurt in Tabrina's eyes, the truth in his own heart—from his memory.

A light mist began to fall and he switched on the windshield wipers, letting their rhythmic *swoosh swoosh* carry his thoughts away. He had loved Tabrina completely. With a true love. He knew that now. And yes, it was Evette he loved now, but what he'd felt for Tabrina back then was also love. Nothing less.

Somehow, he'd allowed his parents to persuade him that marriage to Tabrina—a beautiful, intelligent, vivacious African-American young woman—would ruin his life. They'd convinced him that no amount of love, no amount of good intentions on his and Tabrina's part, could overcome the prejudice they would face in the world as a married couple.

He understood that his parents' advice came from their fears for their son, from their genuine concern for the prejudice he and Tabrina would encounter, and more importantly, the trials any children they might have would no doubt face. But he realized now that the kind of prejudice his parents feared resided within their *own* hearts. Their misguided pride in their "pure" European heritage, their own attitudes—and those of their generation—toward mixed marriage, had cost Judd the woman he loved.

Still, he couldn't blame his parents alone. He could have stood up to them, could have married Tabrina in spite of their protests. He hadn't taken responsibility for his future, and instead he'd caved under the pressure. On a breezy June afternoon, shortly after their junior year of college, he'd told Tabrina he didn't think their relationship could work.

"What do you mean, won't work?"

He hadn't been able to look her in the eye. "I just think we need to break things off. I don't think this is going to work—you and me."

"Judd? I don't understand. Did I do something…say something wrong?"

Remembering the shock on her beautiful face, when she realized he was serious, still made him sick to his stomach.

Tabrina didn't plead with him or even cry…at least not in front of him. She simply got back in his car and asked him to take her home.

She hadn't come back to school the following semester, and he'd never heard from her afterward.

He met Evette at the start of the next school year, and by Christmas they were married. He did love Evette, but he'd finally admitted to himself—never to her, of course—that he'd married her on the rebound.

His parents had approved of Evette from the beginning. He suspected that was only because, at least in their eyes, her skin was the "right" color. Ironically, after he'd given up Tabrina on their account, his relationship with his parents deteriorated to the point that he now barely saw them. They'd moved to Chicago a few years ago, and the extent of Judd's relationship with them was a brief Christmas get-together, and polite phone conversations four or five times a year—usually when Mom called to tell him some great-aunt or second cousin had died. He couldn't blame them completely. It was as much his resentment as their discomfort that kept them at a distance.

The rain fell harder now. Judd passed the sign for his exit and merged into the right lane. He reached into the pocket of his white dress shirt and pulled out the map he'd printed with directions to the hospital. Carla had agreed to meet him there and take him to see Tabrina.

He went a block too far and had to double back, but suddenly the hospital loomed in front of him. He followed the signs to the visitors' entrance and ran through the parking lot without the benefit of an umbrella.

Inside, he brushed in vain at the damp spot on his shirt and paced the waiting area, hoping he'd recognize Carla after all these years.

The woman who came toward him looked the same, except she'd shorn her kinky gray hair close to her head. The style became her, in spite of the dark shadows beneath her deep-set brown eyes. It was easy to see where Tabrina's beauty came from. Carla was taller and thinner than her daughter, with lighter skin. If Tabrina's complexion was cinnamon-mocha, Carla's was weak coffee with a generous portion of cream.

"Judd." She held out a hand.

He took it and held it between his own for a moment. "Carla, I'm so sorry. How is she doing?"

She shook her head, her lips pressed into a harsh line. "It's bad. We didn't find her for two or three hours after she had the stroke. That's the worst thing that could happen."

"What did happen? I never heard."

"She'd been having trouble with her eyes—woke up one morning and could barely see out of one eye—so she made an appointment with her optometrist. She dropped Jolie off at school on her way to the clinic, then apparently she pulled over in a little park along the way. We don't know if she felt the stroke coming on, or if she just pulled over to make a phone call. You know Tabrina… she never liked to use her cell phone while she was driving."

He remembered. Any time he'd called her from his cell phone, her first question was always, "You're not driving, are you?" And she wouldn't talk until he promised he wasn't.

"Anyway," Carla went on, "she never showed up for the appointment. Some woman who came to the park over her lunch hour found Tabrina unconscious in her car. She's been that way ever since. All the tests are saying it was a stroke. Ischemic stroke, they're calling it." She blew out a shaky breath. "The kind that can cause brain damage."

Judd shook his head. "I'm so sorry, Carla."

The way she looked at him, he wondered if she understood that his apology was for so much more than the stroke. It was for not standing up to his parents and for breaking up with the woman he loved. It was for leaving Tabrina to raise their child, though he'd truly had no idea she was pregnant then. But maybe Carla didn't know that.

"Do you want to see her? Tabrina? She won't respond, but…"

"I understand. Yes…I want to see her." *Did he really?* A rush of old feelings swarmed over him. His hands grew clammy and he wiped them on the sides of his khaki pants.

"She's on the fourth floor. This way…" Carla headed for a bank of elevators to her right.

They rode up in silence, and when they got off the elevator, Carla strode past the nurses' station to a room at the end of a long hallway.

St. John's had over eight hundred beds, but one of them held the mother of his daughter. A woman he had once been crazy in love with. A woman who might be dying. What was he supposed to do, to feel?

Carla swept into the room. The bed closest to the door was empty, and she went directly to the far bed.

Judd took a halting step. Tabrina lay on her back in the bed. The black hair she'd always worked so hard to straighten was pulled into a bunch on top of her head, but the wild mass of curls escaped the wide band and spilled onto the pillow. Her skin had an odd grayish cast, but except for the wires and tubes that ran from her body to the various contraptions and monitors surrounding her bed, she looked like he remembered. Her mouth had a crooked tilt to it, as if she'd fallen asleep sitting up in the car on one of their drives from University of Missouri to visit Harry and Carla in St. Louis.

His tongue felt like sandpaper. He started to reach out, touch the slender fingers that lay atop the crisp white sheet. But the IV taped to her hand—and the image of Evette's face that came just then—stopped him. Instead, he gripped the bed rail and looked down at her.

And reality hit him. Tabrina Jackson was not going home to her daughter—to their daughter—anytime soon. Maybe never.

Chapter Seven

Evette stirred and raised her head from the sofa pillow. She heard the kitchen door shut softly, the way Judd closed it when he came home late from an out-of-town ball game, careful not to wake her. She squinted at the clock on the mantel. Only eight-thirty. She felt as if she'd been sleeping for hours. The sofa had been her anchor for most of this day while she agonized over what would come of Judd's trip to Springfield.

She should have gone with him. He would have done the same for her. She knew that and was ashamed.

She heard him tiptoe through the hall and rose up on one elbow. "Judd?"

He appeared in the arched doorway. "You're up."

"Are you okay?"

He nodded and stepped into the room. She got a better look at his face, and was stunned at how shaken he appeared. "What happened?"

He sat down as if his legs wouldn't hold him any longer. "It's not good. She—Tabrina has a long haul ahead of her. If she even makes it."

"Did you talk to her?" She held her breath.

He shook his head. "She's not conscious. She's paralyzed. It was the kind of stroke that affects the brain. Carla said the doctors aren't giving them much hope that she'll recover."

"So…what does that mean?"

"It means there's a little girl who needs a place to live, Evie. *My* little girl. And…I'd like for us to be that place, that home."

She could tell he'd rehearsed exactly how he would say those words. Well, she'd rehearsed some things, too. She had lots of questions before she agreed to let this thing turn their lives upside down.

She sat up and opened her mouth to speak, but Judd put a hand on her knee and took a deep breath. "Let me say something first, babe. Please. I know what I'm asking is not fair and…that it will change our lives. I want you to know that if you say no, I'll understand. I won't force this on you. That wouldn't be right. But I also want you to know how strongly I feel about it."

He swallowed hard, then bowed his head as if he was struggling to collect his emotions. "Evette, all the way home from Springfield I prayed that God would show me a way out of this mess. It…it's been a long time since I've prayed like that. I feel like He was saying there isn't an honorable way out. So I finally started praying that He would show me a way *through* it. I wish I could just write a check every month and feel I was doing the right thing."

She knew what was coming and braced herself for it, physically swinging her legs off the sofa and planting her feet on the floor, tensed for the impact of what he was about to say.

"I'm sorry, Evie, but I just cannot find peace about that. It's not money Jolie needs."

The way he spoke her name made it sound as though he knew and loved the little girl already.

"Did you meet her?"

"Jolie?"

She nodded.

"No. I told you I wouldn't."

"It just…it sounded like maybe you had."

He shook his head. "No, but I will. I'd like you to be there when I do."

She held up a hand. "Judd, I want to support you in this. I do. But we need to talk this over. I don't think you've thought everything through."

A tendon in his jaw went taut. "Thinking everything through is *all* I've done since I got Carla's phone call."

"Okay, then help me with some answers because I don't know what to do."

"I don't have all the answers, Evette. Some things we'll just have to work out as we go."

"Tell me this, Judd. If we do take her in, what will we tell people? How are we going to introduce her? What are you going to tell your team when this little—" she'd been about to say *little* black *girl* "—girl comes to live with us?" She shook her head. Whether Evette wanted to admit it or not, that was one big thing eating at her. It would be bad enough to have to explain that her godly husband had fathered a child out of wedlock. But for that child to be of another race…

She couldn't finish the sentence even in her own mind.

She wasn't prejudiced. She prided herself on that point. But the thoughts that had taken root in her brain over the past few days filled her with shame. Yet she couldn't deny they were there. She could hardly voice them, but surely Judd had entertained some of the same thoughts. He'd been engaged to Tabrina…been in love with her by his own admission. But he'd broken up with her…for some of the same reasons she was now pondering.

She backpedaled. "If we take her in, what will you tell your boys, your players, about this little girl who shows up at the next game calling you 'Daddy'?"

Judd drew back as if she'd struck him. If he'd thought about her question at all, it was obvious he hadn't come up with a satisfactory answer. He took such pride in the team he coached. How often had he told her how grateful he was to have the opportunity to make a difference in his players' lives?

She'd put up with having a bunch of smelly adolescent boys in their house, sweating on her nice furniture and spilling Coke and pizza all over her new carpeting, because it was important to Judd. And she believed he was making a difference in their lives. Would this revelation about their sainted coach undo everything he'd tried to accomplish? She wasn't cruel enough to pose such a question now, but she hoped he'd thought about that.

"I don't know what I'll tell them, Evie. The truth, I guess. I've always told them that the truth is always the right thing."

The truth will set you free.

A little of the steam went out of her. "Okay. And what do you want me to tell my friends—and my parents?"

"I'll leave that up to you. You can tell people as much or as little as you're comfortable with. I'm not going to make up a story that's not true, but I don't think we owe people all the gory details, either."

"And if…if she's still here when the baby—our baby—is old enough to ask questions? What do we say then?" She tried to imagine explaining to her pale-skinned son or daughter why big sister had dark skin. She'd seen a few old photographs of Tabrina. She was a beautiful girl with mahogany skin. Of course, Judd's daughter would be half Caucasian…maybe it wouldn't be obvious that she was half African-American. Many biracial children looked more white than black.

Her conscience screamed accusations. How could she even be thinking such things? Why did it matter to her what color skin this child had? This was a little girl who had all but lost her mother, who had no one else in her life that could take her in. Evette rubbed her temples. The girl was Judd's flesh and blood. Could she not love her for that alone?

Still she could hear her mother now. Bert and Tessa Bryant were good Christians. They were certainly not prejudiced. Why, they had many African-American friends. *Yeah, right.* The "help," as her mother referred to the string of nameless African-American or Hispanic people who'd cleaned the Bryant summer home in Phoenix. The "help" kept the Bryant home spotless, kept her mother's extensive, expensive wardrobe clean and pressed, and kept her garden and the Olympic-size pool immaculate. "We pay those people well," her mother was fond of saying. And the inflection she used when she uttered the words "those people" said it all.

But Evette wasn't like her mother. Was she? Yet, in so many ways she'd catered to the bigotry. Her parents knew Judd had been engaged before, but she'd purposely never mentioned that Tabrina was black. Because that would have brought Judd down a notch in her mother's estimation. Was *she* any better, editing the truth as she had?

Judd cocked his head and eyed her, as if he were reading her thoughts. She dipped her head, feeling shamed at the possibility.

He lifted her chin. "I think our baby will be blessed just to have a big sister doting on him. We have enough bridges to get across. I don't think that's one we need to worry about right now. What else?" he challenged. "What else are you apprehensive about?"

"What am I *not* apprehensive about? Will we be expected to keep her—the girl—in contact with her mother?" She couldn't bring herself to use their names. *Tabrina. Jolie.* She didn't want those to be familiar names. "What about her grandmother? Is she going to want to maintain a relationship? How would all that work?"

"Evette, at this point we don't even know if Tabrina will make it. Or maybe she'll wake up tomorrow and Carla will change her mind. I don't think we can really answer your question. I guess—aside from Tabrina dying—the worst-case scenario is that she lives, but isn't able to care for Jolie. If that happens, of course we'd want to make sure she and Jolie get to see each other."

She forced a wry smile. "You make it sound so easy."

"I don't mean to. Nothing about this is easy. Especially for you. Don't think I don't know that, Evie. I'm just… I want to be sure you know what you're agreeing to."

She wasn't agreeing to anything. She didn't want to be here. Hated being forced into these decisions. But she couldn't tell him that. She *was* here, and there wasn't a thing she could do about it, short of kicking Judd out. Again.

But since she'd quit her job, anticipating being a stay-at-home mom to their baby, she was dependent on him. If she asked him to leave, she couldn't afford to stay in this house. If she kicked Judd out of her life, then she'd be putting her baby in the same position Judd's daughter was in.

Besides, even after all that had happened, she loved this man. She'd be a fool to do anything to drive him away.

Feeling claustrophobic, she jumped off the sofa. "I'm going to make some tea. Do you want anything?"

"No." He followed her across the spotless hardwood floor to the kitchen.

She filled the kettle with cold water from the tap and put it on to boil. She rummaged for her favorite ceramic mug in the cupboard beside the stove top.

"Grab me a cup, will you? I guess I will have something." Judd perched on a bar stool, resting his elbows on the granite countertop.

She pulled down one of the oversize mugs she knew he liked and plopped tea bags in each, then measured two teaspoons of sugar into Judd's cup, the way he liked it.

Finally, she found her voice. "Just put it to me straight."

He raised an eyebrow.

"What are you asking of me, Judd? What do you want me to do?"

He studied her for a long minute before he spoke. "I want to tell Carla that we'll take Jolie in for as long as we need to. That she'll have a place to stay until Tabrina can take her back."

"And if she can't? If Tabrina never can take her back?"

"Then…I'd like to raise my daughter, Evette. I'd like *us* to raise my daughter."

The kettle started a low, mournful whistle. She made no move to take it off the burner, and the sound quickly built to an urgent siren wail. But she couldn't seem to make her muscles cooperate to reach over and turn off the fire.

Chapter Eight

The Caliber seemed to remember the road, and despite the fact that Evette was in the car with him this time, the drone of tires on pavement was the only sound Judd had heard for the first hour of the drive to Springfield. They had another hour to go and her silence made him ache.

He watched her from the corner of his vision. She was just starting to show, and she'd begun wearing looser clothes that emphasized her pregnancy. She cradled her little pooch of a belly, staring out the window as if she'd never seen the Missouri landscape before. The calendar had turned to March, but the countryside was still dressed in drab winter-gray.

He knew Evette was doing her best to accept his decision to take Jolie in, but it was clear she was still struggling to come to terms with the bombshell of Carla's phone call.

For Evette's sake, he would have given his very life to turn back the clock and make this all go away. And yet, even with his hands gripping the steering wheel in trepidation, there was a tiny spark of excitement building inside him. He would meet his daughter today for the first time. *His daughter.*

He could never share these feelings of anticipation with Evette. It felt downright selfish to even be mulling over these thoughts when she was obviously in such pain over what was happening. But he couldn't help wondering…would he be able to see himself in his own flesh-and-blood daughter? Did she have his square jaw? His aptitude for numbers and logic? Would she be a good basketball player?

A new thought hit him. Would he see Tabrina every time he looked at this little girl? Did Jolie have that ornery spark in her eyes that Tabrina had, the sharp sense of humor that had always kept him in stitches? Did her skin take on that burnished cinnamon glow after she'd spent time in the sun? How much would his blood dilute her African-American features? As much as he hoped his daughter had been blessed with Tabrina's uncommon beauty, it would make things easier for Evette if Jolie wasn't too obviously biracial. If she had strong black features, people would probably just assume they'd adopted her. Strangers, anyway. But what about the people they knew?

They'd decided not to tell anyone about Jolie yet. It was still possible this would be a short-term commitment, though growing less likely with every day Tabrina remained comatose. It had been more than three weeks since her stroke now, ten days since the night he'd discovered he had a daughter.

They passed a sign that read Springfield, 56 Miles. He snuck another glance at Evette. Ten days. Would ten *years* be enough to come to terms with what she'd had to adjust to since then? He tried to put himself in her shoes, tried to assess everything she'd sacrificed because of his mistake that long-ago night.

Before they'd left the house this afternoon, she'd hurried around putting last-minute touches on the guest room. Judd had assumed they would put Jolie up in the nursery, that she'd sleep on the daybed they'd bought for that room. "So I won't keep you awake when I have to get up with our Little Bambino at night," Evette had said. She'd furnished and decorated the nursery, next door to the master bedroom, before she'd unpacked the boxes in the living room and the family room off the kitchen. The sunny little bedroom sat ready for a baby even before Evette became pregnant this time.

But last night, to Judd's surprise, she'd taken down the new draperies and pulled off the fancy bedspread in the guest room and replaced them with an inexpensive washable quilt and curtains from the mall.

"What are you doing?"

Fluffing a crisp pink sheet out over the queen-size bed, she hadn't looked at him when she answered. "Getting the room ready."

"Why are you putting her in here?" Just a few months ago, she'd worked so hard to turn the guest room into a haven for her sister and her parents whenever they could figure out a time to come for a visit.

"Where else would we put her, Judd? We can't just stick her down in the basement."

Apparently, the nursery wasn't an option in her eyes. And he wasn't about to suggest that Jolie share a room with their baby. He watched Evette box up the throw pillows and silk plants and scented candles, and knew it killed her to give up that room and—with it—the hope of an overnight visit from her family. Another sacrifice she'd had to make. He'd offered to help her finish making the bed and hang the new curtains, but she brushed him off. And he apologized again for how his mistake had messed up her life.

But lately his words of contrition seemed to be more of a burden than a comfort to her, and he'd made up his mind not to apologize again. Still, the guilt stabbed at him when he thought too hard about all his wife had given up to make this work.

And with basketball play-offs and tax season both looming, things were going to get worse before they got better. Though the extra expenses of these trips to Springfield and getting things ready for Jolie were minor, it was out of the question for him to take time off from either job. At least if he wanted to stay gainfully employed. Now, more than ever, he needed the work, and the medical insurance it provided.

Most of Jolie's care was going to fall to Evette for a while. They'd get her enrolled in school as soon as they saw how she was adjusting. That would free up Evette's days somewhat, but he worried that she didn't have a realistic picture of how much was involved in taking care of a little girl.

It was something he'd worried about with their own coming baby. Evette tended to idealize everything. For all the years they'd been trying to have a baby, he knew her visions of having an infant in the house involved a sleeping or cooing cherub who rarely cried and certainly never made messes. Evette was a bit of a perfectionist, especially when it came to the house. She liked things just so, and he worried that when it came time to baby proof the house she would have some issues. Well, he'd find out soon enough how she would handle it.

"Maybe we can tell people we're adopting her." Evette's voice shattered his reverie.

They'd be at the hospital in twenty minutes. He didn't want to start an argument. "I'm—I'm not sure that would be fair to Tabrina. And how would Jolie feel if she heard us tell someone that? I don't want to lie about this, Evie. We don't have to tell people all the details, but I don't want to lie."

She turned back to stare out the window, and he returned to his troubled thoughts.

It started to rain just as they pulled into the hospital entrance, reminding him of his last visit to Springfield. He parked in the same parking lot as before, then reached into the glove compartment and pulled out the umbrella he'd stowed there. "You want this?"

She took it from him. "Thanks." Her voice sounded shaky. She must have been as nervous as he was.

"It'll be okay, Evie."

Her shoulders heaved as she sucked in a deep breath. She reached for the door handle.

He took a risk and grabbed her left hand. "Can we pray…before we go in?"

She nodded, squeezed his hand and bowed her head.

"Well, God…" His voice faltered and he cleared his throat and started over. "Father, we don't even know what to expect today. But we put this day in Your hands. Help us know how to make Jolie feel welcome, help us to—" He paused. He'd been about to say *help us do the right thing,* but that sounded too much like it was aimed at Evette. He didn't mean it that way. "Just help us, Lord," he said finally. "This is new territory and we don't know what to expect. We're not sure what it is You're asking of us, but we give this day to You and ask Your blessing on everything that happens."

He squeezed her hand and she squeezed back with a whispered *amen*. But she didn't offer her own prayer as she would have…before all this had happened.

He climbed out and went around to her side, waited while she put the umbrella up, then locked the car. He put a hand on her back and she raised the umbrella in invitation for him to come underneath with her. She was doing her best to treat him with dignity. A dignity he knew she wasn't sure he deserved. He wanted to thank her for agreeing to this, for coming with him. But he was afraid of giving her a chance to change her mind.

Instead, he bent his elbow and offered it. "Ready?"

She didn't answer, but took his arm and leaned into him. He didn't dare speculate whether it was merely to stay out of the rain or because she wanted to feel closer to him. Or maybe her knees were weak with fear, like his.

As before, Carla was waiting inside the entrance to the main waiting room. Judd trailed Evette's gaze as she looked past Tabrina's mother and around the room. Except for an elderly couple sitting side by side in a row of attached chairs, the room was empty. He'd expected Jolie to be with Carla. The anticipation was doing a number on his blood pressure.

He greeted Carla with a nod. "This is Evette…my wife." He put a possessive arm around her, hoping she wouldn't shrug him off.

She didn't, and extended a hand to Carla. "It's nice to meet you. I—I'm so sorry about your daughter."

"Thank you." Carla eyed Evette with what Judd interpreted to be suspicion. "So…how you doing with all this? You're okay with taking her in? Even in your condition?" She pointed to Evette's belly.

Evette nodded.

"I've got no choice, you know," Carla said. "It pains me to do this."

Carla had never been one to mince words. Judd had forgotten that about her.

He tried to catch Evette's eye, ready to jump in and answer for her in case she was uncomfortable with Carla's probing.

But she appeared calm and poised, and didn't shy away from Carla's appraising stare. "This must be terribly difficult for you."

Judd wanted to hug his wife. Then he caught her stealing another curious glance past him into the waiting room.

Carla must have noticed, too. "Jolie's up in Tabrina's room." She gave a slight shrug. "I thought it might be best if we talked things over before you meet her."

"Of course." Judd put a hand at the small of Evette's back and ushered her to a group of chairs in a corner of the room. Though the sun still hid behind a curtain of clouds, the room's many windows kept it bright.

Carla followed. "We're trying to get Tabrina into a nursing facility in Lebanon. It's about fifty miles northeast of here."

Judd remembered seeing the exit for Lebanon. "Yes, I know where it is." The town was half the distance of Springfield from the Falls. Judd wasn't sure if it comforted or disconcerted him to think of having Tabrina that close. But for Carla's sake, and for Jolie's, it was good Tabrina wouldn't be too far away.

"Until we find out if her insurance will cover it, we're kind of in limbo, but…" Carla swallowed hard and looked at the floor. "I'd like to be able to see Jolie as often as I can. The doctors say it might help Tabrina to hear Jolie's voice…"

For the first time, Judd realized how terribly hard this had to be for Carla. Not just because her daughter was desperately ill, but because this couldn't help but change her relationship with her granddaughter.

He touched her arm lightly. "We'll do all we can to help." No sooner were the words out than he realized they implied a promise from Evette, too. He couldn't do that to her. But he couldn't very well take back his words, either. He opted for turning the conversation to the even more difficult things they had to discuss before they drove away with Jolie in their car.

They'd agreed not to take any legal action until the doctors determined what Tabrina's long-term prognosis was. There was still an outside chance that she might recover enough to at least have part-time custody of her daughter—*their* daughter. He hurried past that thought. "Do you have Jolie's school records…and her insurance information and medical release?"

Carla dug in the large tote bag over her shoulder and produced a manila envelope. "Everything you need should be here. My phone numbers are in there if you have any questions about anything. But…" She sucked in already hollowed cheeks. "I think it might be best if Jolie doesn't call me for a few weeks—until after she's settled in with you."

Evette shot Judd a look, and he tried to telegraph her a beats-me-why-she-said-that look. He scrambled to think of the questions he knew they'd have about

Jolie once they got home. "How is she handling everything now?"

"If you mean, 'Is she still crying for her mommy every night?' no. She's a well-adjusted little girl, but this has obviously been hard on her. I've spent every spare moment with her or Tabrina since the day it happened. Jolie's been in school, or with Walt most of the time. He's a good man…" She looked at the floor. "But Walt's never had kids of his own, and patience is not his strong suit. You can see why I—" Her voice broke. "I just cannot do this anymore. I tried to keep things together, I tried to do it all, I really did…but it's just not working."

Judd had the sense that Carla was trying to convince herself as much as them. He resisted the urge to put an arm around her, not sure how Evette would take that. But he wanted Tabrina's mother to see the compassion in his eyes. His heart went out to this woman. In spite of the conflict between her and Tabrina when Tabrina was growing up, he could see now that Carla loved her daughter deeply. And her granddaughter. "We'll take good care of her. We'll keep in touch…let you know how things are going."

"Thank you."

Evette stepped forward. "She'll be okay. We'll do our best."

Again, Carla studied Evette as if she wasn't quite sure she could be trusted. But after a minute, she offered a wan smile. "Thank you…Evette, was it?"

"That's right."

Carla turned to Judd and lifted her shoulders to inhale deeply. She blew out a sigh, then brightened. "Now, shall we go meet your daughter?"

Chapter Nine

The elevator rose to the fourth floor and Evette's pulse climbed with it. She had not counted on having to see Tabrina today.

The doors slid open and Judd moved aside to let Carla off first. Evette felt his tug on her sleeve and turned to see a pleading look in his eyes. *Are you okay with this?* he mouthed.

She nodded. She didn't really want to meet the woman, but she wanted to be at Judd's side when he met his daughter. If the two went hand in hand, so be it.

Carla led the way to the room at the end of the hallway. Evette and Judd followed her into the room, past a frail old woman, sleeping with her jaw slack, to the bed by the window. There were two vases on the wide windowsill and Evette's first thought was that they should have brought flowers.

Her second thought, when her gaze fell on the other bed, was that Tabrina looked like she was laid out for burial. Evette shuddered. The railings were up on both sides of the bed and white blankets were mounded over

her, giving the appearance of a coffin. The curtain around
the bed was pushed back on its track so Evette could see
Tabrina's deathly still form. Her mouth had the crooked
appearance of an elderly stroke victim. Curly black hair
was pulled back from her face, and it formed a halo
above her head. Her slender hands were folded over her
chest. Her dark skin couldn't hide the deep purple bruises
on the back of one hand where an IV needle was taped.

Carla had told Judd that Tabrina taught at a small
college in Springfield. It was hard to imagine the
withered woman in the bed standing in front of a classroom.

The curtain rustled and Evette involuntarily took a
step back. A skinny little arm pushed the divider back
between the window wall and Tabrina's bed. Two bright
dark eyes peeked around the edge.

"There you are!" Carla went to the little girl. "Did
you think I forgot about you?" She motioned Judd and
Evette over.

Judd led the way. He looked calm, but he grasped for
Evette's hand as he passed by and squeezed her fingers
so tightly she caught her breath.

Carla knelt by the vinyl chair Jolie was sitting in. She
pressed her back against the wall for support. Jolie sat
on the edge of the oversize chair, her feet six inches off
the floor, legs swinging back and forth. Her thick dark
hair was pushed off her forehead with a wide pink
headband and spilled in tight waves behind her shoulders. Her hair was darker than Judd's, but the influence
of his genes could be seen in its milky-brown shade. And
in her eyes. Not the coffee-bean color of her grandmother's, but a golden brown flecked with green—hazel,
most people would have called them. Like Judd's.

Judd's daughter glanced at Evette, her eyes stopping when they came to her stomach. Her knowing grin told Evette the little girl understood there was a baby in there. Jolie's gaze shifted and lifted notch by notch until she was looking up into Judd's face.

"Jolie, this is Judd and Evette. You'll be going home with—"

"You're my dad," Jolie said matter-of-factly, never taking her eyes off Judd.

Judd had said Carla didn't know what Tabrina had told Jolie about her father, so they'd agreed to introduce him and Evette simply as "your mom's friends" until they knew more about Tabrina's prognosis.

Judd threw Carla a pleading gaze that she returned with a don't-look-at-me shrug.

He met Evette's eyes briefly, then knelt in front of Jolie. "Yes, Jolie. I am." He opened his mouth as if to say something else, but then he caught his bottom lip with his teeth the way he did when he was choked up.

The pain and isolation Evette felt seeing them together took her by surprise. She drew in a sharp breath, waging war against the self-centered thoughts that pushed into her mind. She threw up a desperate prayer for Judd. They couldn't let this little girl see how emotion-charged this moment was. She'd been through enough without having to wonder why meeting her made them cry.

You're my dad, Jolie had said. Tabrina apparently had told her about Judd after all. She'd recognized him on sight. Jolie must have seen pictures of Judd. But why wouldn't Carla have been aware of that?

A question niggled at Evette. Had Judd already met Jolie and not told her? She tried to dismiss the suspicion.

Judd hadn't lied to her before, except about the extent
of his relationship with Tabrina. That qualified as a pretty
colossal deception. She tucked that away to examine
later. This was no time to haul out accusations.

Feeling awkward and out of place, Evette watched
Judd with his daughter. She felt Carla's eyes on her. No
doubt, she was failing every test the woman had devised.
Well, tough. She couldn't make herself care right now.
This was going to be harder than she had thought. There
were too many things they hadn't talked out thoroughly
enough.

If Judd was going to be called *Dad,* who was she to
this little girl? She looked at the woman lying in the bed
not two feet away from them, a silent reminder of how
Jolie had come to be. Even with her mouth drooping and
tubes and wires everywhere, Evette saw how beautiful
she must have been. If Tabrina survived and recovered,
Judd would have a relationship with her—again. Forever,
they would be tied together because of Jolie.

She closed her eyes and pictured graduations and
weddings and school programs and basketball games with
Judd and Tabrina cheering their daughter on while Evette
faded into the background. How could it be any other
way?

In her womb, the baby fluttered. That was happening
more and more recently, and if she and Judd were home,
she'd call him over to see if he could feel it. Evette put
a hand to her belly, but Judd only had eyes for Jolie.

He touched the St. Louis Cardinals patch on the
sleeve of her T-shirt. "I like your shirt. Did you get to
go to a game?"

"Yeah, 'cept the Cardinals lost."

"Oh, that's too bad."

"Mama said we oughta ask for our money back."

Judd threw back his head and laughed. "Oh, I just bet she did."

His laughter was genuine, but it stung Evette to have a memory of Tabrina make Judd smile. Another bond he shared with his firstborn.

It startled her to realize that her first child would not be Judd's firstborn. *Firstborn.* A word she would have to strike from her vocabulary. She blinked. She needed to stop this. It wasn't helping.

She forced herself to look at Jolie with eyes of compassion. It wasn't the little girl's fault she was caught in the middle of this situation.

Judd engaged his daughter in conversation the way he did with his teenage basketball players. He had always been good with kids. Evette loved babies, and the whole idea of being a mother. But if she were honest, the thought of having older children who could speak their own minds, make choices that might embarrass their parents, choose to disobey, scared her to death.

"So…your grandma told you you'd be coming home with us, right?" Judd said.

Jolie's eyes grew wide with apprehension. "Only for a couple of days."

He and Evette exchanged looks, then turned to Carla. She looked away quickly and bent to fiddle with something on Tabrina's bed. What exactly had Carla told Jolie?

"How far is it?" Jolie asked.

"To our house? It's about an hour…" He touched the patch on her sleeve again. "Maybe a little more. We live about halfway between here and St. Louis."

She nodded solemnly. "That's a long, long way."

"Yes, I guess it is," Judd agreed.

He looked over his shoulder at Evette, and she could read his mind. He wanted to tell Jolie that she could visit her mama and her grandma anytime she wanted to.

That wasn't a promise they could keep. Especially not with Judd's coaching schedule and tax season. She took a step toward them, and lowered her voice. "We can talk to your grandma—and your mama, too—on the phone between visits. Maybe you can write some letters, too, or send an e-mail or send your schoolwork so they can see it. Would you like that?"

She wrinkled her forehead. "I'm goin' to school?"

"Sure. You want to finish first grade."

Her chin bobbed. "At my school. With Rebecca and Katesha, ain't that right?"

Evette and Judd exchanged glances again, and she was grateful when he fielded the question. "Well, no, honey. You'll go to Hanover Falls, where we live. There are only a few weeks left before school's out for the summer, but, we'll get you enrolled—signed up—so you can move to second grade next year. You don't want to get behind, do you?"

"But…I won't know anybody at your school."

Carla jumped in. "You will after your first day, now, won't you?"

Jolie dropped her head. "Just for a couple days, right, Grams?"

"We'll talk about that later, girl." Carla became preoccupied with a hangnail.

Oh, dear… Evette felt terrible for bringing up the subject of school. There was so much they still hadn't talked about with Carla—and she and Judd with each other. They should have checked to see exactly what

Carla had told Jolie. Maybe Judd had, but he should have passed that information on to her. And somebody needed to make certain that Jolie understood what was happening. They had to communicate or this would never work.

A nurse in colorful hospital scrubs rolled a blood pressure cart into the room. When she saw the room full of visitors, she drew back with a broad smile. "Whoa! Looks like there's a party going on in here. Can I ask you to take it out to the waiting area for a few minutes while I get this lady's vitals?"

Judd rose to his feet.

Carla looked pointedly at him. "You probably need to be going anyway."

He nodded and knelt in front of the chair again. "Jolie…" Evette recognized the forced brightness in his voice. "We thought we'd stop for supper on the way home. Where would you like to eat?"

"I'm not hungry."

Evette stooped beside Judd. "Do you like hamburgers?"

"Can I have French fries?"

"Sure," Judd said.

"A milk shake?"

"You bet."

"Okay. I guess so…" Jolie slipped off the chair and pushed past them to stand by Carla.

"You go say goodbye to your mama now, girl. You might not see her again for a couple of days."

Evette wanted to strangle the woman for raising the child's hopes. She surely didn't think they were going to make this drive to Springfield every two days.

To Evette's surprise, Jolie went to the side of the bed,

climbed onto the bottom rung of the bed rail and leaned over to plant a kiss on her mother's cheek, as though this were routine.

Tabrina didn't move. Her face remained flaccid, showing no expression. If not for the monitor flashing her vital signs, Evette wouldn't have believed there was any life in her.

But Jolie seemed immune to her state and turned away, skipping toward the door. She couldn't understand the import of this moment, and yet Evette found herself praying that she would remember this time with her mother. Something told her it might be their last moments together.

Jolie blew another kiss toward the hospital bed. "Bye-bye, Mama. I'll see you tomorrow."

No one corrected her. No one said, *No, honey, it won't be tomorrow. Or the next day, or even the day after that.* How did you explain the concept of time to a six-year-old, especially when the adults weren't sure what would happen from minute to minute?

Carla motioned for Evette and Judd to go with Jolie. "I'll meet you down in the lobby. I need to talk to the nurse."

They caught up with the little girl by the elevator. She'd already pushed the down arrow and the doors opened a few seconds later. They stepped inside the car and Judd reached for the keypad, but Jolie beat him to it and confidently pressed the button for the lobby. Sad that she'd become so comfortable with life in the hospital.

They didn't even have a chance to sit down in the lobby waiting room before Carla emerged from the adjacent elevator. She put a hand on Jolie's head. "Come on, girl. Let's go get your things out of Grams's car." She made a beeline for the front doors, suddenly all business.

Judd brought the Caliber around and they transferred

a tiny suitcase and a small tote bag from Carla's trunk, along with the booster seat for the car. Good thing, too. Evette hadn't thought about that.

Judd slammed the hatch closed and turned, waiting, Evette knew, for the two to say their goodbyes.

Carla's jaw worked and she reached to tuck a flyaway strand that had escaped Jolie's headband. "You be a good girl, okay?"

Jolie nodded. "I *am* a good girl."

Carla smiled, but her chin quivered and she gave Jolie a one-armed hug. "Yes…you are. You're a very good girl." Her voice fractured. She rummaged in her purse for something but came up empty-handed—and dry-eyed—a moment later. "Well, you'd better go. Now you be good," she said again.

Evette didn't trust her own voice, so she went to open the back door of the Caliber. She dug the seat belts out of the crevice and tried to figure out how the booster seat was supposed to fit.

"Here, let me get that." Judd's voice came from behind. She ducked under his arm and stood in silence with Jolie while Judd muttered to himself as he worked with the mechanism.

She looked around the parking lot for Carla, but she had disappeared.

Jolie popped her thumb out of her mouth long enough to point. "That part goes right there."

Judd followed her instructions, then looked at her with amusement. "Well, I'll be! You're right." He straightened, and tugged on the strap. "There. That should do it. See if that works." He helped Jolie into the seat, pulled the seat belt around her and locked it in place.

Evette tried to imagine an infant car seat on the other side of the backseat and a feeling of panic built inside her. She wasn't ready for this.

Not for any of it.

Chapter Ten

"Is McDonald's okay with you, Jolie?" Judd turned on his blinker and waited for traffic to thin in front of the McDonald's drive-through. He searched for Jolie's reflection in the rearview mirror, but saw only the top of the backseat.

Alarmed, he turned and leaned around his seat. Jolie sat with her head down, her curly hair forming a dark curtain over her face. Her shoulders heaved.

"Jolie?" He patted Evette's knee to get her attention, but she was already twisting in her seat, her forehead furrowed.

Judd took advantage of a short break in traffic and turned into the McDonald's parking lot. He eased the car between two minivans and cut the engine.

"Jolie? What's wrong?"

Evette reached between the front seats and touched the little girl's knee. "What's the matter, honey?"

She'd been quiet since they pulled out of the hospital parking lot half an hour ago, answering their questions with one-word replies. But now that he thought about it, why wouldn't she be upset? Poor little kid. It had to be scary being sent off with two people you'd never met before.

Please help us reassure her, Lord. Give us the words…

"Are you hungry, sweetie?" Evette unlatched her seat belt and leaned farther between the seats, putting a hand on Jolie's arm.

It touched him to see her be so tender with Jolie. But a moment later, he watched in the mirror as Jolie shook Evette off and buried her head deeper in her lap.

Jolie's tears escalated to muffled wails. "I want Mama. I wanna go back to the hospital."

She hunched so far over in the booster seat, Judd was afraid the seat belt would strangle her. Now what were they supposed to do?

"It'll be okay, Jolie…" Evette retreated from between the seats and shot Judd a look of desperation. "What should we do?" she whispered.

"I don't know." Feeling helpless, he climbed out of the car, opened the back door and squatted down. "Jolie?"

No response.

"Do you want something to eat? We can take it home and you can eat it later if you want."

"I want Mama! I want Grams." Her sobs bordered on the verge of hysterics now and a middle-aged couple leaving the restaurant gave him the evil eye as they walked to their car. What would they think if they could see Jolie?

Not knowing what else to do, he climbed back behind the wheel and started the car. "I guess we'll just go home," he said softly to Evette.

She barely nodded, her lips pressed together hard.

At the drive-through, he ordered burgers and fries and a salad for Evette, then headed back to the highway.

Jolie sobbed for several miles until her cries finally turned to pathetic whimpers. What had they gotten themselves into? This wasn't how he'd pictured things. He wasn't so naive that he didn't realize there would be a period of adjustment, but he hadn't imagined that Jolie would be completely inconsolable.

The sun had barely started its decline into the western sky when they pulled into the city limits of Hanover Falls. He wished it were bedtime so they could all have a fresh start tomorrow. But a whole afternoon and evening loomed ahead of them. He looked at his watch. He needed to head to practice in a couple of hours, but how could he leave Evette with Jolie like this?

He couldn't… But even as the thought formed in his mind, relief swept through him at the prospect of calling someone to cover for him. He knew all too well the *reason* for his relief: it meant one more day he could put off talking to his team about his daughter.

The hamburger bun was tough as cardboard and the fries were frigid—and untouched. "Jolie," Evette coaxed, "do you want me to make you a peanut-butter-and-jelly sandwich?" She did not want to start off on the wrong foot, giving Jolie the impression that she ran a short-order restaurant here, but the poor kid had to be hungry. It had been three hours since they left the hospital, and she didn't know when Jolie had eaten before that.

But the little girl who'd been so cheerful and talkative at the hospital was somber now. Frighteningly so.

Judd carried the cold food into the kitchen.

Evette tagged behind him, keeping her voice low. "She has to eat something."

He shrugged and dumped the McDonald's fare in the garbage disposal. "We can't force her. She'll eat when she's hungry."

"Maybe we should call Carla…"

"What is she going to do?"

"I don't know, but we have to do something."

"We can't call Carla. We'll just have to fig—"

The phone made them both jump. Judd leaned to look at the caller ID. "It's your mother."

"Great…just great." She gave a little growl. "Don't answer it."

"You know her… She'll keep calling until you do. Or she'll call your cell."

Evette rolled her eyes. "Fine…I'll take it in our room."

He glanced toward Jolie. "Don't be long." The look of panic on his face was almost comical. Almost.

She snatched the phone from the base and hurried down the hallway, answering in her cheeriest voice. "Hi, Mother."

"Evette? What took you so long to answer? I hope I'm not interrupting anything…?" For once she was glad her mother never simply came out and asked what they were doing.

"No…we just finished lunch."

"So late? It's almost two o'clock."

"Well, we ate out." She slipped into their bedroom and nudged the door closed with her toe.

"That's nice. Where'd you eat?"

"McDonald's."

Her mother practically snorted. "McDonald's?"

She had walked into that one. "I just had a salad."

Her mother made a familiar clucking noise with her tongue. "You don't eat enough to keep a bird alive. You're eating for two now, you know. We want a fat, happy baby come summer."

"That eating-for-two business is an old wives' tale, Mother." Evette feigned a laugh and changed the subject. "How's Daddy?"

"Oh, he's fine. He's golfing with Merlon. Those two have been out on the driving range until dark every night this week. I don't know how they can hit that silly ball all afternoon and not go stark raving mad. It's not even decent weather yet."

"Have you talked to Annie lately?" She plopped down on the bed and braced herself to hear one of her mother's glowing accounts of her perfect sister with Geoffrey the perfect husband, two perfect sons, perfect house, perfect—

"Oh! I almost forgot. That's why I'm calling. Annie wants to throw a baby shower for you. She wanted it to be a surprise, but I told her it would be impossible to find a time if we had to work around your schedule and Judd's, too."

Evette sent up a silent prayer of thanks that her mother had nixed the surprise party idea. She scrambled for an out, even as resentment crept in. A month ago, she would have loved nothing more than to have her sister throw her an extravagant baby shower. Now... "I really don't know, Mother. Things are pretty crazy around here." That much was true.

"Don't worry, we won't schedule it until after basketball's over."

"Why, are the guys invited?"

"Oh heavens, no! I just figured Judd would come up with you is all. You don't need to be driving by yourself in your condition, but I know basketball is all he's thinking about for a while. Until the tournaments are over."

Basketball was the least of their worries. And she couldn't avoid it much longer. Even if they only had Jolie for a few weeks, she would have to tell her parents about Judd's indiscretion. The minute they made a public appearance here in Hanover Falls with Jolie, word was bound to make its way to her parents in St. Louis. If you so much as sneezed in the Falls, you were likely to land on three prayer chains.

Did Judd plan to call his parents? He hadn't mentioned it, but they'd have to be told eventually. Of course, the McGlins were halfway across the country and not as likely to hear it through the grapevine, especially since they'd become less and less involved in Judd's life over the last few years.

But there was simply no way around it. Her family had to be told, and the sooner the better. She sighed. Then Annie's Geoffrey would suddenly become even more noble and intelligent and wealthy—don't forget wealthy—in her mother's eyes.

"Evette? Are you there?"

"I'm here, Mother. Sorry…you were saying?"

"Are you okay?"

"I'm fine. I just…got distracted. What were you saying?"

"Just that Annie's trying to put together a guest list. Aunt Bertie and Aunt Carol, and Marty Zimmerman… you remember Marty? And we thought we'd invite some of your college friends…"

Ah…*we*. This was probably all her mother's idea in the first place. "I'll have to talk to Judd and get back to you, okay?"

"Are you sure you're feeling okay? You sound a little off."

"I'm just tired."

"You'll feel better in a couple of months. The first trimester is always the hardest."

She was almost midway through her second trimester, but Evette didn't bother to correct her mother. "Can I call you back, Mother? I'll talk to Judd and let you know later in the week."

"Oh…okay. But don't wait too long. We need— Well, Annie's wanting to get this thing planned. Get the invitations out, you know."

"I know. I'll get back to you soon."

Evette sank onto the bed. They had to start telling people. She could put her mother off for a few more days, but they had to decide what they were going to say…how much they were going to reveal.

Looking longingly at her pillow, she rose, smoothed the coverlet at the foot of the bed and reached for the door. What she wanted to do was crawl under the quilts and stay there until this was all over.

Chapter Eleven

"Are you sure you don't want something to eat? I think there's ice cream in the freezer." Judd pulled out a chair and sat next to Jolie at the table in the breakfast nook. She'd been in their care for more than six hours now, and hadn't done more than pick at the meals they'd put in front of her. Could a kid go that long without food with no ill effects?

Head still bowed, she peeked up at him through squinty eyes and shook her head again.

"Okay. If you're sure. But you let us know if you change your mind, okay?"

No response.

With Jolie still seated, he gently scooted out her chair and pivoted it so she was facing him. "Why don't I show you where your room is and we can get your stuff put away, okay?"

She stared at him with the same suspicious look she'd given them at the hospital when they told her she'd be going to school in Hanover Falls. The poor child had to be beyond confused. But what could they tell her? He didn't have any idea how long she'd be with them. None of them did. It might be weeks… It might be forever.

He reached for the little lime-green rolling suitcase and matching backpack she'd brought. They'd unloaded the car and piled all her things by the door waiting for her to finish her lunch.

She slid off the chair and stood there, looking lost and uncertain.

"Here…" He handed Jolie the backpack and pasted on a smile. "Follow me. It's right back here."

At the guest-room door, he motioned her in. "Here you go. All yours." Across the hall, the door to the master bedroom was closed. Evette must have still been on the phone with her mother.

He plopped the suitcase on the floor at the foot of the bed. He probably should wait for Evette. She no doubt had a certain way she wanted things put away. But for lack of anything else to talk to his daughter about, he started opening drawers in the dresser. "You can take everything out of your suitcase and put it in here. Do you want some help?"

She shrugged, but knelt in front of the suitcase and slowly unzipped it and propped the lid open against the bed. She pulled out a black stuffed dog with fur that looked a little like Jolie's hair.

"Who's that?"

"Barksey."

"Hello there, Barksey. I hope you're a well-behaved doggie." He patted the dog's head and eyed Jolie. "He doesn't eat much, does he?"

Jolie ignored him. She pulled the dog away and stroked its head, arranging its floppy ears before setting it on the bed.

The few clothes that were in the child-size suitcase had shifted to the bottom in a jumble. Was this all she'd brought with her? Two or three T-shirts and a couple of pairs of jeans? Something that looked like pajamas, and a pile of socks and underwear. A pair of high-top tennis shoes stuck out from the wad of fabric. That was it. Maybe Carla planned to mail her other things.

He watched her sort through her belongings, touching each item but not removing anything, as if she couldn't decide what to put away first.

He pulled the bottom drawer open a few more inches. "Here, you can put your jeans in this one."

She looked at him, and he thought her expression softened a little.

He plopped down cross-legged on the carpet beside her. She reached into the case and handed him two tiny pairs of jeans. She held up some pink sweatpants. "These, too? They're not jeans…"

"Close enough." He folded each pair of pants in half and layered them in the drawer. "Is that all?"

She nodded.

He closed the drawer and opened the next one. "How about shirts in this one?"

"Uh-huh." She handed him a T-shirt, then another.

He folded each and placed them in the drawer, closing it, too, when she'd put the last one in his hands. "Okay, next? Looks like pj's?"

When they'd finished that drawer he peered into her case. "Okay, socks…and um…undies." He put a hand to his mouth and tried to imitate a first-grader's snicker.

She giggled, and he screwed his face up in a goofy expression that made her laugh harder.

"I think I'll let you put those away." He opened the top drawer. "Right here."

She scooped up the remaining contents of her suitcase and unceremoniously dumped them into the drawer, slammed it shut and turned, pressing her back against the dresser. "Undies?"

"Yep. That's what we call 'em around here."

She wrinkled her nose. "You're funny."

In that moment, he saw Tabrina in her face. The memories came flooding back. Did his daughter have anything of *him* in her? When Tabrina looked at her, had she ever seen a glimpse of him in Jolie's grin, in the furrow of her brow or the crinkle of her hazel eyes?

The old feelings washed over him and he fought them off. Jolie's entrance into his life—their lives—had nothing to do with Tabrina, really. He had to remember that. There was no reason he couldn't love Jolie apart from Tabrina. This didn't have to be a setback.

He pushed the long-ago memories of Tabrina from his mind, forced himself to think about how far he and Evette had come, how far *he* had come in learning to forget his first love and love his wife the way a husband should.

It was a gift, having this chance to get to know his daughter. Astonishing, really, that he'd even learned of her existence. He could treasure that without delving into the past, without examining his emotions too carefully.

"What do I call you?"

He looked up to see Jolie watching him, her head tilted to one side.

"What?" He knew what she was asking, but he was buying himself some time since he didn't know how to answer.

Until this afternoon at the hospital, they hadn't known

that Jolie knew he was her father. Carla hadn't seemed to think Jolie was aware. But apparently Tabrina had told her about him. He might never know exactly what Tabrina had said, and he wasn't sure he wanted to know.

"Do I call you Dad?"

No! Yes…yes, of course. I am your father. "I'm…not sure, Jolie. What do you think your mom would think about that? She told you about me, huh?"

Jolie nodded, but she didn't offer the details he craved. But how could he deny his own flesh and blood the right to call him "Dad"?

"Do you *want* to call me Dad?"

She beamed and wagged her head. The first real smile he'd seen on her face since they'd left the hospital.

"Then I guess Dad it is." He felt like he'd stepped off a cliff, but the plunge was exhilarating.

Until he looked up to see Evette standing in the doorway.

Instantly, he thought of the night Carla called and started this chain of events. Evette had stood in another doorway in this same hallway, with the same pain and fear written on her face.

It didn't seem fair that his mistake with Tabrina was resulting in something very close to joy for him. He had a precious daughter, and he was being offered an opportunity to get to know her.

But the very things that promised joy for him were bringing heartache to Evette. Where was the justice in that? Jolie could rightfully call him Dad, but she already had a Mama. Not that Evette would have welcomed that label.

And how would she feel about hearing someone else's child call him Dad before their own baby could even form the word?

Chapter Twelve

Evette felt like a spy standing in the doorway, watching Judd play doting father to his daughter. Somehow he'd managed to get the sullen little girl to smile, giggle even. Evette had always known Judd would be a wonderful father, but never had she dreamed he would play that role to another woman's child.

Judd looked up and saw her standing there. If she had to give a name to the expression that flashed in his eyes, it would be guilt.

"Hey, babe." He stood quickly, smiling a little too brightly. He zipped Jolie's suitcase shut. "We got all her clothes put away. Didn't we, Jolie?"

"Uh-huh." Jolie didn't look at Evette, but kept her eyes glued on Judd.

"That's good." Evette took the suitcase from Judd and deposited it on the floor of the closet. "Do you want to play in the yard for a while?"

Again, Jolie looked to Judd, as if awaiting his permission, or his assurance that the mean stepmother wasn't luring her with a poison apple.

"Good idea. Let's go outside. I'll show you the yard."

"Do you have a dog?" She looked hopeful.

"No, sorry. We don't even have a cat. Did you and your—did you have any pets? In Springfield?"

"Mama wouldn't let me. She said they were too 'spensive."

"Well, that's true. It costs quite a bit to keep a pet." Jolie trailed him down the hall.

Evette started to follow, but realized that Judd was completely caught up in his conversation with Jolie.

"A hamster doesn't cost much. Katesha got one at PetSmart and it only cost like eight dollars."

"Yeah," Judd said, "but what about the cage and the food and trips to the vet?"

"Man!" Jolie stopped mid-strut and propped her hands on her slim hips, sporting major attitude. "You sound like my mama."

Judd laughed.

"Katesha got a cage and stuff at a garage sale."

"Oh she did, did she? Well, that would help…"

Their voices faded. Evette heard the back door slam, and the house was silent again.

She went to the window and peered out, trying to stay hidden behind the draperies, trying not to feel that she was eavesdropping.

Judd had grabbed a basketball from the garage, and he and Jolie passed it back and forth. He seemed so comfortable and natural with her. As if he'd been her father— her *daddy*—for her whole life.

She pulled the curtains on the scene and went to throw a load of Judd's sweat suits in the washer.

Judd and Jolie came in half an hour later, laughing— giggling—about something. He skimmed by Evette as she came from the laundry room, not offering to let her in on the joke. She didn't ask.

He went to the refrigerator and opened the door. "Are you hungry yet, Jolie? What sounds good? I bet Evette could whip us up a snack."

Oh, sure…good ol' Evette. She can just whip up anything your little heart desires…right after she scours the floors and scrubs the toilets. Resentment simmered, but she pasted on a smile and played along. "Sure. How about some cheese and crackers? Do you like cheese?"

"Do you got that squirt kind?"

"No. Sorry. We only have the kind you slice. Cheddar."

Jolie nodded. "I like that, too."

"Okay. Well, have a seat."

Judd pulled out the chair in the breakfast nook where Jolie had sat earlier. She wriggled into the seat and put her forearms on the table, watching Evette in the kitchen.

Judd pulled a carton of milk from the refrigerator. "You want something to drink?"

"Not milk."

"How about orange juice?" He held up the container.

"Do you got some root beer?"

Judd started to speak at the same time Evette did. "Root beer?" He practically had his keys in hand, ready to run down to the convenience store on the corner for root beer if that would make his girl happy.

Evette overruled him. "Let's have either milk or juice right now."

Jolie smiled. "Orange juice, please."

The "please" went a long way toward tempering Evette's resentment.

Jolie built sandwiches of a short stack of crackers and cheese and devoured them. "Can I have more?"

Evette hurried to answer before Judd could. "We don't want to spoil your dinner."

"What's for dinner?"

Judd laughed and looked to Evette, obviously relieved that Jolie's appetite had returned.

She shrugged. "I haven't thought about it yet. Jolie, why don't you go see what's on TV?" She gestured toward the family room just off the kitchen. She and Judd had already decided they would severely limit how much television their baby watched, but this was different. How else did you entertain a six-year-old?

Jolie nodded and went to stand in front of the TV in the family room on the other side of the kitchen bar.

Judd carried her dishes to the sink, then went to the family room with Jolie. Evette heard the adolescent banter from some after-school show on TV. Probably not the best choice for a six-year-old, but she wasn't going to argue.

Judd came back to the kitchen. "I need to go in to the office later tonight, but how about if we all take a walk before dinner?"

She hesitated. "Where?"

"Just around the neighborhood."

"Judd…do you really think that's a good idea?"

"Why wouldn't it be?"

Evette shook her head. Judd was in some sort of denial. Had he really not thought things through enough to realize that they were going to have to answer some hard questions when they started showing up places with Jolie in tow?

"Fine, introduce her around town." She lowered her voice and hooked a thumb toward the family room, where Jolie sat entranced in front of the TV. "But you might want to make it quick…before she calls you Daddy in front of someone who doesn't have a clue what's going on with us."

His stunned look told her she was right—he hadn't thought about the reaction they might get. But he regained his composure and moved closer. "Then you heard me earlier, telling her she could…call me Daddy." It wasn't a question. "Evette, I didn't—"

She didn't give him a chance to explain. "That was not fair, Judd. How is that going to sound to people?" It seemed that Judd was suddenly happy about everything that had happened. And that made his betrayal all the more difficult to stomach. "Before you get any cozy little fantasies in your head, just know that she's not calling me *Mom.* She has a mother. And it's not me! It can't ever be me. Do you get that?"

"Evette…" He sighed and straightened, pressing his back against the kitchen counter. "I don't know how many different ways I can say I'm sorry. What do you want me to do about it? About any of this?" He looked into the family room, as if he was worried Jolie might hear him. "It kills me to see how much pain this is causing you, but there isn't one thing I can do about it. I can't change anything now."

She was being ridiculous, feeling jealous of a six-year-old. She knew she was. *I'm sorry, Lord. Please help me to have a right attitude about this.* "I know. I know, Judd. I'm sorry."

He held out his arms and she went into them. The baby between them kept her from being able to get as close to Judd as she wanted to—needed to—but she twisted until she was comfortable, then put her head on his shoulder.

He stroked her hair and kissed the top of her head. "We have to tell people, Evie. I have to tell my team and the staff at school…at the office, too. And…and my parents. Did you tell your mom?"

She shook her head against his shoulder.

"We need to let them know, Evette."

She leaned away from him. "We?"

He ducked his head. "I'm sorry… I'll tell them. I…I just didn't want to tell your family without your permission."

"No." She held her hands out like a traffic cop and backed away from him. "Absolutely not. This needs to come from me." Her mother would have her head on a platter if she heard the news from Judd.

"All right…I understand. We should call Pastor Mike and let the church know, too," Judd said.

"The whole church?" Cornerstone Community Church had been their church home for over four years now and they truly felt they'd found a church family, but the church was growing quickly and there were many members they barely knew. "How do you propose to do that?"

"I don't know. We'll ask Mike what he thinks would be best. We're going to need their support."

She shook her head. "Why do we even have to tell anyone, Judd? Not yet. Let's…let's wait and see how she—how Tabrina—gets along. Maybe we can lie low for a few weeks…maybe we won't have to say anything."

"No." He looked at the floor, shaking his head. "Evie…"

She knew that tone in his voice. He was going to say something important. Something decisive. She took another step back.

He reached for her hand, tried to pull her back to him. But when she resisted, he let her go and placed his palms on the counter behind him. She watched the tendons in his forearms tense, then lifted her head to look into his hazel eyes.

He met her gaze. "We can't hole up in here waiting to see if Tabrina gets better. But, Evie…even if she recovers and we're not needed for Jolie anymore, I want to have a relationship with my daughter. And I want you to be a part of that. Please…"

She deflated. She'd fantasized about a phone call from Carla saying they'd found a nursing facility for Tabrina, and that Carla was ready to take Jolie back. In her fantasy, the call came just in time so they didn't have to tell anyone, and they could go back to their lives the way they'd been before. But it was just that—a fantasy.

This wasn't going to go away. One way or another they were in this for the long haul. If she didn't want to lose her husband, she'd better get used to the idea.

"Okay. I understand, Judd. I really do. Then what exactly are we going to tell people? We need to—" She put a hand to her mouth. "I started to say 'We need to get our stories straight,' but that makes it sound like we're coming up with a big lie. I know you want to be honest. But…"

"But do we have to tell everything? Is that what you were going to say?"

She nodded.

"When we say Jolie is my daughter, well, it doesn't leave much to the imagination, does it?"

"No. It doesn't."

"Evie, do you believe God is in this?"

"What do you mean?"

"I think God's hand is on everything that's happened. I'm not trying to whitewash my sin. But since then… getting to be with Jolie today, getting to know her…" He looked at the floor. "I don't know. I found myself glad that something happened so that she'll grow up knowing who her father is. Not that I would ever wish this on Tabrina…I don't mean that…"

"I know," she said.

"But I'm glad that now Jolie will know she has a father who loves her." He beckoned her to his side.

But she couldn't make her feet move.

He didn't force her, but gave her a tender look. "I love you, Evie, and I want you to share this with me. Maybe it's too much to ask, but I want you to love my daughter the way I'm growing to."

"How can you say that already? That you love her? You've only known her for one day. It…it's going to take some time for me, Judd. I'm sorry. You're going to have to be patient with me."

He nodded, his eyes brimming with hope. "I'll give you as much time as you need."

"We don't have as much time as I need, Judd. That's not a luxury we can—"

The doorbell fractured her sentence. She looked at Judd, wondering if he was expecting someone, but he shrugged.

He started for the door, but Jolie darted from the family room. "That's my Grams!"

Again, Evette looked to Judd. He hadn't said anything about Carla coming. His confused expression told her he was not expecting Jolie's grandmother or anyone else.

Jolie flung the door wide and Evette froze.

Chapter Thirteen

"Hey, Coach."

Evette recognized Rafe Clairmont's voice through the screen door.

Judd stepped between Jolie and the door. "Hi, Rafe... James...what's up?"

Since he'd had started coaching, she and Judd had always opened their home to the team. Many a Saturday morning the family room was crowded with a dozen or more gangly teens watching game film with Coach McGlin. But Judd always gave her fair warning if the guys were coming over. He hadn't said anything today.

Surely he wasn't so thoughtless that he'd invited them now?

But he opened the screen door and stepped back to usher in Rafe and James Severn, two of his senior basketball players.

Rafe gave her a glib wave. "Hey, Mrs. McGlin."

James followed suit, except his greeting seemed halfway genuine. Rafe had never been her favorite, though Judd had always had a soft spot in his heart for the kid. "He just needs some direction," Judd had told her more than once.

"Hi, guys. Good game the other night." She tried to catch Judd's eye to signal for him to get rid of these guys. What was he thinking, letting them in?

Jolie chose that moment to peek around Judd's legs.

Rafe looked down and gave an exaggerated scowl when he saw her. He shot Judd a look that said, *Who in the world is that and what is she doing here?*

Judd put an arm around Jolie, drawing her close. "What are you guys up to?"

"We were over at the park shooting…just thought we'd stop by. We missed you at practice." Rafe shifted from one foot to the other, his eyes darting between Judd and Jolie.

Judd shot Evette a look she interpreted as apology, then put a hand on Jolie's shoulder. "Guys, this is Jolie. Jolie Jackson."

To Evette's relief, he left it at that.

The boys uttered identical grunts in greeting. Evette wasn't sure if any six-year-old girl would have drawn the same indifference or if they were being particularly rude because Jolie happened to be black. Knowing Rafe's reputation, she suspected the latter, though he was no gentleman regardless. He'd only greeted her as Mrs. McGlin because Judd had insisted on it in the past.

Jolie stood with one arm wrapped possessively around Judd's knee. If she was disappointed that it hadn't been Carla at the door, she didn't show it. There was only curiosity in her eyes now. She didn't seem to be intimidated by the boys in the least, but stared right back at them, her chin jutting out and one shoulder thrown back.

"These guys are on my basketball team," Judd explained.

Jolie's eyes bugged out and she looked up at Judd. "You play basketball?"

Rafe smirked.

Judd winked at him and patted Jolie's head. "I'm the coach."

"Oh. Cool. Can I go watch TV some more?"

"Sure."

She skipped back to the family room like she'd lived here forever.

Rafe cocked his head in her direction. "You babysitting or something?"

Judd cut his eyes toward Evette. "Listen, guys, I'd invite you to stay, but we're kind of in the middle of something." He took a step toward the door. "I'll see you at practice, okay? We're gonna go after it hard tomorrow. Tell the other guys."

They groaned and Judd laughed as he closed the door behind them.

When he turned to Evette, his expression sobered.

She sighed and closed her eyes. "I guess that about seals it."

"What do you mean?"

His tone told her he knew exactly what she meant, but she didn't call him on it. She slumped into a kitchen chair. "You'd better let John Severn know." It wouldn't do to have James's dad, the high-school principal, find out from his son. "And the firm, too. You know this town. We'll be front page news."

He glanced in the direction of the family room where the TV blared. He came around and put his hands on Evette's shoulders. "I'm sorry, Evette. I wish we could wait. But I'm afraid you're right. I'll need to tell the team for sure, and I can't very well do that without talking to John first."

She shook her head, knowing he was right but feeling completely drained by the thought of having her husband's betrayal on parade in front of the entire town.

He squeezed her shoulders, but she shrugged out from under his touch and stood. Suddenly, his touch repulsed her, even as she somehow longed for him to take her in his arms and promise her everything would be okay.

Chapter Fourteen

Judd paced the locker room from one end to the other, and with every step he changed his mind. The team was so close to the conference tournament. This probably wouldn't be as big a deal to them as he imagined, but still, did he want even the slightest risk that his news would take the team's focus off these next crucial games?

This morning he'd told John Severn, the principal, and James and Rafe had seen Jolie. If he didn't explain things, the team would find out from someone else soon enough. That wasn't an option.

But how much should he tell them? The big question hid in the recesses of his brain, too awkward to explore, and yet too important to ignore. Did he tell the team that Jolie was biracial. If he didn't, James or Rafe would. He knew his players would see her as African-American. To them it would be…well, black and white. If he didn't lay that out from the get-go, there would be repercussions. He knew some of these boys too well to ignore that.

He was trying so hard to convince Evette that the color of Jolie's skin shouldn't matter, but the truth was, if he didn't warn his guys—*tell* them… Good grief. *Warn?* Where had that come from? As if Jolie were some monster they needed to be wary of.

But the truth was, while the rest of the world might have progressed past all this, sometimes this little town seemed stuck in the days before the civil rights movement.

Already he loved his daughter with a fierceness he couldn't explain. The color of her skin didn't matter to him. It truly didn't. He'd worked through all those questions, all those emotions, years ago when he was dating Tabrina. Or had he? Then why had he let his parents convince him that being married to Tabrina would never work? And why hadn't he told them about Jolie yet?

He knew the answer to the latter. His relationship with his parents was already fractured beyond repair. This would be the severing blow for them.

He shook off the question. He couldn't think about that now. He had to focus. The caged clock over the office door ticked off the seconds too fast. The final bell had rung, and Coach Hazen was already out on the floor shooting baskets. Practice started in fifteen minutes. He had to make a decision, and live with the fallout.

The thing was, prejudice was alive and well, maybe more than he wanted to admit. If he only told his players part of the story, the rumors that filled in the blanks were likely to be worse than the truth.

Until now, he'd only dwelled on what they would think of him, how it would affect his witness for the Lord, his marriage, his standing in the community. Now it struck him that people's reaction might hurt Jolie. His heart broke to imagine any harm, any emotional pain coming to his little girl over this.

Randall Hazen appeared in the doorway, tossing a basketball from one hand to the other. "You wanna run 'em first today, Coach?"

"No…" Judd filled his lungs and blew out a hard breath. "I need to talk to the guys before practice, Randall. There's…some stuff going on at home I need to let the guys know about. You, too, of course."

The younger coach's brow furrowed. "Everything's okay with your wife, I hope? The baby?"

"Everything's fine. It's not that. I… We got some news a couple of weeks ago that's put our lives in a tailspin. I guess you could say my past has kind of come back to haunt me."

Randall leaned forward, curiosity thick on his face. Judd knew he'd see that same eager interest in his players' eyes a few minutes from now. He hated having this news to tell. To confess. Hated it with everything in him.

Give me the words, Lord. Help them to understand and forgive. Oh, God…I wanted so much to be a good role model to these kids. I'm sorry…

He motioned toward the double doors that led to the gymnasium. "Let's meet out on the bleachers."

"Sure." Coach Hazen followed him into the gym and helped him roll out a section of the bleachers. A few of the players arrived early and shot around for the first five minutes, but as the rest of the team trickled in from the parking lot, Judd directed them to gather on the bleachers.

The usual good-natured clowning around was absent, and Judd didn't miss the silent questions the guys shot one another.

Coach Hazen sat on the front row below the players.

Watching him, Judd started second-guessing himself. He should have talked to Randall first. But his assistant wasn't much older than his senior players, and he wouldn't have said anything different to Randall than he intended to say to the team.

"Hey, guys…eyes up here." He waited till he had their full attention. "There's something I need to talk to you about before we practice today. This— Man, this is going to be harder than I thought." He rubbed his tennis shoe on the shiny wooden floor, working to control his emotions. "I've always preached to you guys that what you do today matters tomorrow. Well, I guess I should have taken my own advice." He gave a humorless laugh.

His fifteen players sat like statues, faces like granite, all eyes glued on him.

"I made a mistake—a big mistake—seven years ago. That's a long time ago…and you know, I thought I'd gotten away with it. I'd pretty much tried to forget about it, because I wasn't proud of what I did. Oh, I'd asked God to forgive me years ago. And He did. I have no doubt of that. But that doesn't mean we—I—don't still have to live with the consequences of my sin. As long as you live on this earth, you can't escape that. It's just the way it is."

He squatted on the floor in front of the bleachers, put his head down for a minute. "What I did, guys, could happen to any one of you. I pray to God it doesn't. But don't think you're the one guy it won't happen to."

The only sound in the gym was the air-conditioner fans running overhead. The players were speculating, he knew, on the confession their coach was about to make. Better spit it out before they all had him pegged in their minds as a serial killer.

"Seven years ago, I was engaged to get married. My girlfriend was a sweet, intelligent, Christian woman. A beautiful…African-American woman—"

In the second row, Rafe Clairmont scowled and whispered something to James. Judd wondered if already they were guessing what was to come. Rafe stuck his lower lip out and said something Judd couldn't hear, but by the reaction of the players around him, it was crude—and bigoted.

He could feel the eyes of the entire team on him. Rage boiled up inside of him, but he could not lose his cool. Not now. The way he handled this would set the tone for how this whole thing would be treated by the team.

He leveled a stare at his best post player. "Rafe, I don't even want to know what you just said, but I'd better not hear another word out of you."

Rafe's face turned crimson, but he dipped his head and mumbled an apology. "Sorry, Coach."

"Can I go on?"

As one, the players gave a solemn nod.

"My parents weren't too happy about me dating this girl. And—we ended up breaking off our relationship." He realized too late that he might have given the impression that it was a mutual breakup. He didn't correct himself, but went on. "I didn't know it. Tabr—" He caught himself before he used her name. No use dragging her name into this. "My fiancée never told me, but she was pregnant at the time we broke up."

A murmur went up from the bleachers, and the players gave each other wide-eyed looks. Judd held up a hand and they quieted immediately, eager, no doubt, for him to spill the details.

"I might have gone on never knowing that I had…a daughter." He swallowed hard, picturing Jolie's sweet smile. "But her mother got sick a few weeks ago and now it's my responsibility—my privilege—to take care of my little six-year-old girl."

"Oh, man! That bites." Rafe nudged James Severn and Judd knew they were putting two and two together, if they hadn't before. "So now you have to pay alimony?" Rafe asked.

Brent Harper gave him a harmless shove. "Not alimony, you idiot…child support. Alimony's when you have to pay the ex-wife."

Judd gave a rueful smile. "Neither one, guys. It's called being a father. Jolie has come to live with us. We're raising her—my wife and I. At least for now. Until her mother gets better…" He was shocked to realize that his thoughts had shifted dramatically from a few weeks ago when that was his hope…his prayer. Now, much as he prayed Tabrina would recover, he dreaded the day they'd have to pack up Jolie's little green suitcase and take her back to Springfield.

He straightened and attempted to make eye contact with each player. "I never dreamed that one really bad choice—not waiting until I was married—would someday come back to me in the form of a little girl who needs to be taken care of for the rest of her childhood. But it did."

He stopped to let that sink in.

"I want you guys to know that I've asked God to forgive me. I've asked my wife to forgive me…" It struck him that he probably also owed apologies to Tabrina… and Jolie, though she was too young to understand now. But that wasn't any of the team's business.

He started again. "I know some of you are sitting

here right now thinking it would never happen to you. I thought the same thing." He was bordering on getting preachy. He hadn't meant to do that. Time to wrap it up.

"Okay, guys. I appreciate you listening. I just wanted you to hear it from me. You'll probably be seeing my daughter at some of the games. Her name's Jolie. I…I just didn't want you wondering."

He pushed off the floor and rose to his full height, feeling a little light-headed. "Oh, just one more thing. I know how rumors get around a little town like this. I'd appreciate it when you're talking to your friends and your parents, if you'd only repeat what I told you here today, okay? If you didn't hear it from me, it's probably just a rumor."

They nodded solemnly.

"Okay. That's it." He scooped his clipboard off the bottom row of the bleachers. "Now let's get a good practice under our belts. We've got our work cut out for us Friday night."

Brent pushed off the bench, clutching a basketball under one arm. "Thanks, Coach. For telling us…"

A quiet chorus of similar comments filtered down the bleachers as the boys headed past him onto the gym floor.

Coach Hazen clapped him on the shoulder. "Sure 'preciate your honesty, Coach."

Judd felt like the weight of the world had been lifted from his shoulders. Maybe some of his players would even learn from his mistake. *Father, use me to reach them. And help me to reach Evie, too, I'm sorry, Lord, for the pain I caused her.* A cloak of peace settled over him.

He only hoped Evette would feel the same comfort after she'd told the people she needed to tell.

Chapter Fifteen

"How'd it go?"

Evette studied Judd as he deposited the day's mail and two full Wal-Mart bags on the kitchen counter. She couldn't read his face.

He looked through to the family room. "Where is she?"

"She's in her room."

"Why? Is she okay?"

"She's fine. She's just playing."

"With what? There was hardly anything in her bags." He pushed the Wal-Mart bags toward Evette. "I picked up some stuff for her. I didn't know what to get…maybe you'd better make sure this is all okay for her age."

Evette dug through the contents of the plastic sacks and pulled out a large box of crayons, several coloring and activity books, a jump rope, a set of jacks, Play-Doh, a Candy Land game… "You bought the entire toy aisle?"

"Well, I wasn't sure what to get for a girl her age."

"She's fine, Judd. I had those markers we got for the garage sale. She colored with those for a while, and then

I let her play with some dishes. She's in there 'making dinner' for us." She scratched quotation marks in the air.

"You're brilliant." He came around the counter and gave her a quick kiss. "So, you two got along okay?"

She kissed him back, more so she wouldn't have to answer his question than because she was feeling loving. Because she wasn't. Judd hadn't bought one thing for their baby. Not even a little basketball. When Annie was pregnant with their first baby, Geoffrey had practically bought out Toys "R" Us. The kid had a bicycle he wouldn't be able to ride for another two years.

Lately, Judd had barely talked about their baby, let alone shown any interest in buying toys. Now, suddenly, he was home with two Wal-Mart bags brimming with toys for his daughter?

He eyed the clock above the stove. "What did you guys have for supper?"

"We haven't eaten yet."

"Really? Evette, it's almost seven."

"We never eat before seven."

"But…don't kids need to eat earlier than that?"

"She's fine, Judd." Jolie had played quietly in her room most of the day, barely saying two words to Evette, but she wasn't going to tell him that.

"So what are we having?" he pressed.

"There's some leftover casserole from the other night. I thought I'd heat that up. Okay?"

He shrugged. "I guess. We should probably start eating healthier. Do we have stuff for a fruit salad? I could throw one together," he added quickly—guiltily, she thought.

She got apples and grapes from the refrigerator and set them on the counter for him. At least he offered to help. Besides, her curiosity wouldn't let her give him the silent treatment. "How did it go…talking to the team?"

"It went well. Let me change my clothes real quick and we'll talk while we get dinner." He scooped up the Wal-Mart bags and went down the hall.

Evette heard him poke his head into the guest room. "Hey, there. How are you?"

"Hi, Dad!"

Evette closed her eyes and forced herself to unclench her jaw.

When Judd came back to the kitchen a few minutes later, Jolie was tagging behind him. The two of them chattered like old friends. She wouldn't get to hear about Judd's talk with the players until after Jolie went to bed. But he'd said it went well, and he was in a good mood.

She heated up the casserole dish in the microwave while Judd cut apples and bananas for the fruit salad.

"Jolie, why don't you set the table?" Judd said.

"What do I do?"

He turned to Evette. "What dishes do you want to use, babe?"

"The ones we always use are fine." She took three plates down from the cupboard. "Here you go." She placed them in Jolie's outstretched arms. But the dishes somehow slipped through the little girl's hands and clattered to the hardwood floor. Two of the plates broke into jagged, pie-shaped wedges and the third had a fatal crack.

Jolie burst into tears. "I didn't mean to! I didn't mean to!"

Evette put her hands on Jolie's shoulders and steered her away from the sharp pottery shards. "Get out of the way so you don't get cut." She bent and started gathering what was left of her favorite dishes.

Judd dropped the knife he was using, hurriedly wiped his hands on a dish towel and knelt beside her to help. She folded the front of her maternity shirt into an apron and collected the broken pieces in it.

"It was a accident," Jolie whimpered behind them. "They were too heavy. I didn't know they were heavy."

Evette felt her blood pressure soar. "Please…" She spoke through clenched teeth. "Just be quiet until we get the mess cleaned up."

Judd lowered his voice. "It was an accident, Evette."

She looked at him and snapped, "I know it was an accident! Did I say it wasn't?"

He stood and put his hands out, palms up, as if to say "I give up." He stepped around her and she heard him behind her in the pantry, rummaging in the broom closet.

He came back a minute later with a broom and dustpan. "I'll finish up here."

She let him take over. Jolie had disappeared. Evette found her in the family room sitting in an overstuffed chair, her head in her hands. The chair dwarfed her tiny figure. *Lord, help me. I know my attitude isn't right. Please change my heart. Please, God…*

Evette went to her and sat down on the edge of the ottoman.

The little girl almost cowered before her.

Evette felt terrible. The child was terrified. She patted her bony knee. "Hey, it's okay. I know you didn't do it on purpose."

"I'm sorry," Jolie squeaked.

"I know you are. You can be sorry it happened, but you don't owe me an apology. I should have told you how heavy they were. Those old dishes are even too heavy for me if I try to carry too many of them at once.

It's a good thing we weren't having sixteen people for dinner." She pantomimed balancing a tall stack of heavy dishes.

Jolie giggled through her tears. "Then you woulda had to buy new dishes for sure."

"Let's go see if Judd has all the sharp pieces cleaned up. You must be getting hungry."

Jolie sniffed the air and nodded. "It smells good."

"It does, doesn't it?" Evette took her hand. "Come on, let's go eat."

Judd smiled wide when he saw them enter the kitchen hand in hand. "Everybody okay?"

He looked like an overeager puppy and she wanted to slap the goofy, fake grin right off of his face. The image made her giggle.

"What?"

She shook her head. "Nothing."

"What?"

"Nothing. I'll tell you later. We're hungry."

"Great! Everybody sit down. I'll serve you."

His enthusiasm drew another laugh, and he gave her a look that said he didn't have a clue. Well, that was for sure. He didn't. She understood his desire for her and Jolie to get along, but ever since they'd brought his daughter home, Evette had felt pressured. As if he were pushing her off the diving board before she knew how to swim. She had to do this at her own pace, and on her own terms. It took every ounce of energy she could muster just to go through the motions. It wasn't fair of him to expect her to warm up to Jolie the way he had.

They needed to talk. And the sooner the better.

Chapter Sixteen

Judd clicked the remote and the TV went silent. He unfolded himself from the sofa and jiggled Jolie's knee. "Come on, squirt. Bedtime."

Jolie frowned, but she wriggled off the overstuffed chair where she'd been curled up, watching television.

Judd cleared his throat and tried to catch Evette's eye, but she scurried around the room, gathering up their popcorn dishes and Coke cans. "We're heading down the hall, babe," he said, hoping she'd accept his veiled invitation.

He supervised teeth-brushing and waited in the hall while Jolie used the bathroom and changed into her pajamas.

Listening for Evette with one ear, he dragged out the bedtime routine, tucking Jolie in, reading a story and saying a bedtime prayer with her.

But ten minutes went by and he heard Evette still rattling around in the kitchen. It didn't take a genius to know she was using the cleanup as an excuse to get out of helping him with the bedtime ritual. This was only the third night they'd had Jolie, and the first two were not nights he wanted to become the norm, or that he even wanted to remember.

Poor kid. So far Jolie had cried for her mother, then cried for Carla each night. He'd stayed up with her, sitting by her bed, grasping for some way to comfort her. He'd come within an inch of calling Carla and telling her she had to come and console the poor girl. Or at least talk to her on the phone. But Jolie would never adjust if they called Carla every time she got a little homesick. She'd finally quieted down around ten o'clock last night and, as far as he knew, she'd slept through the night.

At least she'd woken up happy. He'd stuck around until about nine—making sure Jolie felt comfortable with Evette—then gone in to the firm late. And left early for basketball practice. Karl had been extremely understanding about his situation so far, but he knew the closer they got to April fifteenth, the crankier and less understanding his boss would be. He didn't blame the guy. The timing couldn't have been worse. He was already pushing the limits with the basketball job. But if it weren't for the money, he would sooner give up his CPA job than his coaching position.

He pulled the covers up around Jolie's chin and gave Barksey the dog a pat. "You have everything you need?"

She nodded.

"I'll see you in the morning, okay?"

Another nod.

"We'll leave the light on in the hall in case you need to get up and use the bathroom, okay?"

"Okay."

She probably ought to have a bath one of these nights. He had no idea how often kids were supposed to bathe, and that would have to be Evette's department. He felt like he was walking on eggshells where Jolie was concerned, but if she didn't bring it up, he would have to.

"Good night, Jolie."

"Good night."

He turned out the light and started to pull the door closed partway.

"Wait! Dad?"

He flipped the light back on. "What is it?"

"Is my mama ever gonna talk to me again?"

Give me the words, God…give me the words. He went to the bed and sat down on the edge of the mattress. "Oh, honey…I hope so."

"And then you can come and live with us, right?"

He sucked in a breath. "I…I can't do that, Jolie."

"How come? You could help Mama get well. And then she could walk and talk and play with me like she used to."

He patted her foot on top of the blanket. "Oh, sweetie. I wish it was that easy." He took another deep breath and whispered a prayer as he blew it out. "Your mama and I never got married, so I can't…" He grasped for the right words. "I can't be with her. I'm married to Evette, Jolie. I love her. We're going to have a baby. Did you know that?"

She nodded solemnly. "And then you won't be my dad anymore." She said it as if it were a simple truth.

"No! Of course not. I'll always be your daddy. And even if your mama gets better and you get to go back to Springfield and live with her, I'll still be your dad. Now that I know where you live, I'll want to come and visit you whenever I can. But for now, you have a home right here—with me and Evette. Okay? You'll always be safe here."

"Uh-huh."

He wasn't sure she was convinced, but she rolled over on her side and closed her eyes. And she looked peaceful.

He patted her feet again. "Good night, sweetie."

She giggled.

The sound alone made him smile. "What's so funny?"

"I like that."

"What?"

"When you say 'sweetie.'"

"Well, okay then, sweetie."

She giggled again.

"Good night, silly. Sleep tight. Don't let the bedbugs bite."

She sat up in bed, her eyes twinkling. "That's what Mama always says."

A memory steamrolled over him. He'd taken Tabrina home after a date. They were newly in love, in that honeymoon period before his parents had started in on them. He'd kissed her good night at the door of her apartment, wanting like crazy to go in with her, glad at the same time that she didn't invite him in. "Good night." He kissed her again, stroked his finger slowly down the bridge of her nose. "Sleep tight." He kissed her one last time. "Don't let the bedbugs bite."

She'd laughed at him. "Where do you come up with this stuff?"

"What? You never heard that before?"

"*Pffft*. You made that up."

"No, I did not."

"Liar."

He wasn't sure he ever had convinced Tabrina that he didn't make up the silly rhyme. He didn't have a clue where *he'd* first heard it. Probably his mother.

Did Tabrina think of him when she tucked Jolie in with those words? He'd trained himself to push thoughts of her away. He needed to do that now. But how could he, with their daughter looking up at him with that same ornery gleam in her eyes?

He reached to turn out the lamp on Jolie's nightstand and pulled her door halfway closed.

Evette was waiting for him in the kitchen. "Is she asleep?"

"Headed that way."

"That was easy. I hope we don't have another sleep-less night."

Her comment irritated him. He'd been the one to stay with Jolie until she fell asleep last night. He stared at her. "Oh? You didn't sleep last night?"

His question apparently hit the mark. She looked sheepish and answered him in a quiet voice. "I just mean that it took her so long to get to sleep…."

He let it go. They didn't need anything else to fight about. And—he kept having to remind himself—Jolie was *his* daughter. He really had no right to expect Evette to take equal responsibility. With him working, right now she was doing more than her share. He'd just hoped that she would be beside him more fully in this.

"So…do you want to hear about how it went with the guys?" He gave her a short version of his talk with the team. "You know, it really wasn't as bad as I thought it would be. Except for Rafe—and I wouldn't have expected any less from that kid—they all seemed really under-standing." *Unlike you, Evette.* He couldn't seem to let it go.

"Well, I'm glad. Now that you've told your whole world, I guess I'd better tell mine." She wiped off a counter that she'd already cleaned twice in the space of five minutes.

"I think it'll be the same for you. When you tell people, I mean."

She bit the corner of her lip. "Don't push it, Judd."

"I'm not. I'm just saying…" Her reluctance disappointed him. She was acting like a child. If they ended up with Jolie permanently, his daughter wouldn't be able to help but sense Evette's resentment.

Cross that bridge when you come to it.

He didn't know if the thought was his own conscience, or if the Lord was trying to tell him something. Either way, he chose to ignore it. Always a bad decision, but right now he didn't care. He needed to get some things off his chest. He picked up a dish towel off the counter and idly wadded it into a ball, tossing it from one hand to the other as if it were a basketball.

"You know, Evette." He paused, knowing, *knowing* he'd be sorry later for the things he was about to say, but he plunged ahead anyway. "I understand this is hard for you. I know you feel put-upon—or put out, or whatever you want to call it—because of all this, but you're going to have to let it go at some point. I can take it, but it's not fair to punish Jolie."

"What?" She acted as if she had no clue what he was talking about. "What are you talking about? You know, I can't make this work if I don't have some ownership, Judd. You're her fun, toy-buying, play-in-the-yard dad. But I can't be your counterpart. I can't be Mom because she already has a mom living just up the interstate." She jabbed a finger toward the back door.

"You say you want ownership, but you won't *take* ownership!"

"What do you mean?"

"You've left everything to me…from unpacking her suitcase to making sure there were toys in the house, to tucking her in at ni—"

"Hold on just one minute, buster. You had the suitcase unpacked before I knew what happened. And there were plenty of things in this house for her to play with. You didn't need to go buy special toys for her. She was perfectly happy with the markers and the dishes I got out for her. And while we're on the subject, I'd like to know why it is you haven't bought one thing—not one toy, not one item of clothing, nothing—for *our* baby?"

"What are you talking about?"

"Just what I said, Judd. You practically bought out Wal-Mart for your daughter, but you haven't bought one thing for our baby. Not one thing! You barely talk about our baby—especially since *she* came." She pointed down the hall where Jolie slept.

"Evette, don't be ridiculous. We have five months before our baby—"

"Four and a half months," she corrected.

"Fine. Four and a half months before our baby even arrives. Last time I checked, babies didn't start playing with toys until they were at least a couple months old." He forced his voice down an octave. They were both on the verge of being out of control. "Jolie is here now and she came with nothing. I didn't think it would hurt to get her a few toys. Besides, I knew you were going to be the one entertaining her most of the time. I thought you'd appreciate it."

"Oh, well, aren't you thoughtful, thinking of me the whole time." Evette spit out the words with venom. "Maybe you should have been so thoughtful seven years ago."

He threw the dish towel down hard on the counter. "Okay, that is enough. If you're going to throw that back in my face every single time we try to have a civil discussion about this, then just forget it." He turned and started to walk away.

"Judd…Judd, I'm sorry." Her voice shook and became soft, contrite. "That was uncalled-for. Please forgive me."

He faced her again, regretting that he'd goaded her. "Listen, Evie…I know this is hard for you. It's hard for me, too, okay?"

"That's just it, Judd. It's *not* hard for you. You act like you've been a father half your life. You've fallen into the role like you were born to it. You're in love with Jolie as if you've known her forever." She put a fist to her mouth, tears welling in her eyes. "I can't do that! You want something from me that I just can't manufacture. I'm trying, okay? I'm really trying. But you're going to have to give me some time. I don't know how to conjure up love like that. I…I just can't forget everything she stands for, okay?"

He nodded slowly. He did understand. And she was right. He wanted so desperately for her to love Jolie the way he did. For her to mother her the way he imagined she would their baby.

The truth was, he'd started to worry about the kind of mother she would be to any child. Sometimes she seemed so cold…so detached from Jolie. He feared she would be the same way with their child.

But he couldn't tell her that. Not now.

Chapter Seventeen

Evette took a sip of decaf and looked at the to-do list in front of her. It made her head swim just to think about everything she had to accomplish. She'd thought she had a lot to do to get ready for the baby before, but with Jolie here, her priority list had changed drastically, and it seemed everything needed to be done at the same time.

At least after next week, Jolie would be enrolled in school and gone for the better part of the day. Then maybe Evette could accomplish some of the other things on her list, foremost of which was informing people about this drastic change in their lives.

Her parents—well, her mother anyway—was going to have a conniption when she discovered that Evette had known about Judd's daughter for two weeks now, and that Jolie had been living with them for four days. There was nothing her mother hated more than being "out of the loop." In her own defense, Evette had started to dial her parents three times in the past two days, but each time, Jolie needed something or came into the room just as she pushed the first buttons.

As if Evette's thoughts had summoned her, Jolie wandered into the kitchen, still in her pajamas.

"Good morning," Evette said.

"Morning." She rubbed her eyes. "Where's my dad?"

"He's already at work. Do you want some cereal or toast?"

"Can I have jelly on toast?"

"Sure."

"Okay."

Evette set the list aside and went to pop two slices of bread in the toaster.

She poured orange juice for Jolie, and poured herself a second cup of decaf while she waited for the toast to pop up.

Judd's daughter seemed to be adjusting fairly well. She was a little weepy at bedtime, and quite often Evette would catch her staring off into space with a sad look on her face. Judd seemed to be able to joke her out of her doldrums, and get her to sleep each night with silly songs and sweet words. If the circumstances had been any different, she would have been falling in love with her husband all over again. Even though Judd had always been good with the boys he coached, his easy way with Jolie surprised her. And touched her, even as it filled her with sadness that she wasn't witnessing these things for the first time with their own child.

She spread butter and jelly on the toast and set it in front of Jolie. "We need to do something with your hair right after breakfast. Do you have a special brush you use?"

"Mama's pick, but Grams said I couldn't take it 'cause Mama needs it."

"Okay. I'm sure I have something we can use. And

then maybe we can stop and buy what you need when we go to the school to enroll."

She glanced at the calendar. Oh! She'd almost forgotten she had an appointment with her obstetrician this afternoon, too. How would she ever get everything done? The hands on the clock seemed to be spinning out of control. Like their lives.

She didn't dare hope that Judd might take off early and come with her to her appointment. Then he could watch Jolie. But this afternoon was the last practice before tomorrow night's first game in the conference tournament. There was no way he'd miss that.

She hadn't decided yet if she would go to the game. People would wonder why she wasn't there, but they'd do plenty more wondering if she showed up with Jolie.

She looked at the list again. Judd had called Pastor Mike and set up an appointment to talk to him on Sunday afternoon. Judd had explained their situation, and Mike said his teenage daughter would be at the church to entertain Jolie so they could talk in private. Evette didn't know what to expect of that meeting. She supposed it would be part confessional, part counseling session, but mostly she thought Judd intended the meeting simply to tell their pastor the whole story, to ask for prayer, and to get Mike's advice on how they could best inform the congregation. No matter what happened, it would be a humiliating experience.

Jolie pushed her plate away and scooted back on her chair. "Can I be 'scused?"

Evette smiled. "Yes, you may. And let's go get your hair washed."

She followed Jolie back to the guest bathroom and filled the tub. "Test that water and make sure it's not too hot for you."

Jolie stuck a hand in the water and shook her head solemnly. "It's not too hot."

"Okay. Get your jammies off and hop in then." She felt awkward playing mommy to this little girl.

But Jolie didn't seem to notice. She slipped out of her pajamas and climbed into the tub.

"Can you wash your own hair or do you need help?"

She shook her head. "I don't get the soap out good. Mama washes it…I mean, she did." Jolie tossed her head and made a face. "You know what I mean."

"I know what you mean." Evette forced a smile. From the looks of it, the girl's hair hadn't been washed in some time. "Okay, then…what's the best way to do this? Do you lie back in the water or use a pitcher to pour, or what?"

"Cup. Mama gets a great big Cardinals cup and dumps it on me."

"You and your Cardinals," she teased. "Okay, hang on…" She searched through the cupboards beneath the sink but didn't find anything.

"Let me run and get a cup. You stay right here." Was it okay to leave a six-year-old in the bathtub for a few seconds? Wasn't this knowledge supposed to come naturally to women? What was she going to do when she had her own baby—one who couldn't talk her through the steps of giving a simple bath and shampoo?

"I'll be *right* back." She raced down the hall, grabbed one of the giant soft-drink cups Judd was always bringing home from some ball game or another, and sprinted back to the bathroom.

Jolie was trailing her hands through the water, singing to herself. A song Evette didn't know.

"Okay…I can't do Cardinals, but how does—" she

turned the cup around to read the logo "—the Crimson Tigers sound?"

"What's that?" Jolie wrinkled her button nose.

"Tigers? You know what a tiger is, don't you? Haven't you ever been to the zoo?"

"No, not tiger. That other one." She pointed to the cup.

"Oh. Crimson?"

"Yeah, that."

"Crimson is red."

"Red tigers? I ain't never seen a red tiger."

Evette cringed at the grammar. "Haven't."

"Huh?"

"Say 'I *haven't* ever seen a red tiger.' Not ain't."

"Why?"

"Because it just isn't good grammar. It's not the proper way to speak English." Why was she making a big deal about grammar all of a sudden? *Because you're afraid of what people will say when they meet Jolie and she sounds…black.*

She ignored the answer her conscience gave. "Okay… close your eyes…let's get this hair washed."

Jolie squinched her eyes shut. "Grams says Mama's *all* about good grammar."

"See there. It's important to speak correctly." Judd had talked about how intelligent and well-spoken Tabrina was. She'd noticed that it was when Jolie was around Carla or the African-American nurses who spoke in their black dialect that Jolie slipped into speaking that way, too. She wondered if Tabrina would have corrected Jolie. Probably, from the little Judd had told her about Tabrina. Regardless, there was nothing wrong with expecting the girl to speak correctly and use good grammar.

Evette squeezed shampoo into her hand and rubbed

it into Jolie's tight curls. It seemed to take forever to go through the routine of shampooing and conditioning and rinsing it all out of the masses of long curls that seemed to turn even coarser once they were wet.

Later, with Jolie wrapped snug in a towel, Evette tried in vain to comb out the damp tangles.

"Ouch!" Jolie clutched at her head and pushed away the hand that held the comb.

"I'm sorry, honey, but we have to get those tangles out." She tried again, doing her best not to yank.

"Ouch! Owie! Stop! That hurts!" Jolie jumped up and down on one foot. "You hafta put stuff in it. Tangle stuff. And that's not the right comb!" She pointed an accusing finger at the fine-tooth comb Evette held.

"Let me go see if I can find a different one." She went to the master bath and rummaged through her vanity drawer, but all she came up with was a round brush her hairdresser had talked her into buying when she first started wearing her hair shorter.

She took it back into the guest bath. Jolie stood in front of the mirror shivering, the towel pulled up to her chin.

"Let's go get you dressed, and then we'll see what we can do with your hair."

She let Jolie pick an outfit from her dresser and waited while she painstakingly pulled on each item of clothing. Evette checked her watch. At this rate, they'd be lucky to make her afternoon doctor's appointment on time.

Finally, they were back in the bathroom again, this time armed with a round brush and a blow-dryer. But she hadn't gotten the brush through Jolie's shoulder-length hair one time before it snagged on the bristles and got hung up in a strand of curls. Jolie yelped and tried to yank the brush out.

"Stop, Jolie. You're only making it worse. Let me get you untangled."

The little girl finally settled down so Evette could start the tedious process of releasing her hair from the grip of the brush. But Evette's efforts only seemed to wrap Jolie's hair tighter around the barrel.

Her screams of pain dissolved into sobbing. "I don't want that brush! Get it out!" And then, echoing Evette's fears, "We'll never get it out. Never. Why did you hafta wash my hair in the first place? Mama only washes it sometimes."

"Honey, you can't just not wash your hair. It's been at least four days…"

"So?"

She made her voice stern. "Jolie." She hadn't seen the sassy side of Judd's daughter yet, but this was exactly what she'd feared before she'd ever met her. She pushed the anger down. This was no time to get in a shouting match with the girl. They had to somehow untangle the brush from her hair and get her hair combed and dried so they could get to the school and clinic.

She assessed the hairbrush situation. "I think I'm just going to have to cut the thing out. I don't know what else to do."

"No! Don't cut it! Don't cut it!"

"Then you're going to have to let me get it out of there." She reached for the brush, but Jolie tore out of the bathroom and down the hall.

"Jolie! Get back here!"

She had a sudden image of trying to handle all this with a baby crying in the nursery. Feeling heartless and guilty, she tossed a prayer up to heaven—that Jolie would be gone by the time her baby came.

Chapter Eighteen

The principal's office contained only one extra chair and Jolie stood, red-eyed and fuzzy-haired, beside Evette. Evette had finally had to insist that Jolie let her cut the brush out of her hair. She'd hurriedly blow-dried Jolie's hair, but the more it dried, the wilder it got, until her head looked like one of those British lawyers' wigs. An attempt to tame it into twin braids had failed miserably and brought on more tears.

They'd managed to corral most of her hair into a thick plume on top of her head, but already tufts were slipping out of the ponytail holder and flying around her head like cotton. Jolie had put together a presentable outfit from the few items she'd brought with her, but they'd need to go shopping for clothes before she started school.

She'd practically dragged Jolie, kicking and screaming, to the car. Frankly, she didn't blame her for not wanting to be seen in public, looking the way she did. But they'd barely had time to run a few errands before coming here to enroll in school.

After a ten-minute wait, the principal finally appeared, looking frazzled. "The district office said you'd be stopping by. Sorry to make you wait." She dispensed some hand sanitizer from a container on her desk and rubbed her hands together vigorously. "We've had an outbreak of the flu recently," she explained.

Evette wished the woman would offer her and Jolie some of the germ-killer, but she didn't, taking the large chair behind her desk. "I'm Patricia Wayne, by the way."

"Evette McGlin." She handed Ms. Wayne the sheaf of papers the district office had sent with them. "And this is Jolie Jackson."

"Let's see…" The woman slid on a pair of reading glasses and shuffled through the documents. "You are Jolie's legal guardian?"

"Well, not exactly." She'd dreaded the explanation and had practiced how she would word things in the car. She glanced at Jolie, who was running her hand along a row of encyclopedias lined up on a shelf against the wall. "Jolie is my husband's daughter. Her mother is in the hospital…we're not certain for how long. She's staying with us indefinitely."

"But your husband has legal guardianship?"

"Not yet. We may only have her for a short time." She pointed to the papers spread on the desk. "You'll see Jolie's maternal grandmother has left medical release forms and insurance information. It was my husband's understanding when he talked to the district office that you wouldn't need anything else until permanent arrangements are made."

"If that's what they told you…I'll give Dr. Johnson a call, but in the meantime, we'll go ahead and get her set up here." She turned to Jolie. "Let's see…Jolie Glynn Jackson. Did I say that right? Jo-lee?"

Jolie squirmed, but she looked the woman in the eye and nodded.

"What do you like to be called?"

Jolie stared at her.

"Do you want them to call you just Jolie?" Evette prodded.

She shook her head. "No. Jolie."

"Just Jolie?"

"Uh-uh. Jolie. Not 'just Jolie.' *Jolie.*" She emphasized her name with a bob of her chin.

The principal laughed and Evette joined in. Jolie looked embarrassed, but she smiled.

Poor girl. She'd had a rough day. Evette's heart went out to her. This had to be scary. A wave of remorse picked her up and deposited her in a pool of regret. She certainly hadn't made things any easier for a little girl who'd been through so much. *Forgive me, Lord.*

Evette put an arm around Jolie's narrow shoulders. "She goes by Jolie."

"That's a nice name," Principal Wayne said.

After a barrage of questions for each of them, the principal turned them over to an aide, who gave them a brief tour of the school and let them peek into the classroom that would be Jolie's. The students were out at recess, but the teacher was at her desk. Hope rose in Evette as the pretty African-American woman strode to the door to greet them.

"This is Mrs. Markham, Jolie," the aide said. "She'll be your teacher."

"Welcome, Jolie. Nice to meet you. And is this your mother?" Mrs. Markham gave Evette a conspiratorial smile. "I'm Brandi Markham."

"No, she's—"Jolie looked at Evette as if sizing her up. "She's just Evette."

"Hi, Evette," Brandi Markham extended a hand to Evette and then Jolie.

"I'm Jolie's…stepmother." It was the first time she'd spoken those words.

"Welcome to Hanover Falls Elementary…both of you."

"Is there any certain place you'd like to sit, Jolie? You don't wear glasses, do you? Do you need to sit up front?"

Jolie shook her head.

"How about if we put you right here?" Mrs. Markham pushed one of the desks into the second row. "Will that be okay?"

She nodded and scooted closer to Evette.

"You don't need to be shy, girl." Mrs. Markham laughed. "We have all kinds of fun here. You'll see. Will you be starting right away?"

Jolie looked to Evette for the answer.

"We thought we'd give her a week or two to get settled in. She'll be here…probably a week from Monday."

A spark came to Mrs. Markham's dark eyes. "Good. That'll give you time to do something with this hair." She winked at Jolie and tugged on a tuft of the cotton candy hair. "Let me guess…Evette did your hair?"

Jolie rolled her eyes and nodded.

"Girl, you've got to do something about that before you come to school."

"She had to cut off some of my hair to get the brush out."

Little tattletale! But Evette laughed and hid her eyes behind one hand. "I guess I didn't have the right kind of brush, and when we tried to dry it, it just got… frizzier and frizzier."

The teacher laughed. "Do you know where the flower shop is downtown?"

"Sure…" What did flowers have to do with Jolie's hair?

"Right next door is The Hair Boutique. You ask for Maisie. She comes over from Rolla on Mondays. Tell her it's an emergency. She does my hair, and, honey, if she can get this head of hair to behave, she'll have Jolie looking beautiful in no time." She reached out again and pulled a strand of Jolie's fluff through her fingers. "You've got good hair. Just needs a little help from Maisie."

"Maisie. Got it." Evette turned to Jolie and copied the teacher's wink.

Mrs. Markham ran her palm down Jolie's arm, as if she were petting a cat. "You should rub on some lotion, too, girl. You're turning ashy."

"My mama's in the hospital," she said, as if that explained everything.

"Well, maybe Evette can help you. You need to get some lotion on that skin before you turn as white as her. And get some Pink oil for your hair."

Jolie nodded as if she knew exactly what the teacher was talking about.

Evette felt they were speaking a foreign language. "Pink oil?"

"You just tell Maisie. She'll get you fixed up."

Evette nodded. "Okay. Next stop, The Hair Boutique. Thank you, Mrs. Markham."

"Happy to help." She turned to Jolie, shook her head and clucked her tongue. But there was a glint of mischief in her eyes. "Girl, just be glad you found me."

The smile Jolie returned to the teacher brought an unexpected lump to Evette's throat. It was the first time she'd seen genuine happiness on the little girl's face.

* * *

"You're almost too big to ride in the cart." Evette tucked her purse beside Jolie in the child's seat of the grocery cart.

"Mama said I hafta walk when I'm seven."

"I'm not sure you'll fit in the cart that long. You don't turn seven for a while." She steered the cart toward the produce aisle.

"October!" Jolie grinned. "That's my birthday. And I'm gonna have a party and invite Rebecca and Katesha and Teacher and—"

"Mrs. Markham?"

"Uh-huh. And Mama and Grams and Dad. Oh, and... who else?"

Evette shrugged.

"Oh! And you! *You* can come to my party, too."

Gee, thanks. She feigned a smile and tuned out the chattering. What would their lives look like by October? She couldn't imagine.

The day's errands had exhausted her, but she had accomplished a lot. Jolie was enrolled for school, and they had an appointment to get her hair braided. Evette had seen the doctor and the baby was fine. Now if they could get the cupboards filled at home, she'd feel better about her to-do list. Jolie had regained her appetite and Evette couldn't believe what a difference one more mouth to feed had made in their grocery bill.

She checked her list and looked up to see Barbara Pembroke, a former coworker from the furniture store, not twenty feet in front of her. Barb was engrossed in filling a produce bag with apples. Holding her breath, Evette tried to turn the cart and get away before Barb spotted her. But Jolie's weight and the thick mats in front of the vegetable display cases made the cart difficult to steer. Before she could make her getaway, Barb looked up and recognition lit her face.

"Evette? Is that you?" The woman's eyes darted between Jolie and Evette and back again, the question obvious on her face.

She pretended to be surprised. "Oh, hi, Barb. How's it going?"

Barb bent to speak to Jolie. "Hi, there."

Jolie smiled and mumbled hello, but then grabbed Evette's arm and buried her face.

"Just look at you, Evette!" Barb gushed, reaching to splay a hand briefly on Evette's belly. "You look wonderful. I forget…when's the baby due?" Again, the woman's eyes darted to Jolie.

What would she tell her? Barbara was a fountain of gossip…the last person Evette wanted to explain Jolie to. "I'm due in August, but big as an elephant already." She put a hand over her stomach to demonstrate.

"Goodness, no! You look fabulous."

"Thanks. How's everything at work?"

"Same ol', same ol'. Jerry still hasn't replaced you, so we're all overworked and underpaid."

"Sorry." Evette cringed, even while she was grateful for something to talk about that might move the spotlight away from Jolie.

But Barb couldn't keep her eyes off the child. Now she bent and touched Jolie's knee. "And what's *your* name?" Barb asked.

Jolie burrowed deeper and Evette hoped Barb didn't explode from curiosity.

"This is Jolie. And…" Evette cast about for an excuse. She finally resorted to looking pointedly at her watch. "If we don't hurry, we'll be late for an appointment."

Jolie pushed back and looked up at her with a groan. "We have *another* 'pointment?"

Great. Caught in her lie. She ignored Jolie's question and backed the cart up. "It was sure good to see you, Barb. Tell everyone at the store hi for me, would you?"

"I'll do that. You let us know when that baby comes."

"Oh, I will." Evette couldn't push the cart fast enough. She kept her head down and rushed through the rest of her shopping, ignoring Jolie's questions about their next "appointment." She just hoped the child didn't tattle to Judd about her little white lie.

Brent Harper dished the pass off to Rafe Clairmont and he went up for the shot. Judd held his breath as the last tenth of a second ticked off the clock and the buzzer sounded. He whirled to watch the referee's call.

Good! The shot was good! Hanover Falls High had won the game. They were headed into district play-offs with a conference championship under their belt. He joined his players as they lined up to shake hands with the opposing team.

At the end of the line, he shook the hand of the Brennan Valley coach. "Great game, Coach." His words were sincere. The Broncos had given them a whale of a game.

Headed to the locker room, he looked up in the stands again. The spot on the bleachers that Evette usually occupied was still empty. She hadn't come. He wasn't surprised, but he was disappointed.

He'd called her on the way to the game this afternoon, but he'd only gotten the answering machine. She hadn't called him back, and she didn't answer her cell phone. She'd had a doctor's appointment this afternoon. His pulse pounded out an extra beat. What if she'd gotten bad news?

He joined the celebration in the locker room, but he couldn't get Evette out of his mind. He gave the boys a shortened version of the speech he had planned and while they dressed, he went into his office to call her.

She answered on the first ring. "Hey, babe. Did you win?"

"We did. By two. At the buzzer. Where were you? I kept watching for you…"

"I'm sorry, Judd. We had a big day. I just couldn't… I wasn't up to coming."

"Is everything okay? Your appointment went okay?"

"Everything's fine. They'll do another ultrasound next time. We can find out what we're having then…if we want to."

"We'll talk about it when I get home. Jolie's okay? You got her registered for school?"

"Yes. I'll tell you about that, too. I told them she'd probably start a week from Monday."

"Good. Okay…I'll let you go. I just—I missed you. I hate it when you're not here. And I wanted the guys to meet Jolie."

"I'm sorry, Judd. Next time, okay?"

"Yeah, okay. I'll be home in a little bit. Is she in bed yet?"

"She went down about eight-thirty. She was worn-out."

"Big day, huh?"

"Yes. Big day. We'll talk later. You go celebrate with your boys."

He hung up the phone. He tried not to be angry with her. And in truth, what he felt was probably more disappointment than anger. But Evette knew how much it meant for her to be up in those stands. Especially for the big games like this one.

Calm down, buddy. Her life has been turned upside down thanks to you. She's had to make a lot of changes. You can't expect to have everything your way.

Sunday afternoon they'd meet with Mike at the church and maybe that would help Evette accept things for what they were. Something had to change. They—*she*—could not go on as if this was all going to go away.

Chapter Nineteen

Evette pushed open the door to The Hair Boutique and ushered Jolie inside. Three stylists worked at identical stations along the wall. A fourth chair was empty. The salon stank of perm solution and hair spray.

Jolie wrinkled her nose and a faraway look came to her hazel eyes. "Mama got her hair made straight at a place just like this. When I was five."

"You remember that?"

Her head bobbed. "Keisha gave me a lemon sucker. But it got hair stuck on it and Mama made me throw it away."

"You've got a good memory, kiddo."

"Keisha put stuff on Mama's hair and it got all straight—like yours." She pointed at Evette and made a smoothing motion at the sides of her head. "Grams didn't like it, though."

Tabrina's hair had been in a kinky ponytail when they'd seen her in the hospital, but in the photos Judd had shown Evette years ago, she'd worn her hair straight and long and looked like a supermodel.

A middle-aged redhead with a seventies' updo looked up from the foil-wrapped head she was working on. "Good morning! Somebody will be right with you."

"I called earlier…for her." Evette looked down at Jolie. "Brandi Markham recommended Maisie."

The woman looked from Evette to Jolie. "Oh. Sure. Well, you might as well make yourselves at home. She's doing braids, right?"

Evette nodded.

The beehive lady put down her comb and came to where they were standing. She picked up a hank of Jolie's hair and inspected it. "Her hair won't be too bad to do. If you want to go shopping or something, feel free. She'll probably be done around noon. We can call your cell phone when she's finished."

"Noon?" Evette looked at her watch. Jolie's appointment had been for nine o'clock and it was five minutes till. "We'll just come back later. What time do you think you can get her in?"

"Oh, Maisie's here now. She can start right away."

Evette felt her jaw drop. "It takes that long to do braids?"

"Long? Honey, that's short. If we were doing extensions, you'd be here till supper. You go on, though. Run some errands if you want. She'll be all right here. We'll give you a call when she's ready."

Evette blew out a breath and looked down at Jolie. Her narrow shoulders were tensed, and she had the hem of her T-shirt wadded in one hand.

"I'll stay," Evette told the woman. She wished she'd brought a book to read.

"Maisie! Your braid's here." The woman went back to her station, and Evette led Jolie to a row of chairs by the window that overlooked Main Street.

A minute later a large black woman emerged from a door at the back of the shop. She waddled over to where they were sitting. "You Jolie?"

Jolie nodded.

She did the same thing the beehive lady had done—lifted a handful of hair and inspected it as if searching for lice or something. She shook her head and made a disgusted face. She turned to Jolie, but threw her head back in Evette's direction. "She do this to you?"

Jolie nodded.

"You her mother? Or *tryin'* to be?" She clucked and let go of Jolie's hair like it was a wad of dryer lint. Come to think of it, that's about what it looked like.

"Excuse me?" Evette could hardly believe the woman's gall. She opened her mouth to defend herself, but Jolie saved her the trouble.

"My mama's in the hospital."

Maisie eyed Evette and her demeanor softened a little. "You gotta get some moisture in this girl's hair. Her body, too, for that matter. Look at her."

"Excuse me?" she said again. She didn't have to take flak from this woman.

"You gotta keep lotion on this skin. You see how ashy she looks? Lotion. Oil. Every day. Maybe twice a day for a while. She's bone-dry."

Maisie walked over to a display case filled with product and came back with a large plastic bottle and a smaller squeeze bottle. "You two come on back here." She pointed at Evette. "You can do lotion while I try to salvage this head of hair. When you last wash it?"

"A couple of days ago. It…it might have been four days before that."

"Four days? Girl, what you doin' washin' her hair after four days? No wonder she look like cotton candy on a stick." Maisie led the way back through the door she'd come out of, down a hallway and into a small room with a sofa and a couple of sling chairs.

"Come here, little girl. Sit right there." She flapped a fleshy elbow in the direction of the sofa and handed Jolie a tray full of beads and tiny rubber bands. "You pick out some colors you like and we'll get you fixed up. Don't your mama use Pink oil on your head?"

"She uses somethin'. I don't know what it's called. She never said…pink."

"Hang on." Maisie rummaged through a deep desk drawer and came up with another bottle, the elixir she called Pink oil, presumably, since the bottle was pink.

"Sit down," Maisie ordered Evette, pointing to the other end of the sofa.

Evette did as she was told. She was half afraid of this woman, and half mad that Maisie seemed to wield the power to make her do whatever she commanded.

Maisie handed her a lotion bottle and pointed to Jolie. "Take your jeans off so we can get to your skinny legs."

Jolie looked at Evette like the woman was crazy.

"It's okay. Ain't nobody gonna come in here. You can keep the rest of your clothes on."

Evette hesitated, then nodded, and Jolie stripped off her shoes and socks, and then her blue jeans.

"Okay, now…sit right here." Maisie patted the sofa. "Lean back on the arm here." She pulled a low stool to the side of the sofa and bare arms jiggling, she started combing and oiling and dividing Jolie's hair.

Evette sat down at the opposite end of the sofa. Feeling awkward and out of place, she feigned interest in what was written on the back of the bottle. Finally, she touched Jolie's bare leg tentatively. "You ready?"

Jolie nodded. Evette cupped a hand and squirted out a generous dollop of the creamy lotion. She rubbed her palms together, picked up Jolie's stick-thin leg and started rubbing the oily lotion into her skin.

Jolie didn't seem to be the least uncomfortable, but it felt oddly intimate to be touching Judd's daughter this way. Evette's mother had not been overly affectionate toward her and Annie. Even now, it was a strain to hug her mother. And while Evette fantasized about having an infant to cuddle, she'd never thought about what it would be like when their baby was six years old—or a teenager. She pumped another handful of lotion, rubbed her hands together and slicked the lotion down Jolie's calf to her foot.

Jolie giggled. "That tickles!"

Maisie craned her thick neck and looked over Jolie's head. "It might tickle, but you look a far sight better already. See there?" She tossed Evette a towel. "Put that on your lap. It'll keep your pretty clothes from getting ruined."

Evette couldn't tell if Maisie was giving her a compliment or chiding her for wearing nice clothes to this appointment. But she spread the towel over her lap and lifted Jolie's legs onto it. She pumped the lotion again and started in on her arms and hands.

The hairdresser propped open a back door with an upturned plastic bucket, and the sounds of the back alley filtered in through the door.

Maisie hummed old, familiar hymns while she worked, stopping only to boss Evette around. "Put an extra dose on those knees and elbows. You see how they need that moisture?"

Every half hour or so, Maisie stood and stretched and made Jolie do the same.

The little girl's skin glowed from the oils. She did look better, but Evette was already devising a lesson to teach her to take care of her own skin. This wasn't exactly something Judd would be comfortable doing—nor would she want him to—and she didn't have time for the routine every night. Especially not after the baby got here—if Jolie was still with them by then.

Jolie entertained herself playing with the beads and rubber bands, arranging them in an intricate pattern on the tray, handing them to Maisie as she requested. After two hours, Jolie fell asleep under Maisie's deft ministrations.

Evette was about to doze off, too, when a teenage girl poked her head in the back door. Jolie opened her eyes, taking in the visitor with a curious glance.

"Mom, I need your keys." Maisie's daughter was as slender as Maisie was wide. She had a creamy brown complexion and wore her hair in beaded braids like the ones Jolie was getting.

A smile nearly split Maisie's face when she turned to the girl. "What you doin' up so early, girl?"

She rolled her eyes. "Daddy made me get up. I need the keys," she said again.

"What for?"

"Daddy needs the car."

"What he need the car for?" Her voice held mild annoyance.

"I don't know." The girl matched her mother's tone and flipped her head, making the beads at the end of her braids clack together. "Daddy just said come get the car, so I came and got the car."

"Don't you be lippin' off to me, girl."

"I'm not lippin' off to you." She mimicked her mother's inflection. It was the first time she'd sounded "black."

Watching her, Evette could see what Jolie might look like when she was a teenager. She tried to imagine what it would be like if Jolie was still with them ten years from now.

"This here's my daughter. Betsy, this is Jolie and Evette." Maisie nodded at them in turn.

The girl lifted a hand, suddenly looking shy. "Hi."

"You help me finish up this head. Then I can come home with you."

"Mom…" Betsy rolled her eyes and spoke through gritted teeth.

"Come on. We can have this girl outta here in twenty minutes if you help."

Betsy gave an exaggerated sigh, but she straddled the arm of the sofa and went to work on the opposite side of Jolie's head. Mother and daughter bantered back and forth, and even Jolie got in on their chatter.

Feeling very much out of place, Evette laid her head on the back of the sofa and pretended to sleep. But she listened, fascinated, to the running conversation between the women as they worked.

Would she ever have such a rapport with a daughter? With Jolie? It was hard to picture.

Twenty-five minutes later, Jolie was tossing a head full of tight, shiny—Pink-oiled—beaded braids.

"Looks good," Betsy offered.

Maisie handed Jolie a round mirror.

Jolie tilted her head and studied her reflection.

"Now, ain't that better?"

Jolie caught Evette's eye in the mirror. "Evette says you're not s'posed to say 'ain't.'"

Evette froze. "Jolie—!"

Maisie glared at her but, to her relief, said nothing.

Evette blew out a shallow breath. She tugged on one of Jolie's new braids. "You look good, kiddo." She turned to the hairdresser. "How long will these stay in?"

"You take care of 'em—keep her scalp nice and oiled in between the rows—they'll last five or six weeks before they start lookin' ratty. Her hair's not too nappy…might last a little longer on her. You call me when it needs doin' again."

"Thank you… Do I pay at the front?"

"That's right."

Evette hated to guess how much this was going to cost. She slipped two ten-dollar bills from her purse and gave one to Maisie and one to Betsy. "Thank you. I really appreciate you getting us in on such short notice."

"No problem."

Betsy stood by the door, tapping her foot, rolling her eyes at her mother. But she lifted a hand to Jolie. "'Bye, Jolie."

"G'bye." Jolie grinned, obviously pleased at the teen's attention.

"Wait till Dad sees my hair, huh, Evette?"

"Yeah. He'll think you look gorgeous."

"What's that mean? Gorgeous?"

"Beautiful. Lovely. Pretty." Evette winked.

Jolie tilted her head again. That distant look they saw so often in her hazel eyes was there again. She must be remembering something about Tabrina, about her mother.

Evette prayed it was a happy memory.

Chapter Twenty

"Hey, Coach, great game Friday night!"

Judd shook Mike Mitchard's outstretched hand. "Yeah, it was a close one, that's for sure. Thanks for being there, Pastor. I sure appreciate the support." He regretted the words almost before they were out. He truly hadn't meant his words to rub it in that Evette *hadn't* been at the game, but as sensitive as she was these days, she was sure to take it that way.

But if she was offended, her face gave nothing away. She gave Mike a warm smile and shook his hand.

Mike bent to Jolie's eye level and put a hand on her shoulder. "And this must be the young lady you were telling me about."

Judd stepped forward and put a matching hand on Jolie's other shoulder. "Yes, this is Jolie. She just enrolled in school this week."

"Well, hey, that's great. Welcome, Jolie. My daughter will be here in a few minutes. Mandy can show you around the church and—" Mike's bubbly daughter popped her head in the door just then, knocking after the fact. "Ah, there she is now. Mandy, this is Jolie. Why don't you give her a tour, and then you guys can hang out in the youth room until we're done talking."

Jolie looked up at Judd, her eyes seeking permission. "We'll be right in here," he said. "You let Mandy know if you need anything, okay? We won't be too long."

Jolie smiled shyly and tagged behind the girl, the little beads at the ends of her braids bobbing. She looked cute as all get-out. She had on the bright-red Cardinals T-shirt she'd been wearing the day they'd first met her.

Mike chuckled as Mandy's chattering faded down the hallway. "Jolie won't be able to get a word in edgewise."

Judd smiled. "She probably won't mind. She's pretty quiet."

Mike's expression turned serious. "We missed you in church this morning."

Judd nodded. "We missed being there."

"So, how are you all adjusting?" Mike motioned toward the sofa across from his desk. "Have a seat. Can I get you guys some coffee? Or water?"

Judd and Evette waved off his offer and sat at opposite ends of the sofa.

The pastor took a seat in a wing chair facing them. "If I had to guess, I'd say it's been a little stressful…." Mike left the words to hang between them.

"A little," Judd admitted.

Evette laughed the way she did when she was nervous. "A lot."

"That's certainly understandable. Under the best circumstances, bringing a child into your home to live is stressful. What would you say is the toughest part so far?"

Mike was looking at Evette, and Judd waited for her to answer.

"I guess…for me…I'm still trying to deal with the news that Judd *has* a daughter. Jolie's a great little girl. She has some issues—who wouldn't in her shoes?—but I'm having a little trouble separating those issues from the fact that my husband has a child that I…didn't know about."

"I didn't know about her, either." He'd addressed his comment to Mike, but again, once the words were out they sounded defensive, even to his own ears, as if he were arguing with Evette.

Mike shifted in his seat and turned to Evette. "Judd told me about the situation on the phone…and that he's wanting to introduce Jolie to the congregation. Is that right, Judd?"

Judd hesitated. "We just wanted everyone to know our situation. Since Jolie's biracial and Evette's pregnant… people will have a lot of questions, and we'd rather they hear the truth from us than whatever the rumor mill is going to say."

"I understand," Mike said. "Do you want to have a few minutes during our sharing time next Sunday?"

"Whatever you think would be best. I don't know how else to handle it."

Mike studied Evette. "Are you comfortable with Judd introducing Jolie in church?"

She nodded, but her face was pinched and drawn and Judd knew she was struggling not to reveal her true feelings to the pastor.

Mike thought for a moment. "Maybe…since Jolie will be with you in church, it would be better to put the introduction in an all-church e-mail? We could say something like…" He steepled his fingers and thought for a moment. "We could say, 'Judd and Evette McGlin ask for your prayers as they bring Judd's daughter into their home while her mother is recovering from a serious illness.' Something like that?"

Judd nodded, relieved at this alternative. It did seem simpler, though it meant there would still be some stares and whispers when they showed up in church with Jolie.

Mike leaned forward. "What does Jolie know about the whole situation?"

Judd thought about the day he'd first met her when Jolie had recognized him immediately. "She knows I'm her father. Apparently, her mother has shown her pictures. But at six, I doubt she understands what exactly that means—in relation to Evette, I mean." He reached to touch her arm.

"No, probably not," Mike agreed. "And what about Evette?"

Judd furrowed his brow. "I'm not sure what you mean."

"Have you thought about how this might feel for Evette, having the whole church know about your daughter? Your past?" Mike held a hand out to Evette. "I don't mean to speak for you, Evette, but I can imagine this has made you a little uncomfortable. Maybe I'm wrong…"

Evette bowed her head briefly before answering. "No. You're not wrong. I feel like—like Judd will essentially be telling the whole congregation that—" tears welled in her eyes "—he cheated on me and—"

"Evette, I didn't cheat on you. I would never cheat on you." He turned to the pastor, feeling the need to explain. "I didn't even meet Evie until after I broke up with Tabrina." Praying she wouldn't pull away from his touch as she had so often recently, Judd reached for her hand.

She let him take it, even as she wiped away tears with her other hand. "I'm just saying that's what some people will think. I want to be supportive of you in this, Judd, I really do. But Jolie's come into our lives so suddenly I haven't had time to process it." She looked up at Mike.

"Judd and I haven't really had time to talk about it because she's there. And—" She closed her eyes. "As terrible as this might sound, it really complicates things that Jolie is…that she's black."

"Why do you feel that complicates things, Evette?" Mike was in full counselor mode now. Maybe they could finally get some things straightened out.

"I guess…I guess because—right or wrong—around here, people are going to talk. When it's just Jolie and me together at the store or wherever, strangers assume she's adopted, or that I'm married to a black man. I ran into a friend the other day and…I just had no idea how to explain things to her."

"So what did you say?"

She shrugged at Mike. "I never did explain. I finally just said, 'This is Jolie.'"

Judd remembered feeling the same way when Rafe and James had stopped by that day.

"It was awkward," Evette said. "I know my friend wondered what was going on. It was my own fault, I know that…and I know I'm bound to get some looks. I— I'm not prejudiced…at least I never thought I was. I'll be honest, though… This has made me wonder."

"I don't know either of your extended families, but are each of your parents accepting of Jolie?"

Judd took a deep breath. "They don't know yet."

"Oh?" Mike drew back in surprise. "They must not live around here."

"My folks are in Chicago." Judd rested an ankle across his knee. "I don't have much of a relationship with them. They—" He gave a sideways glance at Evette, knowing his words would sting, but wanting to be honest. "My parents are the reason I broke up with Jolie's mother."

Mike looked at Evette, too, as if he was checking to see if Judd's words had wounded her. He must have thought she was okay, because he nodded and turned back to Judd.

"I still think it would be a good idea for you to tell them. It seems that would be the only fair thing for their sake. If they react badly, that's another matter, but at least you'll have done the right thing. What about you, Evette?"

"My parents live near St. Louis, but they winter in Florida. They just got back to Missouri. They came back early so they could watch Judd's team in the play-offs."

"But you haven't told them about Jolie? I'm curious why…"

Evette sighed. "I guess…" She glanced at Judd as if unsure whether she should continue.

He nodded, giving her tacit permission.

"Because I know they'll be disappointed in Judd. My mother won't be happy about Jolie. For a lot of reasons. She has very high standards." She stopped and shook her head. "That didn't come out right. I didn't mean…"

Mike reached to pat her arm. "It's okay. We know you didn't mean anything by it."

She pushed up from the sofa and paced in front of Judd. "That's just it, though. That's what this whole thing has caused. Every word is loaded. I find myself having to edit even my thoughts. I'm trying not to let prejudice be a part of this at all. It shouldn't be. I know that. But it seems to be all I can think about."

Mike acknowledged her words with a nod. "Judd, how about you?" Mike moved his chair back a few inches and continued. "I really didn't mean for this to turn into a counseling session, but I think this might be helpful. Are you two okay with the direction this conversation is going?"

Evette nodded and Judd echoed her, grateful she'd agreed. It did help to have Mike guiding the conversation.

"So, Judd, have you felt some of the same struggles with the racial issues? How long were you with Jolie's mother? If that's not too personal a question."

"We dated for about two years. I didn't know she was pregnant when we broke up."

"So you were the one who broke things off?"

"Yes, because my parents practically disowned me for dating Tabrina."

"Because she was black?"

He nodded, feeling the anger rise up in him again.

"So you didn't necessarily want to break up with her?"

"No." Judd didn't dare look at Evette. "I loved her."

"How do you feel hearing Judd say that, Evette?"

"Oh, we've talked about it. It was a pretty big bump in our marriage early on. I felt jealous of a woman I didn't even know…though Judd swore it was me he loved now. I thought we'd worked through it, but now, in some ways, I feel we're back to square one."

Mike rubbed his hands together and his vigorous nod said, *Now we're getting somewhere.* "Judd, do you think there's any reason for Evette to feel this way?"

He started shaking his head. "No. This really doesn't have anything to do with Tabrina. Like I've told Evette, now that I know I have a daughter, I can't help but love her. It doesn't mean my feelings for Tabrina have come back." That wasn't completely honest...the memories of what he'd felt for Tabrina had certainly returned. In full force. But he was dealing with them, mostly successfully, and there was no reason to hurt Evette or cause her to worry.

"Do you believe that, Evette?"

"Yes, I do. I just need a little time. This all happened so suddenly. I haven't had time to get used to any of it. To know what to tell people when they see the three of us together."

Mike nodded and scratched his chin. "Evette, I think what I'm hearing is that, in a way, your main fear is what people will think. Am I right?"

She eyed Judd as if she thought he'd tattled on her. Then, in a whisper, she said, "Yes, I do worry what people will think. I don't want people to think things are falling apart between Judd and me."

"Are they?" Mike looked from one to the other. "Do either of you feel your marriage is in jeopardy because of this?"

"No. Of course not." Judd leaned toward Evette, who was far too quiet. "Evette?"

Her chin quivered and she pressed her lips into a tight line, her head nodding almost frantically.

Judd shifted on the sofa to face her. "Why?" Mike faded from his vision, and it was as if he and Evette were alone in the room. "You wouldn't leave me over this, would you?"

"Me? You're the one... I'm afraid I'll lose you." She

was sobbing now. "I'm so afraid that if I can't get over my fears and quit blaming you…that you'll take Jolie and leave me. That you'll choose her over me."

Judd gathered her into his arms, not caring that Mike was a watchful audience. "Evette, that would never happen. I'm not going to leave you. I'm not. Good grief, babe, I love you!" Speaking the words, he felt the matching emotions swell inside him, and he was grateful beyond words. He did love her.

Mike straightened in his chair. "I'm going to give you some unusual advice, but I think it's wise in this case. I suggest you not come to church next Sunday. At least not here at Cornerstone. Maybe you can just have your own little worship time at home. Take a week or two to get some things worked out, pray about this together before you come back…with Jolie, of course. Meanwhile, I have a couple of assignments for you, okay?"

With his arm around Evette, her head heavy on his shoulder, Judd waited to hear Mike out.

"First, I really think you both need to talk to your parents before we send out an e-mail to the congregation. They may live a distance away, but these things have a tendency to get out to the very people you don't think will hear."

As one, Judd and Evette nodded in agreement.

Pastor Mike went on. "I also think you need to sit down with a pen and paper and decide some things. How much are you going to tell people, and what exactly are you going to tell them? If you talk about your responses in advance, you'll be on the same page and it won't be as difficult. Evette, Judd is doing, in my opinion, the godly, heroic thing. Can you support him in this?"

When she didn't respond, Mike went on, "You've obviously agreed to have Jolie in your home, at least for now. Can you, for Judd's sake, try to put aside your jealousy and look at Jolie as if she were your own?"

"Yes, I'll try."

Judd reached for her hand again. He squeezed it, a silent thank-you. She didn't respond, but neither did she pull her hand away.

"Judd…" Mike turned to him now. "Can you agree not to push Evette to feel something she may not feel yet for Jolie? Can you be content that she has agreed to bring your daughter into her home, even though the two of you have a baby coming soon…?" Mike's eyes challenged him. "Can you give her time to grow to love and accept your daughter? To let God work on her heart in His time?"

If he didn't know better, he'd be suspicious that Evette had talked to their pastor beforehand. Or maybe he was so thickheaded he just hadn't seen what any dunce could see. He squeezed Evette's hand again, his eyes never leaving hers as he answered Mike's question. "Yes, I'll give her time."

This time, she pressed her hand tighter into his and he saw the love shining in her eyes that hadn't been there for a long time.

Chapter Twenty-One

The sense of anticipation Evette usually felt on the drive to visit her parents and sister was there, but certainly not in the usual way. She couldn't identify the emotion surging through her as anything besides elation.

Part of it was just the chance to get away by herself. To have this time on the road to process everything that had happened to her and Judd over the past few weeks. Before she hit the road this afternoon, Judd had called Carla to ask how Tabrina was doing. It crossed her mind, as she watched him punch in the number, that maybe Carla would have good news—a dramatic change in Tabrina—and she could cancel her trip and leave her parents none the wiser.

But Carla's news was not good, and only reinforced her need to talk to her parents as soon as possible. They were moving Tabrina to a nursing center in Lebanon next week. She was breathing on her own now, but there'd been no appreciable change in her condition and her doctors said it was unlikely there would be. Carla wanted Judd to take Jolie to visit her mother as soon as possible.

Jolie spoke with Carla on the phone, but their exchange had been short and rather one-sided, with Jolie mostly nodding into the phone, her face more serious than any six-year-old's ought to be. Jolie hung up and trudged back to her room.

When Evette came to say goodbye, Jolie was sitting on her bed looking so glum it broke her heart. As she pulled out of the driveway, she'd prayed for Jolie—and for Judd, that he'd know how to cheer her up. It shamed her to realize she'd never really done that before. Prayed for them.

She'd done plenty of praying for herself. Her own comfort, her own convenience. Now, she offered up everything, including her attitude, to God. *Oh, Father…I give You permission to work in my life however You desire.*

It scared her to pray that kind of a prayer, and even as she formed the words, she knew she was still holding onto something…something she couldn't quite let go of yet. Still, it was a start. She hoped the Lord would honor that.

This time alone brought back memories of the years she and Judd had waited in anguish for God to grant them a baby. Since she'd passed the two-month mark—the point when she'd miscarried before—she'd begun to take the miracle of her pregnancy for granted. Now, in the quiet of the car, she thanked God again for allowing her to carry this child in her womb. Judd's child, who carried his blood just as Jolie did. It was a startling thought.

She navigated the streets of St. Louis, wishing this trip was for carefree lunches and shopping with her mother and sister, chess with her dad in the evening. She was eager to get this day behind her. After talking to Mike, she recognized that she'd worried more than she realized about announcing the news of Jolie to her family.

She'd taken the back roads instead of I-44, and somewhere on the two-hour stretch of narrow highways that snaked from the Falls to St. Louis, she'd decided it didn't matter what her family thought. She knew in her heart what was right, and it was time she grew up and quit worrying so much what people thought. It had hurt to have her pastor nail her problem on the head last week when she and Judd sat in Mike's office. But he was right.

She tapped the steering wheel and let out a sigh. The minute she walked into her parents' house, her resolve would weaken. She knew that. Especially if Annie was there. But she was determined to say what she needed to say, and to not be swayed, even by her older sister.

When she was buzzed through the gates to the Bryant estate twenty minutes later, her mother practically accosted her at the door. "What's wrong, Evette? Is everything okay with the baby?" She parted Evette's unzipped jacket and put both hands on the small mound of her stomach as if it were a crystal ball.

"The baby is fine, Mother. The doctor says it's a textbook pregnancy."

"Something's wrong with Judd?"

"Why would you think that?" Her mother was going to force her to spill everything before she even got her coat off.

"I could hear it in your voice when you called to tell us you were coming. And why isn't Judd with you?"

"You know he can't get away so close to the playoffs."

She harrumphed. "I can't believe he let you come by yourself—in your condition."

"I'm pregnant, Mother. It's not a 'condition.'"

"I would have called you on the road to make sure you were okay, but I was afraid you'd get in an accident trying to drive and talk on the phone. So what is it?"

"What do you mean?"

"Something is wrong. A mother knows these things."

Evette sighed and slipped her arms out of her jacket and hung it over the back of a kitchen chair. "Let me get my things from the car and we'll talk."

"I knew it. I just knew it." She reminded Evette of a heroine in an old movie, pacing and wringing her hands. "I told your father you weren't just coming for a visit."

Evette laughed. "I do have something to talk to you about, but it's not nearly as bad as you're making it out to be." She hoped her mother would agree with that assessment once she'd shared her news. She'd hoped to wait until her father was there, so she could tell them together, but Daddy was golfing and she knew better than to think she could hold her mother off until he got home.

By the time she got her things in from the car, tea was set at the gleaming mahogany table in the breakfast room. She stirred sweetener into the tea her mother had poured and looked around the elegantly appointed room. Except for crisp new linen curtains and wallpaper, the room was exactly as it had been when she and Annie were little girls. She was astonished to realize that this room was the epitome of what she'd been looking for when she and Judd were searching for their house. Except after the multitude of homes they'd wandered through in pursuit of the perfect, yet affordable, home, she realized that any ordinary family would have had children's crayon drawings and school papers tacked to a bulletin board, a sloppily dated calendar on the wall and toys scattered across the floor.

There'd never been a room in Mother and Daddy's house like that. Even the playroom she and Annie had shared as children had been professionally decorated, and every plaything, every book, even, was hidden behind a polished cupboard door and put away immediately after use. She wondered now how her Mother had managed that. Already, what few toys Jolie possessed were scattered from one end of the house to the other. Of course Mother had always had someone to help with the house, and a nanny until she and Annie were both in school.

The midday sun poured through sparkling windows, and fresh roses and Earl Grey fragranced the room. Yet somehow it lacked warmth. She'd never noticed that before.

Her mother flitted back and forth from the large kitchen, setting sliced nut bread and a fruit compote in front of Evette. "Help yourself and I'll send what's left home for Judd. I don't dare eat a bite if I'm going to fit into the gown I bought for the charity ball." She pulled out a chair and sat primly on its edge, waiting.

Evette took another sip of tea, wanting to get this over with, yet unsure exactly how to begin. "Well, you're right, Mother. I didn't just come for a visit." She toyed with the silver spoon on the saucer. "We got some rather…shocking news a couple of weeks ago. Three weeks ago, actually." It surprised her to realize it had been that long.

Her mother's face fell. "Not the baby?" She looked heavenward. "Oh please, Lord, no."

"The baby's fine, Mother. I told you that. No, it's…"

She smoothed the napkin in her lap. "You remember that Judd was engaged? Back in college…before we met?"

Her mother's perfectly groomed eyebrows went up.

"He didn't know it, but my his fiancée was pregnant when they broke up. He hasn't seen her since," she added quickly, "but…Judd has a child. A six-year-old daughter."

"Oh, Evette." Mother's head dropped to her chest. "And I suppose this woman is trying to take you for everything you have now?"

"No, Mother. It's not that. Actually, she had a stroke. She's very ill. She may never recover enough to take care of Jolie."

"Jolie? Have you met the child?" She stared through narrowed eyes and Evette could see her mind conjecturing.

"Yes. She's…a very sweet girl. Naturally this has been terribly hard on her. She doesn't have anyone—"

Her mother's hands went up. "Don't tell me Judd is thinking about taking her in."

"There isn't anyone else. Tabrina never married and Tabrina's mother can't take care of both of them."

"Tabrina? What kind of name is that?"

Evette opted to play dumb. "What do you mean?"

"Did you say *Tabrina?* Who would saddle their child with a name like that? It sounds like a *black* name, for heaven's sake!"

The emphasis she put on the word made Evette want to shake her. "It *is* a black name, Mother." It took everything in her to keep her voice even. "Jolie's mother is African-American."

"You mean—Judd?" Her hand flew to her mouth. "Oh, dear God."

Evette didn't think she meant it as a prayer.

Her mother stood and began to pace again. "Well, I certainly hope he doesn't expect you to get involved."

Evette closed her eyes. This was going to be harder than she thought. "That's why I'm here."

A little gasp escaped her mother's throat. "You've left Judd. Well, who could blame—"

"No! I haven't left Judd. Of course not." Evette stirred her untouched tea. "Actually, Mother...Jolie is living with us. Maybe permanently."

Her mother plopped back into the chair across from her. "You can't be serious? Evette! With the baby coming? You have your whole future ahead of you. I can't believe Judd would even ask such a thing of you!"

"Would you expect him to let his own daughter go into foster care?"

"Under the circumstances, yes, I would." She pinched the bridge of her nose. "I most certainly would! There has to be another solution, Evette. You can't raise your baby under these circumstances."

"What circumstances? What do you mean?" But she was afraid she knew exactly what her mother meant. A deeper wave of shame laved over her. Maybe Tessa Bryant had more integrity than she did...at least her mother was giving honest voice to her prejudices—the same prejudices Evette had entertained when she'd learned of Jolie's existence. She'd merely couched her thoughts in more "acceptable" guises.

Now she found herself offering the same arguments Judd had presented to her. And he was right. She saw that now. How could she have been so selfish and short-sighted? Blind.

She took a deep breath. "No, it wasn't easy to learn that Judd had a child. He was as shocked as I was."

Her mother rolled her eyes. "Well, he had to have some inkling." Then she wilted. "Oh, Evette…what will you do? This couldn't have possibly come at a worse time. Just when you finally have a baby on the way."

Her mother moved her chair out and started clearing the things off the tea table, her take-charge attitude back in full force. "Maybe she'll be gone by the time the baby comes. You could come here until then, I suppose. No one has to know—"

"Mother! What are you talking about? Jolie is a precious little girl who has had something terrible happen in her life. Judd is hap— Judd and *I* are happy to give her a place to call home…for as long as she needs it."

She heard herself speaking the words Judd had said to her and was chagrined to realize that she was answering some of the very questions she'd used to argue with Judd. But there was something emancipating in the conviction and passion in her own voice, in the realization that she meant every word.

Her mother stared at her as if she'd lost her mind. "You would put your own child at risk by taking this…this love child of your husband's into your home?"

"I can't believe what I'm hearing." She pushed her chair back and stood, gripping the back of the chair for support.

"Well, hear this." Her mother's eyes pierced her. "Do not expect one cent of help from your father and me if you decide to go through with this. When you come to your senses, you will see that this is a terrible idea. A monumentally terrible idea and I want no part of it."

Evette stared at her mother in stunned silence. "I didn't come here asking for your help. I came to tell you what I've been dealing with, what Judd and I are going through. All I wanted from you was understanding and support. This isn't easy for us, but we are determined to do the right thing, whether we have your support or not."

"And if you think the right thing is welcoming that child into your home…your family—" her voice quavered "—then that husband of yours has brainwashed you more than we thought."

Blinded by tears of rage and disappointment and shock, Evette followed her mother into the kitchen and yanked her jacket from the back of the chair. Stuffing an arm into one sleeve, she stumbled to the hallway.

Her mother tagged along after her, her voice strident. "What are you doing?"

"I'm going home." She picked up her suitcase and grabbed her purse.

"Evette, don't be ridiculous."

Hitching her bag up on her shoulder, Evette swiped at the tears that wet her cheeks. "I'll call you later. I…I can't talk now."

"Evette. Please." Her mother's tone changed one hundred and eighty degrees, suddenly all softness and contrition. "Honey…please. Stay. We'll talk this out. Your father will know how to handle this. You are in no mental state to drive. You'll have an accident."

"I can't stay. I'm sorry."

"What about Annie…the baby shower? Don't leave, Evette…"

"I'll call you when I get home." Numb, she slammed the door behind her and went to the car.

She drove for almost an hour, unaware of her surroundings, of the passage of time, weary with shame and sorrow, and something akin to grief. She only wanted to be home. And right now she wasn't sure where home was.

Chapter Twenty-Two

Judd hung up the telephone feeling like a wrung-out dishrag. His call to his parents had gone about as he expected. His father had stopped short of saying, "I told you so," but not of saying, "You've made your bed, now lie in it." His mother had spent most of the short call weeping. He'd told them both he loved them before he hung up. And he did. But he was finding it difficult to respect them.

But he'd done his duty. They knew now, and he could quit worrying that they'd find out from someone else. He checked on Jolie once more before heading in to catch the six-o'clock news. He'd just gotten comfortable in his recliner when the telephone rang.

He groaned, set his soda glass on the end table and went for the phone. Alarm surged through him when he saw the name that caller ID displayed: Bertram Bryant. Evette didn't usually call him when she was at her parents'.

He picked up the phone. "Hello?"

"Judd?" Tessa Bryant's voice was shrill with panic.

"Oh, Judd, Evette's not answering her cell phone and I'm worried sick. Bert hasn't come in off the course yet and I can't get hold of Annie, either."

"Hang on…calm down." He felt anything but calm himself. "Evette's not there yet?" She should have arrived in St. Louis hours ago. Her parents knew what time to expect her. Surely they would have called him before now if she hadn't arrived.

"She's been here and left already. She was so upset. She wouldn't listen to reason. Judd, you've got to do something!"

"What happened? Why was she upset?"

For a minute he thought the phone had gone dead. Then Tessa's voice came through. "Why do you think? She told us everything, Judd." She spit the words as though she were tattling on Evette.

"Yes…that's why she came. Why was she upset?"

"We got in an argument…and—" Her words came out in big gulping sobs. "She was upset with my reaction and said she couldn't stay here. I'll never forgive myself if anything happens to her."

"Evette is a careful driver, Tessa. She won't do anything to put the baby or herself in danger. Just tell me what happened and maybe I can get hold of her."

Evette's mother launched into a windy account of what had happened, and by the time she was finished Judd could read between the lines and envision exactly how everything had gone down. He felt proud of Evette, even as he worried about where she might be now. And why she hadn't called him. According to Tessa, she'd left St. Louis almost three hours ago.

He hung up the phone, promising to call the minute he heard from Evette. He tried her cell phone, but it went straight to voice mail. He went to the kitchen counter where his cell phone was charging and left her a text message.

Sighing, he went back to the family room, picked up the remote and punched the TV off. She'd probably taken the back roads home and stopped for coffee and a sandwich, time to think. He wasn't overly worried, but he would be if she didn't call soon.

He slumped to the edge of the recliner and put his head in his hands. "Lord," he whispered under his breath, "keep her safe on the road. Surround her car with Your angels and bring her home safe. Comfort her, Father. I know how much she cares what her parents think. Please just impress Your truth on her heart. Show her what's right. Give her strength…"

Evette had always cared too much what people thought. One glance around their home testified to that. She'd decorated it with the best she could get her hands on, and she'd done everything to her mother's and sister's specifications. If Annie got a new blue settee, that became the item Evette coveted. If Annie got new draperies, Evette started campaigning for them. When Annie had her babies, Evette's longing for a child was magnified.

He just hoped Annie didn't ever get a new husband. Of course, Geoffrey was perfect in every way—at least to hear Tessa Bryant tell it. For all he knew, when they spoke of him to Geoffrey, he shone like the sun. But he doubted it. He didn't keep Evette in palatial surroundings the way Geoffrey kept Annie. And he didn't have the "credentials" Geoffrey Stanton had—Ivy League degree, white-collar job, parents with a pedigree.

He shrugged off the thoughts like an itchy jacket.

Still, he felt bad that it was his actions that had flung Evette from her parents' good graces. All the more reason for her to resent Jolie—and him.

He picked up the phone and tried to call Evette again, but while the phone was still ringing, he heard the garage door go up. He walked through the kitchen and into the garage, he waited while she parked the car, then went around to open her door for her.

"Your mother called. Things didn't go so well, huh?"

He expected her to sag into a weepy heap in his arms—or storm away from him. Instead she hugged him tight and cradled his head in her hands. "Oh, Judd. Am I like that?"

He pulled back and looked into those cornflower blue eyes that were calm as a glassy pond. "What happened?"

"What did my mother tell you happened? That should be interesting."

He repeated a short version of his conversation with Tessa. "I need to call her. She's worried about you."

"Call her, but I don't want to talk to her right now."

"Okay."

Together they carried her things into the house. Evette slipped out of her shoes and jacket and slumped into a kitchen chair. "I'm beat. Can we talk in the morning?"

"Absolutely. You want me to run you a bath?"

"That would be really nice." She hesitated, and turned serious. "As long as you're doing it because you love me, and not because I'm a prima donna who expects the world handed to me on a silver platter."

He didn't know what had happened to his wife over the past ten hours, but whatever it was, he silently thanked God for it. He went to stand behind her and kneaded her shoulder blades gently. "Definitely because I love you."

"Mmm." She leaned back into his massage. Beneath his fingers, he felt the tension drain from her. But after a few minutes, her shoulders began to shake and he realized she was crying.

He knelt beside her chair and put his arms around her. "Pretty bad, huh?"

"Oh, Judd…it's not that. I just… I saw too much of myself today." She swiped at her cheeks with the back of her hands. "How can you stand me sometimes?"

He pulled her close. "I love you, Evette."

She laughed through her tears. "Good answer. Nice save, buddy."

He laughed. It was good to see her able to laugh at herself. In the music of her laughter, there were glimpses of the old Evette—the woman he'd fallen in love with at a time when he was floundering, wondering who he was, and what he really believed in after the breakup with Tabrina.

Tonight, the tiniest glimmer of hope shone through the mist of the despair he'd felt since the day the phone rang and he learned about Jolie. Tonight he could dream that their marriage might survive this after all, that they'd find a way to work it all out.

He drew his wife close, took her hand and led her down the hall to the bath.

Chapter Twenty-Three

Jolie was silent in the backseat, and Judd couldn't help but remember that first time driving home from Springfield—almost a month ago now—when she'd sobbed her little heart out.

Judd had come along with Evette and Jolie for this visit with Tabrina, but basketball season was coming to a head and then he would be hard-pressed just to find time to eat a meal with them. But when Carla reported that the doctor thought it might help Tabrina to hear Jolie's voice as often as possible, Evette surprised Judd by insisting they take Jolie to see her.

"I don't know how to explain it," she told him, "but it's as if I'm seeing everything through such different eyes than before."

She bent her head, and it took a minute for her to collect herself enough to speak. "Can you ever forgive me, Judd? I'm ashamed of how selfish and cold-hearted I was."

"Evette, what happened…it required a lot of you. I understand. I think anyone would. But yes, I forgive you. Of course I forgive you. You forgave me, and there was a lot more to forgive."

Judd felt a tap on his arm and turned around to see Jolie leaning forward, stretching the seat belt as far as it would reach. He sought her eyes in the rearview mirror. "What do you need, squirt?"

"Is Mama awake?"

He and Evette exchanged glances. "No, sweetheart. Not yet. We'll just have to keep praying for her. That she'll wake up." Oh, how it tested his faith to speak those words. What if Tabrina never woke up? How would he explain God's silence to this little girl?

"I am," she said, "'cept I forgot to pray last night. That game got me too 'cited."

Judd hid a smile. They'd taken her to the first game of the sectionals last night and it had indeed been exciting. "God understands. He knows you're praying in your heart every minute."

"How does He know?"

For a six-year-old, she asked some of the hardest questions he'd ever tried to field.

"He just does." He scrambled for a better answer. "God knows everything."

"He knows," Evette said, "because He's the one who made you. The one who made you probably knows *everything* about you, don't you think?"

Well, duh. Why didn't he think of that?

Jolie nodded, seeming satisfied, and Judd looked at Evette in amazement. There had been a transformation in his wife over the past three days since she'd come back from her parents' home. She'd told him about their conversation, and about the epiphany of sorts she'd had on the way home. Her eyes had been opened to some of the prejudice she'd been raised with, and she'd seen the ways she was like her parents. But Judd had a feeling she hadn't told him everything, that there might be more she hadn't revealed yet.

Last night's game had been their first time to take Jolie into the community. He hadn't introduced her to his players like he'd thought he would…it just hadn't seemed the right time with the team so pumped about the game. But the evening had been a success as far as he was concerned.

Evette told him afterward that the cheerleaders had come up to where she and Jolie were sitting at halftime. "You should have seen her, Judd. The girls fawned over her…teased her about her loose tooth and fiddled with her hair. They told her she looked exactly like you…except for the braids." Evette had laughed at that. "She ate up the attention, and she was a little charmer. Just like you." A *charmer.* Evette's word. It meant Jolie had charmed *her,* too.

"What are you smiling about?" Evette was looking at him with a quizzical glint in her eyes.

He hadn't realized he was smiling. "I was just thinking about the game." That was true. He didn't want to push Evette. God had worked miracles in her heart when he finally backed off and quit trying to be her conscience.

"I just have a feeling you're going all the way to State."

He loved her confidence in him, in the team he coached. He nodded slowly. "If we keep playing like this, I think we just might."

Jolie fell asleep in the backseat half an hour out of Hanover Falls, and Judd talked about the game for a while. Evette humored him, letting him ramble about strategies and play-by-play. She didn't even argue when he dared to broach the subject of going back to school to take the education classes he'd need to teach. She usually bristled when he mentioned the possibility of quitting his CPA job.

As they neared Lebanon, Evette navigated with the road atlas spread open on her lap—or what was left of her lap.

She traced a finger over the route. "Unless there's something on the map I can't see underneath here—" she patted her blossoming middle "—I think you take the next exit."

"We have the big ultrasound next week, don't we?"

She nodded. "Have you decided if you want to find out what we're having?"

Before when Evette had been pregnant, he'd been certain he wanted a son, but now he didn't care so much. Jolie was every bit as much fun as he imagined a son might be, and it might be nice for her to have a sister. He'd leave that decision up to the Lord. "You want to know, don't you?"

"Definitely. You know I do."

"Why?"

She looked at him as if he were missing a couple of marbles. "Because we live in the twenty-first century and we *can*."

He laughed. "That's like saying you would open your presents before Christmas just because you can."

She shot him a smug grin. "And I probably would if you ever had my gifts wrapped before Christmas Eve."

"Well, now I have a good reason not to. Seriously, though, what will it change if you know earlier?"

"Well, it might keep me from bringing your son home from the hospital in pink."

He made a face. "Good point. Well, what if I don't want to know? Can you keep a secret?"

"I'll do my best. If I slip up and say 'he' or 'she,' I'll just pretend to slip up the other way…keep you guessing. Deal?"

"I'm still deciding. I've got till Monday, right? What time's the appointment?"

"Two. I'd really like you to be there, Judd…since you missed my last one."

"I'll be there." Monday's practice was an important one. He hoped the appointment didn't take too long. "I can just cover my ears and sing really loud when they tell you the baby's sex." He took his hands off the steering wheel and demonstrated.

Evette laughed, but then she gave a little gasp and pointed through the windshield. "You just missed your exit."

He got off at the next turn and the lighthearted moment was lost. They would be facing another encounter with Tabrina just minutes from now. He worried how Jolie would handle it—whether it would upset her and cause a setback.

And would seeing Tabrina again undo the progress Evette had made? It would be easier if they didn't have to deal with Carla or Tabrina. But that wasn't fair.

Evette patted Jolie's knees gently, trying to wake her, and Judd took a deep breath, steeling himself to see the mother of his child again.

Unlike the hospital, the nursing home's smells weren't clean and antiseptic. Evette wanted to plug her nose the way Jolie did, but she resisted. She hadn't thought about this being a retirement home—full of elderly residents, most of them here to die.

Was that why Tabrina had been sent here? How sad

that this was where she would spend the next weeks—maybe years—of her life.

Carla Greene wasn't waiting for them this time, so Judd asked at the front desk where Tabrina's room was.

The young African-American nurse with braids like Jolie's gave him the room number then, noticing Jolie on the other side of the desk, she broke into a smile. "You must be this Jolie we been hearing 'bout. All the time Tabrina's mama be sayin' 'Jolie this' and 'Jolie that.' So we finally get to meet this Jolie, huh? How you doin', girl?"

"Fine," Jolie muttered. She gave a shy grin and looked at the floor.

"Well, you better get down there and see your mama. She's been missin' you like you would not believe. You go on now." She waved pudgy hands like she was shooing chickens.

Judd looked at the nurse with a question in his eyes. Surely Carla would have told them if there'd been a change.

Evette leaned over the counter, keeping her voice low. "Is she…awake? Has she regained consciousness?"

"Oh, that's not what I meant. Sorry." The nurse looked flustered. "I just mean— Well, if *I* was her mama, I'd sure be missing her."

Evette nodded, teetering between disappointment and relief over the nurse's news about Tabrina's condition.

Judd put his hand at the small of her back. "You ready?"

She nodded. He took Jolie's hand and Evette followed them down the hall.

Carla was in the room, fussing over Tabrina's bedcovers. Thankfully, the bed next to Tabrina's was empty, but Evette couldn't imagine it would stay that way for long.

"Grams!" Jolie threw her arms out and flew to her grandmother. Evette wondered if she hadn't noticed Tabrina in the bed yet, or if she'd just given up hope of seeing her mother alert and awake.

"Hey, baby girl!" Kneeling on the tile floor, Carla hugged Jolie, then rocked back on her haunches and looked her up and down. She held her away and inspected her, tugging on one of her bead-tipped braids. "Just look at you, girl, all fancy with your braids. Who did that?" Carla looked at Evette, skepticism plain in her dark eyes.

Evette laughed nervously. "Not me, I'm afraid. We found a woman in town who does braids."

Barely acknowledging Evette, Carla aimed her reply at Jolie. "Looks good on you. Your mama used to do her hair like that before she took to ironing it out." She threw a look at Judd as if that was his fault, but she didn't wait for his defense before turning her attention back on Jolie. "You doing okay?"

Evette knew what her real questions were. *Are they treating you well? Are you happy at your father's house?*

Jolie nodded, sending the beads in her braids clacking again.

Carla grabbed the end of the bed and grunted, hauling herself up from the floor. "You come on over and say hi to your mama. You talk to her now, you hear? The doctors say she can hear you. She'll be wanting to hear all about you."

Jolie looked back to Judd, asking permission with her eyes. At his nod, she approached the bed timidly. "Hey, Mama…"

For the first time, Evette took a good look at Tabrina. Her wrists and hands already showed signs of atrophy, jutting at odd angles on top of the white blankets. Bony fingers clutched rolled-up washcloths, and she wore braces of some kind on her wrists and forearms.

She'd deteriorated dramatically in the month since they'd seen her. Her jaw hung slack and her face was pale and ashy. Not, Evette thought, from lack of lotion. There was still a scant trace of the beauty Evette knew had once been there. But it was fading, almost before their eyes.

Jolie reached to touch her mother's shoulder. "Mama?"

Carla bustled over to the bed and stood behind Jolie. "She still can't talk to you, baby, but don't let that stop you. You just keep talking. Maybe you'll get through to her. Maybe hearing your voice will help her wake up."

Judd took a step toward them. "Jolie, can you tell your mom where we were last night?"

Jolie's face brightened and she turned back to her mother. "We went to a basketball game. Dad's team won! But they almost didn't. Me 'n' Evette thought they was gonna lose for sure."

Judd winked at Evette and she had the decency to blush.

"That's good, Jolie." Carla patted her hand. "You keep talking. Just like that."

Jolie looked up at her with a panicked look on her face, but just as quickly turned back to Tabrina and gingerly touched the straps on the wrist braces. "How's come you got that on your arms, Mama? Does it hurt?"

A lump formed in Evette's throat, and she prayed Tabrina would somehow respond to Jolie's efforts.

But she lay deathly still, her face an emotionless mask.

Carla backed slowly away and motioned for Judd and

Evette to join her on the other side of the room. For a few minutes, the three of them stood in silence watching Jolie's sweet, one-sided conversation with her mother.

Finally, Judd spoke in a low whisper. "How is she doing, Carla?"

Tabrina's mother shook her head. "Not good. They're having a terrible time managing her diabetes. And it's obviously not good that she still hasn't regained consciousness." She ran a hand over her close-cropped, graying curls. "My job is already at risk because of all the time I've taken off to be here. I simply cannot afford to lose it, either. If I lose my insurance, Walt's medicine will eat up everything I'm spending to keep Tabrina here. And if you think this is bad, you don't want to see where they send people like her without insurance."

"I'm so sorry," Judd said.

Carla leveled her gaze at him. "The doctors—and Tabrina's physical therapist, too—feel she needs to hear Jolie's voice…on a regular basis."

Evette's mind whirled. What was Carla asking?

Judd glanced over Carla's head to where Jolie continued to chatter to her mother, gesturing animatedly with her graceful hands, gathering steam as she told some fanciful story. This had to be good therapy—the best therapy—for Tabrina Jackson.

"I know I've already asked a lot of you, Judd—of both of you…" She included Evette with her intent stare. "But for this, I'm begging you. Tabrina needs to see Jolie—hear her voice as often as possible. I just know it's her only hope of getting better. You read stories all the time about people in comas. They can hear, they know who visits them, and what people say about them when they're in the room." She waited, a hopeful look in her eyes, as if she thought Judd would save her from pleading on her knees.

He stood in the middle of the room, his expression unreadable.

Carla's voice broke. "Judd, please. I know it's asking a lot, but it might—in the most real sense of the word imaginable—mean the difference between life and death for my baby."

The way she called Tabrina "my baby" sent an electric tremor up Evette's spine. In all the time they'd been dealing with the results of Judd and Tabrina's sin, she hadn't really considered how very personal this was for Carla. This was her daughter, her baby girl in the same way Jolie was Tabrina's baby. And Tabrina was her only birth child, according to Judd, though she did have stepchildren in Walt's two grown sons. Carla had demonstrated such a take-charge, almost cool attitude when Evette had met her at the hospital in Springfield, that she hadn't fully understood the tragedy this woman had experienced with Tabrina's stroke.

And of course, in a very real sense, she'd lost Jolie, as well.

Evette knew what Carla was asking. Understood the sacrifice it would take to comply with her wishes. Hours on the road between Hanover Falls and Lebanon—a three-hour round trip in itself. More hours spent in Tabrina's presence, in this place that carried the stench of hopelessness and death. Helping Jolie through what would surely be traumatic encounters.

Carla couldn't come and get Jolie, or she'd lose her job. Judd couldn't lose his jobs, either. They depended wholly on both his position as an accountant and the extra money coaching brought in. His insurance was vital with the baby on the way.

There was only one logical person who could get Jolie to Lebanon every week and encourage her as she spoke to her mother. Evette was that person.

Of course, Jolie needed to be with her mother every bit as much as Tabrina needed her daughter—more than once every few weeks, too.

Evette knew what she was being asked to do. Not for Carla's sake. Not for Judd's. Not even for Jolie's. But out of obedience to the Lord, to whom she'd given her life over in a new and deeper way on the way home from St. Louis.

How could she say anything other than yes? The only question she really had to answer was this: Was she going to do it begrudgingly, or could she do it with a servant's heart?

One week ago, the answer would have been a resounding *no.* Before the eye-opening time with her mother, she could not have taken on such a task. But she was different. Something had changed on that narrow road between St. Louis and Hanover Falls—her personal road to Damascus. Now she knew she had a choice.

She bowed her head and in the quiet of her heart, Evette said yes. She would put on the heart of a servant. She would do it because she loved her husband, because she loved her Lord, because it was the right thing to do.

And she would do it—she realized with joy—because a cute little six-year-old named Jolie Jackson had wormed her way straight into her heart.

Chapter Twenty-Four

The church was almost full this morning, and as the worship team took the stage, Evette had a sudden image of Jolie swaying and clapping and waving her arms in the air like the African-American choirs she'd seen in the movies. Oh dear. What would they do if she started. *Please, Lord...please don't let that happen.*

Immediately, she felt chastened. How could she sit here and *pray* such a thing? Who was she to judge whether that form of worship was acceptable or not? Still, as it was, she felt every eye in the sanctuary on them. They didn't need anything else drawing attention to them.

Jolie had seemed comfortable and familiar with bedtime and mealtime prayers, and when Judd asked her if she and Tabrina attended church, Jolie nodded with enthusiasm. But they'd laughed when he asked her what church they went to and she replied, "The white one." Judd went through a list of denominations, and she shook her head at each one. "It's just called *church*," she insisted. It was something they needed to ask Carla about the next time they saw her.

The guitarists began to play softly and people settled into their seats, but everywhere Evette turned, she saw eyes quickly averted or people whispering behind their hands. They would definitely be the talk of the town at dinner tables and restaurant booths all over the Falls today. Funny thing was, she knew if it had been anyone else, she would have been just as guilty of staring and whispering and starting that dinner-table gossip.

She bowed her head briefly and asked forgiveness for the times she'd been thoughtless in the past, and asked for a strong dose of compassion and sensitivity for the future.

When the worship leader asked the congregation to stand and join them in singing, Jolie stood without prompting. She looked at the words on the overhead, but she wasn't reading well yet and didn't seem to know the song.

A minute later when the drummer started in and the tempo sped up a bit, Evette saw her little foot tapping and her hands drumming the back of the seats in front of her. She held her breath, praying the next song was another slow one.

When the worship team sat down, Pastor Mike asked the congregation to greet one another. Another moment Evette had been dreading. But in the murmur of cheerful greetings, she and Judd were suddenly surrounded. On every side there was someone to tell them they'd been missed and prayed for. And someone to take Jolie's hand and welcome her.

Jolie scooted between Judd and Evette and gripped Evette's skirt as if it were a lifeline, but she grinned at everyone who greeted her. Judd beamed. When Mike began to read the announcements and people gravitated back to their seats, Evette sat down with Jolie between her and Judd and she realized that here, she felt safe. Here, there was a haven for them.

It was a good feeling.

"I can't find my shoe!" Jolie's panicked voice carried down the hallway to the kitchen where Evette was making oatmeal. First-day-of-school jitters—on the first day of April. She just hoped Judd didn't try to pull his usual April Fool's joke. She was in no mood.

"I put them right at the end of your bed," Evette hollered back. "Judd? Can you help?"

No reply, so she turned the burner down under the pan and started to go help Jolie search for the missing shoe. Halfway down the hall she heard Judd running interference. "Where did you have your shoes last?"

"I don't 'member."

"Well, think, Jolie. Don't just start hollering about it. Mommy—Evette—is trying to make breakfast." Judd stumbled over his words, and Evette knew his slip had surprised him as much as it had her.

Mommy. He'd called her *Mommy* to Jolie. It warmed her all the way through. But just as quickly a chill chased the warmth away. She'd have to talk to Judd. What he'd said wasn't fair to Tabrina. Whether Tabrina could ever again be an active parent to her daughter, she was still Jolie's mother. They had to remember that. She had to make sure Judd honored that.

She went to turn on the heat under the oatmeal again. Stirring, she strained to hear the fatherly lecture Judd was delivering.

"If you're going to be a big schoolgirl, you have to start taking responsibility for your things."

"What's that? 'Spons-ability?"

"It means taking care of things for yourself, and not always making me or—Evette take care of it for you. Do you understand?"

Silence, but Evette could imagine Jolie's solemn nod. She would take her father's counsel to heart, too. At the school counselor's advice, they'd decided to give Jolie a few weeks to settle in with them before starting school. But despite all she'd had been through recently, Jolie was a well-behaved, well-adjusted child. Tabrina must have been a wonderful mother. The kind of mother Evette hoped she would be.

The baby somersaulted in her womb and Evette whispered a prayer that it would be so.

An hour later, walking Jolie down the hall to her classroom, Evette knew what it must feel like to drop a kindergartner off at school for the first time. If she could've come up with any excuse to turn around and take Jolie home— or stay in the classroom with her—she would have.

But Mrs. Markham met them at the door with a smile, and practically shoved Evette out the door.

"We'll have a great first day, won't we, Jolie?" the teacher said.

Evette knew she'd been dismissed. A lump lodged in her throat and she stooped and put her arms around Jolie. "You'll have a wonderful time," she whispered.

The uneasy smile she received in return made it all the harder to let go. "I'll pick you up right out front as soon as school's out, okay?"

Jolie's gaze went past Evette to the labyrinth of hallways they'd come down.

Mrs. Markham seemed to read her mind. "Don't

worry, Jolie. I'll walk everybody to the pickup zone when the bell rings."

Jolie's shoulders relaxed and Evette briefly cradled the back of her head. "Have a great day, sweetie." She backed out of the room, waving and fighting to stanch the tears that pressed behind her eyelids.

Jolie waved and edged closer to her teacher.

Evette felt a strange emptiness as she navigated the hallways back to the parking lot. Just a few days ago, she'd looked forward to this day as a respite from what she'd viewed as the ultimate crucible.

What a difference a few sunrises and sunsets—and a trip to St. Louis for an attitude adjustment—made. *Thank You, Father. Thank You.*

The tears flowed then. But they were no longer tears of shame for how self-centered she'd been. Instead, they were tears of joy because she'd been changed—well, mostly. She still felt the pangs of her selfishness more often than she cared to admit, but now she recognized it for what it was, and she knew what medicine would cure her faster than any drug. If she'd been home, she would have taken a dose right now. But that remedy—time on her knees, on her face before God—would have to wait until she got home.

Today was the day they were supposed to find out whether she was carrying a boy or a girl. Judd was meeting her at the clinic for the ultrasound and then they were heading to lunch to celebrate, whether it was a boy or a girl. Judd still hadn't decided if he wanted to know, but she intended to try to persuade him to stay and hear the verdict, and then go shopping for something pink or blue afterward. She did not want to have to keep the baby's gender a secret from him. There'd been enough secrets between them recently.

Her thoughts wandered to a darker place and she forced them back to the present. Things had been good between her and Judd these past few days. They were adjusting to having Jolie in their home, and it wasn't nearly as disruptive as she'd feared. The whole thing with her mother—and hence her father and her sister—hung over her, unfinished business. She'd left a message on her parents' answering machine the day after she got back, letting them know she was home safely and that she'd call them soon.

Her mother hadn't responded, but Evette hadn't expected her to. She was surprised Annie hadn't called after Mother gave her an earful, as Evette knew she would. She planned to call all her family this evening after Jolie was in bed. News about her checkup with the obstetrician would no doubt smooth things over with her mother, and Daddy would be happy if Mother was happy.

To her own surprise, she wasn't terribly concerned about what Annie thought. She loved her sister, but she'd spent a lifetime in competition with her, and far too many years letting Annie's opinion guide her choices, and too often mislead her. Maybe Evette Bryant McGlin was finally growing up…just in time to be a mother.

She hit the drive-through for a decaf latte and ran a few errands, killing time before her appointment. When she got to the clinic, she was surprised to see that Judd's Caliber was already in the parking lot. The clock on her dashboard said nine-fifteen. Hmm…with things at work being so crazy, he'd warned her he might be a few minutes late. Instead, he was fifteen minutes early.

She parked in the empty space to the right of Judd's car and looked over to see him still behind the wheel. He waved and smiled, then got out of the car and opened the Caliber's back door. When he came around to meet her, he held a beribboned silver gift bag.

"For you." He held the bag out, looking decidedly uncomfortable.

"Me?" She tilted her head. "What's the occasion?"

"Well, for Bambino, actually." He shrugged. "Open it."

She looked around the parking lot. "Here?"

"Unless you want to wait."

She laughed. "Are you kidding? I'm so curious, I think I might die."

"Well, then, you'd definitely better open it."

She untied the loose ribbon holding the handles of the bag together and peered into the large bag. There were two identical wrapped boxes inside. "Does it matter which one I open first?"

He shook his head, looking rather smug.

Her curiosity ratcheting upward, she tore the wrapping off one of the boxes. Inside was a pair of tiny blue booties. She looked up at Judd. His tongue made the side of one cheek puff out. What? Did he know something she didn't know?

She handed him the box to hold and opened its twin. Taking off the lid, she started giggling. This box held an identical pair of booties, except in pink. "So does this mean you *do* want to know what we're having?" she said, still laughing.

"I do. I don't think I could stand it if you knew and I didn't. But let's keep it our little secret, okay? Just between you and me."

"I'd like that." Her throat swelled with emotion and she reached up to cup a hand to his face.

He covered her hand with his own, then took the booties from her and put both boxes back in the gift bag. He set the bag on the hood of her car and gathered her in his arms.

"I love you, Evie. I can't wait to see the precious gift God has in store for us in August." The emotion in his voice warmed her in a way she hadn't felt in so long.

"I love you, too," she murmured.

They stood there in each other's arms for a long minute. Finally, Judd stepped back and put his hands on her shoulders. "Okay, Mrs. McGlin. Let's go find out which pair of those booties we'll be needing."

"Who knows…?" She raised her eyebrows and tried to look mysterious, as if she knew something he didn't. "Maybe we'll need both pairs."

He started to nod, then did a double take. "What did you say?"

"Just kidding."

He gave her shoulder a playful punch. "Would you cut that out!"

She cracked up and soon Judd joined in. Their laughter floated on air that held a breath of spring, and as they walked to the clinic arm in arm, Evette thought she could actually feel the rift between them healing.

Chapter Twenty-Five

In the high-school commons, Judd piled his plate high from the table overflowing with casseroles, salads and desserts. His players' moms knew how to fill hungry bellies, but his stomach growled more from nerves than hunger.

He always wished he could give these pregame talks before the meal so he could eat without a knot of nerves tangled in his gut.

Tomorrow night's game was the most important of his life since the State tournament his own senior year of high school. If they won the game tonight, the Hanover Falls Hawks would be headed to the State play-offs for the first time in eleven years.

Team spirit was at an all-time high and the whole town had rallied behind them.

Waiting in line at the dessert table, he looked over to the head table where Evette was helping Jolie cut up some meatballs. Randall and Michelle Hazen sat across the table from her, and his five senior players filled out the table. They were horsing around and snarfing food as if their forks were shovels.

Evette caught Judd's eye and gave him a look that said, "Hurry up and get over here."

She'd always been happy to have the guys over for pizza or to watch a ball game, but for someone who'd managed people and worked in retail, she could be downright shy when it came to making small talk.

He nabbed one of the last slices of a lemon-meringue pie—Rafe's mom's, if the kid's bragging was a clue—and a couple of cookies. These dinners were murder on the physique, but a highlight of his culinary year nevertheless.

Two senior moms were pouring drinks at a cart beside the dessert table. "Congratulations, Coach," they said in unison.

Brent Harper's mother handed him a plastic cup of lukewarm lemonade.

He thanked her and made his way to the head table. As soon as Jolie spotted him, she waved her hands. "Dad! Hey, Dad! Sit here!" She climbed up on her chair and motioned to him. "I saved you a place."

The commons grew quiet as people turned to see who was yelling. Evette shushed her, tugging at the sleeve of Jolie's T-shirt.

Jolie sat back down, but repeated her invitation in a stage whisper. Some of the players and parents seated at the rows of tables laughed good-naturedly. But Judd didn't miss the inquisitive looks on a few faces, and the whispers and fingers pointed at Jolie. Apparently, not everybody in town had heard about Coach McGlin's daughter, but the good ol' gossip mill would take care of that tonight. He wondered if Evette had noticed. She seemed preoccupied, trying to settle Jolie back in her chair. Judd suspected that was merely a way to avoid the unwanted attention she and Jolie were receiving.

He set his plate down on the other side of Jolie and bent over Evette. "Do you need anything else?"

She gave him an affected smile that left no doubt she knew they were being watched. He hoped this evening wouldn't be the catalyst for another argument.

He mentally chided himself. Evette seemed truly changed. Not that everything was perfect…they still had plenty of issues to work through. But she'd completely surprised him on the way home from Lebanon the other night after visiting Tabrina.

With Jolie asleep in the backseat of the car, Evette had turned to him wearing a serious expression. "There's no reason I can't bring Jolie to see her—to see Tabrina— once or twice a week. I think it would be good for Jolie, too. I…I've made this all out to be such an inconvenience, but when it comes right down to it, it's not that hard."

For a minute, he'd thought she was being sarcastic. But her expression said otherwise. "What do you mean?"

"Well, here I am, privileged to be home full-time." Looking over her shoulder at Jolie, she'd lowered her voice. "Tabrina needs to see her, hear her voice. It's a small thing, really, for me to help that happen."

He wasn't sure he'd heard her right at first. Even for her to speak Tabrina's name showed a shift in her thinking. He hated that he was so preoccupied with the tax workload at the office and even more with the basketball play-offs. He kept telling himself that once tax day was past, he'd aim all his attention at Evette and Jolie. That somehow he would show his wife how much he appreciated everything she'd done for him and for Jolie.

Quickly finishing his meal, he went to the front of the

commons and turned on the mike. He began with a welcome to the team and parents and a heartfelt thanks to everyone who'd provided the delicious meal. "I've seen how these guys eat, so believe me, I know it's no small investment of grocery money and hours in the kitchen to keep this team fueled."

Laughter trickled through the room.

"More than the food, though, I thank you for loaning me your sons for this season and the seasons leading up to this past incredible week."

The audience of less than fifty erupted with the enthusiasm of five hundred. If they won tomorrow night and went to State, the Falls cheering section could very well be five hundred strong, but these were the core Hawks fans and he wanted them to know how much he appreciated every one of them.

Judd waited until they'd settled down before he continued. "Coaching the Hawks has been a real privilege for me, and a highlight of these last few years of my life. I couldn't be more sincere when I say that this could not have happened without the support of the parents and families of these players. Without the long hours in the gym and all the other sacrifices these guys have made for the good of the team, we would not be here tonight. We would not be headed to Calimont tomorrow night and, God willing, to Columbia next week for the State tournament."

The team and the cheerleaders roared again, whooping and whistling at the top of their lungs. The parents in the audience laughed, but Judd could feel their excitement building, too. This might really happen.

It was doubtful few in this room remembered Hanover Falls' last trip to Columbia for State. Oh, how he would love to be the one to bring this fairy tale to life. What a great memory for his five seniors, and what great motivation for the team he'd build for next year.

This season had been everything a coach could hope for. He waited for the cheers to run their course and when that didn't seem to be happening, he picked up the mike again. "Hey, hey, guys…don't use up all that energy tonight. Save it…save it…"

That made them laugh and settle down a little. He leaned out over the podium, looking to his left to catch Evette's eye, and launched into the same speech he'd given at every end-of-year banquet the past three years. "You all know my wife, Evette. No coach could ask for a more supportive partner. I'm not kidding when I say that without Evette, I could not hold down this job I love—*or* the one that pays the bills," he deadpanned.

That drew more laughter and a smattering of applause.

Judd turned serious and continued. "This year especially, with a six-year-old in the house—" he smiled at Jolie "—and a baby on the way, Evette has truly held everything together. Thank you, babe." He wanted to honor Evette publicly, but admittedly he'd also worded his remarks carefully with the intent of diffusing the situation with Jolie.

Evette dipped her head and gave him a shy smile as the audience applauded politely.

"And by the way, we found out at our last doctor's appointment that this baby is a future basketball player." He pumped a fist in the air and waited for the response he knew would come.

"All right! A boy! Yeah!" James Severn, Judd's point guard, punched Rafe in the thigh. "See, told ya! It's a boy! You owe me ten bucks, man."

The cheerleaders at the end of the table—who'd made no secret that they were all hoping for a girl—made pouty faces at one another.

"Hang on, hang on…" Judd laughed into the microphone. "I said a future basketball player. Maybe I meant a *female* basketball player."

He raised his eyebrows comically, and the cheerleaders whooped while his players groaned. Judd had been dodging questions about the baby's gender for weeks. Now he relished having a secret to keep with Evette. Instead of *from* her.

"Actually, I told my wife I didn't want to know whether we were having a boy or a girl." The players groaned again, and Judd lifted a hand to silence them. "So I guess you'll have to try to pry the secret out of her. And good luck with *that*."

Evette laughed and winked at him, and he warmed at their brief exchange.

Jolie wiggled in her seat beside Evette, a familiar "dance" that meant she needed to go to the bathroom. Judd shuffled his notes and started to speak again, hopefully to take the spotlight off Evette and Jolie. But too late.

"But I have to go *baaad*." The excellent acoustics in the commons amplified Jolie's whispered plea.

The audience laughed.

Evette bent to whisper something in Jolie's ear.

"But I have to go now!"

The laughter built and Evette colored and scraped her chair back then helped Jolie out of hers.

Jolie skipped between two banquet tables, squealing and holding herself as if she were about to have an accident. Judd joined the good-natured snickers and racked his brain for a clever remark that would ease Evette's embarrassment. Drawing a blank, he stumbled through an awkward transition to the next part of his speech.

Evette and Jolie never came back to the commons, and he assumed Evette had taken her out to the playground at the elementary school across the street from the high school.

But when they still hadn't appeared after the program ended and the crowd dwindled, he followed some of his players out to the parking lot. The car wasn't where he'd parked it. Evette must have taken Jolie home.

He turned on his cell phone and checked his text messages.

Can u get ride? J peed pants. We r hm.

He laughed. Apparently, Jolie's gyrations hadn't been an act to get her out of a boring "meeting." He hoped Evette wasn't upset. He would have been embarrassed in her shoes, too. In the grand scheme of things it wasn't a big deal, but he'd prayed for things to go as close to perfect as possible where Jolie was concerned—for Evette's sake. She'd been a trouper these past few days. It seemed the least God could do under the circumstances was keep things running smoothly. He shot up a prayer saying as much.

He turned back toward the school building, trying to remember if he'd seen Randall and Michelle leave yet. Maybe he could catch a ride with them. Just then, Rafe Clairmont's mother came through the door, juggling two empty pie plates and a small picnic basket. Judd jogged to get the door for her. "Can I carry something for you there?"

She smiled up at him. "Thanks, but Rafe can help me." She nodded back in the direction of the commons. "Tom ducked out early, so I'm riding home with Rafe."

"Yeah, my wife ditched me, too."

Karen Clairmont laughed. "I saw her leave with…your little girl?" Her voice rose like it was a question, but she didn't wait for him to answer. "Kids, huh?"

He shrugged. "Yeah. My poor wife…"

"And you're just getting started. Sounds like you're going to have a houseful in short order."

Rafe burst through the double doors, stopping short when he saw them. "Hey, Coach."

"Hey, Rafe. Heading straight home for a good night's sleep, right?" Judd teased, thankful to have the topic of Jolie short-circuited.

The teen rolled his eyes. "Don't have much choice. Don't exactly want to drag Main with my mom."

Rafe's mother giggled.

"Listen," Judd said, remembering that the Clairmonts lived a few blocks past him on Bramblewood. "Would you mind if I caught a ride?"

"Of course not," Karen said. She pointed to the south end of the parking lot. "We're parked right over there."

"You sure I can't carry something there?" Judd nodded at the load she carried.

"Rafe, take these," Karen chided, sliding the pie plates off the basket and thrusting them at her son.

He took the mostly empty plates, running his finger through a dab of lemon pie filling stuck to the side of one. "This is all that's left?"

His mother patted his back. "Don't worry, there's another whole pie at home. Unless your father got into it."

Rafe's eyes got big. "Oh, man! That's probably why

Dad cut out early." He took off jogging for the car, leaving his mother and Judd laughing.

"It really was a great pie," Judd said, as they walked to Rafe's car.

"Oh, it's my specialty. I'll have to make you one all for yourself sometime." She laughed at him and moved closer, until she was almost touching him. Judd sidestepped and switched his huge duffel bag to the opposite shoulder, putting some distance between them. As they neared the car, he saw that Rafe was in the backseat. He regretted now that he'd asked for a ride. Karen Clairmont had always been a bit of a flirt, but he'd only seen her operate in a public setting where no real harm could be done. Now there was no way he could bow out gracefully.

He opted not to open her door for her, and instead took his time loading his gear in the back beside Rafe. He did take the basket from Karen, holding it on his lap and imagining how he could use it as a shield if she got any bolder. Thank goodness it was only a few blocks to his home.

Judd kept up a running conversation with Rafe all the way, or tried to, over Karen's chattering. When she parked in his driveway, he set the basket on the seat, thanked her for the ride and gathered his things as quickly as he could.

Opening the garage door, he felt a little foolish and wondered if he'd imagined things. It didn't matter. He was just glad to be out of that miserable situation. The last thing he needed was some woman coming on to him.

Chapter Twenty-Six

"Get up, Jolie. Time for school." Evette jiggled the little pink-bottomed toes peeking out from the quilt.

Jolie moaned, plumped her oil-stained pillow and pulled the covers over her head.

"Come on. You need to hustle because Dad's dropping you off at school this morning."

"Why do I hafta go with Dad? Can't you take me, Evie?"

Not for the first time, Evette pushed away a twinge of bitterness that remained over Judd's status as Dad. Jolie had taken to calling her "Evie" the way Judd did. She hadn't been crazy about it at first, but it had grown on her. It was better than having a six-year-old call her by her full first name—or call her Mrs. McGlin.

"Come on, squirt, get up. We're running late. Get up before I have to tickle you up."

Jolie squirmed out from under the covers, rubbing her eyes. With eyes still squinched shut, she stumbled to the hall bathroom—the guest bath that was now decorated with St. Louis Cardinal towels and a SpongeBob tooth-brush holder set.

Evette pulled up the quilts and started to make the bed. Judd thought she should be teaching Jolie to do this, but six seemed a little young to be saddled with a chore like making the bed every morning. Of course, what did she know? She'd never made a bed in her life until she married Judd. All the more reason Judd was probably right. She sighed and reached for a pillow, but before she could fluff it, a scream came from the bathroom.

"Jolie!" Heart pounding in her ears, Evette flew into the hall. "Jolie! What's wrong?"

Jolie stood on the little red bench they'd bought, leaning into the mirror and screaming at the top of her lungs.

Evette couldn't see any blood and Jolie was standing on her own two feet, limbs intact. "What is wrong?" She tried to pick her up, but Jolie shrugged out of her grasp. The screaming stopped, but with her eyes open as wide as her mouth, she kept looking into the mirror, whimpering all the while.

"What happened? Tell me what's wrong, Jolie…" Evette forced calm into her voice.

"Look! Jutht look!" Jolie turned to her, mouth still agape, as if she were sitting in a dentist's chair.

"Oh!" Evette looked at the wide gap in the middle of the row of tiny white teeth. She couldn't help smiling. "You lost your tooth!"

"Where is it? Where is it?" Jolie wailed, looking back to the mirror as though the tooth might magically grow back.

"It must have come out while you were sleeping."

"Get Dad!"

"He's in the shower. Come with me." She hustled Jolie back to her bedroom. "Your tooth is probably under the covers somewhere. Or maybe you swallowed it."

"No!" Jolie gasped. "The tooth fairy won't come then!"

"Shh…it's okay. Help me look. Here…" She pulled the quilt back carefully, running her hand over the wrinkled sheet. Jolie stood beside the bed watching wide-eyed.

Evette picked up a pillow and something fell and bounced on the sheet.

"There it is!" Jolie pounced on the tooth.

Evette sat on the edge of the mattress and held her hand out. "Let me see."

"It'th tho tiny." When her words came out in a lisp, Jolie's eyes bugged out. Evette burst out laughing and that sent Jolie into spasms of giggles.

"Say, 'Sister Suzy sat on a satin pillow,'" Evette urged when she could finally speak again.

Jolie got three lisping words out before they fell onto the bed laughing again.

They were still at it two minutes later when Judd popped his head in the door. "What in the world is so funny, you two? We need to be in the car in twenty minutes, you know…"

Evette put an arm around Jolie and turned her about-face so Judd could see. "Smile at your dad."

Jolie complied and Judd's eyes went wide.

Jolie grinned and scooped the tooth up from the nightstand where Evette had put it for safekeeping. "Thee, I lotht my toof, Dad!"

The giggling started again. And for the first time, Evette felt they were a family—the three of them. The baby squirmed inside of her.

Make that the *four* of them.

Evette stood just outside the doorway to Jolie's classroom, waiting for Brandi Markham to notice her. She'd called the school and sent a note to Mrs. Markham with Jolie yesterday, letting them know she'd be taking Jolie to visit Tabrina, so she would need to be dismissed early.

Her nerves prickled just thinking about it.

Judd had questioned her again last night. "You're sure you're okay with this, babe?"

She'd assured him she was. But what choice did she have? With the final game of the district tournament coming up Friday night and tax day just around the corner, Judd was swamped with both of his jobs.

Now, knowing she'd be alone with Tabrina and Jolie in just a couple of hours, she wasn't so sure.

Yet there was peace about her decision. She knew she was doing the right thing. For Jolie, and for Tabrina. That didn't mean it would be easy for her.

Mrs. Markham stood copying something from a book onto the blackboard. Evette scanned the desks, searching for Jolie. She spotted her beaded braids hanging over a desk three rows back in the middle of the classroom. She had her head down on her desk, her hands grasping a large textbook that was tented over her head. Was this supposed to be naptime? None of the other children was napping. Three boys had their desks pushed together and whispered over what looked like a science experiment. The rest of the children were reading or writing quietly at their desks. Mrs. Markham appeared to be grading papers now.

Evette cleared her throat softly. Jolie popped up, her book falling off the desk with a thud.

Evette started when she saw Jolie's face. Her eyes were red and dark streaks obviously left by tears trailed her cheeks. What was going on?

She slid from her desk and came over to Evette,

pressing close. "Were you sleeping?" Evette asked, testing.

Jolie shrugged, her face expressionless.

Mrs. Markham finally seemed to notice Evette. She smiled and turned to Jolie. "You have your homework assignment, right?"

Jolie nodded.

"Okay, then you can gather up your things."

Obediently, she went to the rack where several dozen small jackets hung on pegs. Evette followed her and slung Jolie's backpack strap over her own shoulder atop her purse. She started to help her into her jacket, but remembering Jolie's pea-size bladder, she held the jacket away and nodded toward the restroom around the corner. "It's a long drive to Lebanon. Do you need to go potty before we leave?"

She watched Jolie's response, trying to determine if she was still upset.

Jolie nodded and hurried to the door marked Girls. She seemed to be okay, but something had happened earlier to make her cry.

Taking advantage of Jolie's absence, Evette went to the teacher's desk. "Did something happen today to upset Jolie? She looks like she's been crying."

"Nothing that won't be forgotten by morning." Mrs. Markham rolled her chair back from her desk and stood, still clutching the turquoise gel pen she'd been marking papers with.

"What happened?" Evette pushed, *not* satisfied with the teacher's answer.

"Just a little tiff between the girls. You remember… three's a crowd when you're this age."

"She was being left out?" Evette suddenly felt like a lioness whose cub had been threatened.

"Some of the girls were playing a board game. Jolie asked to play, but they'd already started. She got her feelings hurt. It'll be okay."

"Well, did she ever get to play with them?" Was Jolie being ostracized because of the color of her skin?

"Not today, but she will next time."

"I don't understand." Evette didn't know anything about Brandi Markham, but judging by her perfect diction and refined speech, she hadn't grown up in Harlem. Surely she knew what it felt like to be left out.

Mrs. Markham shook her head and frowned. "And I don't understand what you don't understand."

"Did you give Jolie a chance to get in on the game?"

"No… Like I said, by the time Jolie asked to play the girls had already chosen their game pieces and the game was well underway."

"They could have started over."

The teacher looked at her askance. "Why should they have had to?" But she must have recognized that Evette was upset because her expression softened and she held up a hand. "I'm not meaning to be argumentative, Mrs. McGlin. But those are the rules for our classroom. I realize Jolie's new here, but I believe she knows the rules. And if she didn't, well, now she does."

The teacher laughed, but something about her attitude made Evette want to slap her. How could Brandi Markham, of all people, let Jolie be treated like that? Why hadn't she done something about those girls? Jolie was one of only a handful of African-American children attending Hanover Falls Elementary. Evette looked around the classroom. Except for the little Chinese girl the post-

master and his wife had adopted from China—Mai Lee,
Evette thought her name was—Jolie was the only non-
white child in the room. And like Mai Lee, most of the
other ethnic children in the schools were part of white
families—either by adoption, or as foster children.

Jolie had been in a large school system in Springfield.
She'd never been such a minority the way she was in this
little town. It was something Evette had worried about,
something she'd tried to explain to Judd. But he hadn't
seemed to share her concern.

"Please…" Her voice wavered and she fought to
steady it. "Be straight with me. Is Jolie being picked on
because she's black?"

Mrs. Markham arched a penciled brow. "I'm not sure
why you think Jolie is being picked on at all."

"She was crying just now. Or didn't you notice?"
Gritting her teeth, Evette silently counted to ten.

"She was crying because she didn't get her way. Because the rules didn't go her way. Would you have me bend
the rules of the classroom for Jolie because she's black?"

"No, no, of course not," Evette sputtered.

"Look, I understand your concern and your desire to
protect Jolie, but she's doing fine. If you invent problems
for her, believe me, they will oblige. But if you—"

"Don't…patronize me." She strained the words
through clenched jaws. Her blood hadn't boiled this hot
since…since the night Judd had told her about Jolie.

The teacher drew back, mild shock on her face.

Evette held up a trembling hand. "I'm sorry. Forgive
me. I'm upset. I didn't mean to—"

Brandi Markham laughed softly, a deep, rumbling
laughter that made her sound older than her years. "You
remind me of *my* mother not so many years ago."

Her blood pressure leveled out, and feeling a little embarrassed at her outburst, she smiled at Jolie's teacher. "I'm sorry. It's just…Jolie has so many strikes against her right now. We're trying to do everything we can to make things a little easier."

"I understand. She's adjusting very well, Mrs. McGlin. It takes time, but she'll be fine."

Evette glanced toward the restrooms, wondering what was taking Jolie so long.

"Mrs. McGlin?" Mrs. Markham looked at the floor, fidgeting with the turquoise pen. Her confident demeanor of a moment ago was gone and she looked young and unsure of herself.

"Yes?"

"I'm sure prejudice exists in the Falls. I'm not immune to it myself, but for the most part first graders *are*. I try not to make trouble where it doesn't exist. If the world could learn fairness and equality from six-year-olds, we'd all be a lot better off." She laughed her deep laugh again.

Evette nodded. "You're right, I'm sure. And I apologize. I was just—"

Mrs. Markham put a hand on Evette's arm. The contrast between their light and dark skin wasn't lost on Evette. "You were just standing up for your baby. I understand. I imagine Jolie's nervous about seeing her mama today…that probably made her a little oversensitive to the girls telling her she was too late to get in on their game."

"Of course…" Evette had been so nervous herself that she hadn't thought about how Jolie must be feeling.

A door creaked behind her and she turned to see Jolie coming from the restroom. Evette went to her and helped her get her backpack adjusted on her shoulders. "You have everything you need?" she whispered.

Jolie nodded. The edges of her sleeves were damp and the tear streaks on her cheeks were gone. She must have washed her face in the bathroom.

Mrs. Markham bent at the waist, coming eye to eye with Jolie. "You have a nice visit with your mama. We'll see you tomorrow, okay?"

"Anything I need to know about her homework?"

Mrs. Markham shook her head. "She'll only miss spelling. Just work on the words with her a little. She can take the test tomorrow."

Jolie's shoulders slumped and she eyed two girls with their heads touching over a desk near the window— no doubt the girls who'd shunned her. "Do I hafta stay in at recess?"

Evette shot a pleading look Mrs. Markham's way.

The teacher caught it and shook her head. "I think you can get it done before then." She patted Jolie's backpack. "You have your list in here, right? Go over your words with your ma—with Evette."

She'd been about to say "with your mama."

Evette steered Jolie down the hall and out to the car, but she couldn't quit thinking about Brandi Markham's slip of the tongue. And for some odd reason, it filled her with pride.

Chapter Twenty-Seven

The soles of their tennis shoes squeaked on the freshly mopped tile floors and Jolie squeezed Evette's hand until it pinched. Evette was overcome with shame. How could she have been so intent on her own discomfort at the prospect of seeing Tabrina—without Judd along to temper things—that she hadn't considered how scary this visit might be for Jolie?

Evette sighed. She had so much more to learn about selflessness. No matter how she tried, her thoughts always seemed to turn back to her own needs and desires. Would she ever learn to be truly selfless?

She wound her way through the waiting room and the hallway to the nurses' station where they'd checked in before. "Do you remember when we were here before?" she asked Jolie.

Jolie nodded and squeezed Evette's hand tighter.

"Are you a little nervous?"

"What's that?"

Evette smiled. "Kind of like scared. Not sure what to expect…"

Jolie nodded. "Will my mama be awake now?"

Evette's throat filled and she shook her head. "I don't think so, honey. I'm sure the doctor—or your grandma—would have called us if she woke up."

"Is Grams here?"

"Probably not today. I think she's at work." Judd had tried to call Carla late last night and again this morning to check on Tabrina's condition. Both times he had gotten an answering machine with what he called "a grumpy man's voice," presumably that of Carla's husband, Walt. Evette wasn't sure if Judd had left a message or not.

A few weeks ago, it would have made her nervous not to be able to reach Carla. Now she realized she was almost hoping Carla might just ease out of Jolie's life. But there she went again, only thinking of what was easiest for Evette McGlin, forgetting that Jolie didn't need any more loss in her life. *Forgive me, Lord.*

At the nurses' station she asked quietly about Tabrina, cutting her eyes toward Jolie, hoping the aide sitting there had the sense not to report bad news in Jolie's hearing.

"No change," the young woman said, giving Evette a look that said, "Why do *you* want to know?"

"She's still in…?" Evette tried to remember the room number.

"One-twelve," the nurse supplied.

"Thanks." She fingered one of Jolie's braids, making a mental note to call for an appointment to have them redone at the salon Mrs. Markham had told them about. Or maybe she could get up the courage to have Brandi Markham teach her how to braid Jolie's hair. "Okay, punkin…let's go see your mommy."

Jolie looked at her askance. "I'm not a punkin."

"You're not? Well, by the looks of those teeth I thought maybe you were a jack-o'-lantern."

Jolie flashed a cheesy smile, showing off the space that seemed far wider than the tiny tooth it had produced. "You're silly, Evie." Her grip on Evette's hand loosened. Good.

But as they neared Room 112, Evette wished she had Judd's hand to cling to. It seemed silly to be so nervous about a woman who probably wouldn't even know they'd been here. Still, her palms grew clammy and she had to remind herself to breathe deeply.

"Here it is, sweetie."

Jolie stopped outside the door and looked at the sign. "One, one, two. I thought that nurth—" She rolled her eyes at Evette and held her tongue the way Judd had shown her last night to say the *s* sound without benefit of a front tooth. "I thought that nurse said one-twelve?"

Evette smiled. "One-one-two *is* one-twelve. See…" She covered the first number with one hand.

"Oh. One, two…twelve. I get it."

The door to the room was slightly ajar and Evette took in a breath and pushed it open, putting an arm around Jolie.

There was an elderly black woman sitting up in the bed by the door. She leaned forward, reaching out, but she was tethered to the bed with some sort of straightjacket-looking vest. Her eyes were open, but they were glazed over, almost blue with thick cataracts. "You come, did ya?" She called out so loudly that Evette and Jolie both jumped.

"I hear ya now. Don't you go tryin' to fool me. I'll call the police on ya, don't think I won't."

Evette put a protective arm around Jolie. "We're just here to visit Tabrina."

"There ain't no Tabrina here," the woman said. "You just get on now. Be on your way and nobody will get hurt."

Jolie looked up at Evette.

"It's okay…" she whispered, whirling a finger by the side of her head, not sure if Jolie would recognize the sign for *crazy*. "She's not quite right in the head," she whispered.

"I'm as right in the head as a cock-a-doodle-doo and don't you think otherwise." The woman started crowing like a demented rooster.

Evette skirted around the end of the bed, putting herself between Jolie and the woman. The crowing grew louder and a nurse's aide appeared in the doorway. "Essie? Are you causing trouble again?"

"I ain't causin' nobody no trouble, no how."

The young aide sweet-talked the woman named Essie and after a few minutes she finally quieted down. If Jolie didn't have nightmares tonight, it would be a miracle. Evette thought she might have them herself. What a horrible place for Jolie's mother! Did she have to listen to this crazy old woman twenty-four hours a day? Why would they put Tabrina in a room with someone who was obviously out of her mind?

Did Carla know about this? And if so, why hadn't she insisted they move Tabrina to a private room? Of course, private rooms weren't cheap.

Evette wanted to pull the curtain between the two beds, but she was afraid that might start the "rooster" on her rampage again. So she pulled a chair from the corner of Tabrina's side of the room and put it beside the bed for Jolie, with her back to Essie. But when Jolie crawled up in the chair, even sitting on her knees, she could barely see over the bed rails.

Evette lifted her up and sat down on the chair herself, helping Jolie get situated in her lap. "Can you see now?"

Jolie nodded, the beads on her braids clacking. But she sat on Evette's lap in silence.

"Aren't you going to say hello to your mama?"

Jolie's thumb went in her mouth. Evette hadn't seen her do that for a while. Since the last time they were here.

"It's okay, Jolie. Your mom's sleeping, but remember the doctor said she might be able to hear you."

Jolie popped out her thumb. "You firtht." This time, she didn't bother to correct her lisp.

Evette reached out her hand, but something within her wouldn't let her touch Tabrina's skin. Instead, she ran her hand briefly over the blanket tucked at her side. "Hello... Tabrina. Jolie is here to see you." Suddenly, she understood how hard it was to try to carry on a "conversation" with someone you knew wouldn't—couldn't—respond.

Jolie turned and looked up over her shoulder at Evette, a bemused expression in her eyes. Evette nodded encouragement.

"Hi, Mama. It's me, Jolie."

Silence.

After a minute, Evette nudged Jolie. "Tell her about your tooth."

Jolie gave a little gasp. "Oh, yeah!" She leaned over the rail and tapped Tabrina's arm. "Mama, I lost my toof...my tooth." Again, she looked over her shoulder, obviously seeking Evette's approval.

She nodded. "Good. Tell her how it happened."

That seemed to open the floodgates and Jolie launched into an animated telling of the tooth story. "Me and Evie was laughin' tho hard we 'bout thplit a gut, and then Dad started laughin', too. You shoulda been there…it was tho funny!"

Evette tensed at the way Jolie lapsed into Carla's lingo. The lisp didn't help matters any. Jolie's diction had become almost flawless within a few days of moving in with them. Judd credited her dialect to Carla. Apparently, Tabrina had prided herself on speaking with perfect diction and without an accent of any kind. "She used to say that on the telephone, nobody had a clue she was black. I always razzed her about that," he'd told Evette. "I told her she needed to get some black pride. And she told me I needed to get a life." Judd had also told her that sometimes when he and Tabrina were being silly, he would launch into his Scottish brogue and Tabrina would affect thick Ebonics. "Boy, did we turn heads then."

Evette had a feeling they turned heads more because Tabrina was drop-dead gorgeous and she and Judd made a striking couple, than because of their feigned accents. A tiny tremor of jealousy still went through her whenever she thought of Judd and Tabrina together.

It startled Evette to realize that while she'd seen Tabrina several times now, she had never heard her voice, or seen her mannerisms. But she could imagine—both from what Judd had said, and because, even with her mouth drooping and her limbs atrophying—there was an elegance about the beautiful woman in this bed.

Jolie finished her story about the tooth fairy, but it fell flat with her unresponsive audience. Evette felt sorry for her little comedienne. She leaned in, addressing Tabrina. "It really was hilarious…Tabrina. You should have heard this girl scream! You would have thought she'd seen a ghost in that mirror."

Jolie looked up at her with a grin. "Not a ghost. The tooth fairy."

"And tell your mom what happened with the tooth fairy?" she prompted.

Jolie bounced on her lap, making the bed rails squeak. "The fairy brought me a whole dollar!"

A feeling of sadness overwhelmed Evette. Tabrina had missed this rite of passage in her daughter's life. One that could never be recaptured.

Evette could only imagine how she would feel if she were to miss such a milestone in her own child's life. She decided then and there that she would write these things down for Tabrina, take photographs of these moments that would never come again. It wouldn't make up for the loss, but maybe it would help.

Carla, too, had missed so many moments with Jolie. Judd had tried to call her twice so Jolie could tell her Grams about losing her tooth. But Walt had answered the first time and didn't know where his wife was, and the second time, they'd ended up having to leave a message on her answering machine. At least she would have the recording of Jolie's account.

She had to wonder at Carla's absence in Jolie's life. It had been almost two weeks since they'd seen Carla here in the nursing home, and she'd only called once since.

Evette considered walking down to the nurses' station to ask when Carla had last been in, but she was afraid to leave Jolie in Tabrina's room alone. She shifted in her seat to watch Tabrina's roommate from the corner of her eye. Essie appeared to be sleeping, her eyes closed, jaw sagging. But if she woke up and started ranting again, she didn't want Jolie to be here alone.

They stayed for over an hour, sitting by Tabrina's bed. Evette read to Jolie from some tattered children's magazines she found in the waiting room, and made a mental note to stop by the library before their next trip to Lebanon. She couldn't say she looked forward to another trip like today's, but she had no doubt that she was doing the right thing, both for Jolie and for Tabrina.

But could she do this indefinitely? In one short hour, she was worn-out from prying "conversation" out of Jolie. What would they talk about next time?

It was more than a little unsettling to imagine that Tabrina might actually hear them. What must she think? If Tabrina knew who she was, would she be bitter—as bitter as Evette had been when she'd learned about Judd and Tabrina's relationship?

She imagined trying to explain this to her mother and shuddered at the thought. She'd only left that brief message on Mother and Daddy's answering machine since her trip to visit them in St. Louis. But she couldn't avoid speaking to them forever. And she needed to get in touch with Annie about the baby shower she wanted to throw.

They all needed to know that Jolie was part of her family now.

Looking down at Tabrina, watching the monitors flash over her bed, she realized that this was forever. Jolie was with them to stay.

She put her arms around Judd's daughter on her lap and hugged her close. She wasn't sorry.

Chapter Twenty-Eight

Judd slammed a palm into the locker door, trying to get some of his frustration out before he spewed it on his team. He took a deep breath and turned to face his players, who were slumped on two rows of benches in the locker room. "What is wrong with you guys? Do you *want* to lose this game? Because that's exactly what's going to happen if you don't start playing like you're capable of playing."

The starters hung their heads while the underclassmen stared at him as if he'd grown another head. They'd been up by eighteen points halfway into the second quarter, but two bad passes for the Hawks and a string of three-pointers by their opponent had put them on the defensive. They weren't used to being on this side of the scoreboard, and it was messing with their minds in a big way.

This was where, in Judd's opinion, coaching won or lost a game. He was in the hot seat, but he couldn't seem to find the words to get them out of their funk.

He grabbed his clipboard and knelt in front of the

bench. "Okay. Listen up, guys. Here's what we have to do." He doled out assignments, taking some risks, giving responsibility to kids he thought might step it up, but who hadn't gotten a chance this year to prove themselves.

He had no choice. Rafe was getting hammered under the basket and even when they got the ball to him, his shot was off. James was taking up some of the slack, but he simply didn't have the brawn to pull it off against Lindmayer's big team. They were going to have to start shooting from the outside. It wasn't their best game, but it was all they had tonight, unless Rafe could cut his head in and make something happen under the basket. Brent had been pretty hot from the top of the key the first quarter, but even he'd cooled off in the second quarter.

Losing this game was not an option. They'd worked too hard to get where they were tonight to lose in sectionals to a team he knew they could beat.

He said every motivational thing he could spit out and said a prayer for good measure. Evette would have reminded him that there was bound to be somebody on the other team praying just as hard as he was to win. She was right. He changed his prayer to one that left the results in God's hands, but requested the best that every player had to give. It was all he could do.

The team huddled at the locker-room door and Judd raised his voice above their cheers. "Okay. Let's get out there and do the job we came to do!"

"Hawks! Hawks!" A cheer rose from the huddle, but to Judd it sounded slightly anemic. Something wasn't clicking tonight.

He caught a glimpse of Evette in the stands as the teams took the floor again to shoot around before the buzzer. Jolie wasn't with her, but Evette seemed unconcerned. Jolie was probably playing with her friends from school.

He looked up at the scoreboard clock and motioned the boys off the floor. *Lord, give me the words that will light a fire under these kids.*

But when the final buzzer sounded, the Hawks were three points shy of a win. Rafe—on the bench for most of the last quarter with four fouls—buried his head between his knees.

"Hold your heads up, guys. You played a good game." That wasn't exactly true, though they had rallied in the last five minutes. But it was too little, too late, and no one hated their defeat more than Judd.

"Come on, line up, guys." Judd clapped Rafe on the shoulder.

He sat there, head down, acting as if he didn't hear.

James and Brent stood and the underclassmen followed their lead, trudging through the line to shake hands with the victorious Lions.

Rafe didn't get up until Judd took his elbow and spoke low in his ear. "Get up now. Come on. Take it like a man, Rafe."

Rafe growled something that was probably a curse, but Judd couldn't hear through the roar of the Lions fans and, besides, this wasn't the time to make an issue of it. No one else had heard.

Judd shook the Lindmayer coach's hand. "Good game, Coach."

"Yeah." The man swaggered past him, accepting Coach Hazen's congratulations with the same cocky grunt. Judd wanted to clock him. He knew how Rafe felt. They'd been handed a huge disappointment. The season was over and they'd be going to State only as spectators.

He'd wanted this so bad he could taste it. But for whatever reason, this wasn't their time. Still, he felt especially bad for Rafe and James and his other seniors. Until tonight, they'd given him their all. They deserved to win.

Of course, the Lindmayer coach was thinking the same thing about now. Judd tried to gather his thoughts, think what he would say in the locker room. The words he spoke tonight would set the tone for next year. He could fire up next year's leadership, or he could turn this into a dirge.

He stood at the locker-room door and waited while the guys filed in and plopped on the benches. The seniors wore the glummest expressions. Rafe sat with a towel over his head, probably crying, but he wouldn't let anyone else see that.

Judd remembered the feeling. He'd had a similar experience his senior year, except they'd made it to State, then dropped the first game, thanks to a couple of missed shots and a couple of blind-as-bats refs. These were games you never forgot as long as you lived. He still relived a key missed three-pointer in his dreams—and practiced from that spot whenever he shot around with the guys, just in case he ever got a chance to redeem himself.

He gave the guys a few minutes to grieve and then he propped a foot on the bench, rested his elbow on his thigh, and spoke from his heart.

When the team finally emerged from the locker room in defeat, Evette and Jolie were waiting for him in a corner of the commons where everyone gathered after games. He just wanted to get out of here. It was no fun being a defeated coach.

He started across the tile floor toward his family. A few fans called out words of regret and disappointment, but most of the people gathered outside the gym avoided his eyes.

A few of the underclassmen's parents patted his shoulder as he passed.

Bradford Rooney's dad stuck out his hand. "Tough luck, Coach."

Judd shook his hand and attempted a smile that felt more like a grimace. "Brad played a great game," Judd told him. "He really stepped it up when Rafe got in foul trouble. We wouldn't have been in the game as long as we were without him."

"We'll get 'em next year." The man's face glowed with pride and Judd knew there would be some secret rejoicing—and lots of talk about next year's team—at the Rooney house tonight.

He waved at Evette. She waved back, making an exaggerated sad face. She knew how much this game had meant to him. Jolie broke away from Evette and trotted across the commons to him.

He scooped her into his arms. "Hey, you. You ready to go home?"

"Did you win, Dad?"

He laughed. "'Fraid not, punkin. We lost a tough one."

"Oh. Sorry."

"Yeah, me, too. But we'll get 'em next year." Somehow Mr. Rooney's optimism didn't sound as good coming from his own mouth.

He caught Evette's eye, but as he headed toward her

with Jolie in his arms, Tom Clairmont cut him off. Judd extended a hand to Rafe's father, but he ignored it, glaring at Judd.

"Nice job, Coach. Way to ruin my son's senior year."

Judd was too shocked to be angry. He sputtered a few unintelligible syllables before he finally muttered, "I'm sorry you feel that way, Tom."

"Yeah, well, *sorry*'s a good word for tonight. We would've won that game if you'd put Rafe in. There was no reason for him to be riding the bench the last quarter."

"He was in foul trouble. And Brad was doing a good job."

"Apparently not good enough. I want to know why you sat Rafe out. Did he do something?"

Judd shook his head. He got plenty of complaints about playing time—to his face and behind his back. He'd always been willing to talk to a disgruntled player or parent, but he'd decided when he first started coaching that he would not have these discussions in public. "I'll be happy to talk to you about it in my office, Tom. Just call and make an appointment."

"It's a little late for that, don't you think?"

"We can talk about—"

Tom dismissed him with a grunt. He pushed past, shoving his shoulder into Judd's arm. Judd had to side-step to keep from losing his balance.

"Was that man mad at you, Daddy?"

Judd shook his head, still in disbelief over Clairmont's accusations. "I don't think he wanted to give me a medal."

"I'll give you a medal." Jolie held up a finger. "First place. Okay?"

Touched, Judd tugged on the end of a braid. "Thanks, toots."

He hitched Jolie up on his hip and crossed the commons, keeping his eyes straight ahead. He felt like a leper. In the corner of his vision, he saw Clairmont heading for James Severn's parents. Great. The guy was rounding up the troops. There'd be a line outside his office come Monday.

Chapter Twenty-Nine

Evette picked up the phone in the kitchen and dialed Annie's cell phone. Jolie was in bed and she prayed Judd wouldn't come home until she was done talking to her sister.

With only three days till tax day, he'd been working late every night. But he'd been in the dumps since losing sectionals. He couldn't seem to put the loss behind him, and almost every night since the game, he'd come home to rehash how he could have coached differently or to seek her reassurance that it hadn't been his fault that the Hawks lost the game. Apparently, a couple of the parents blamed the loss on Judd, and he was taking it hard.

She never had understood what the big deal was. Basketball was only a game. It didn't seem worth the life-or-death importance Judd—and half the world, it seemed—gave it. But she'd done her best to be a good coach's wife and listened to endless replays of the game and kept him fed while he sat in front of the TV and watched tape from the game over and over and over again.

Annie's phone rang half a dozen times and Evette was just about ready to hang up when she heard her sister's voice.

"Hey, Annie. Am I catching you at a bad time?"

"Evette! Hey, we were just talking about you."

"Uh-oh. Who's we?"

"I'm over at Mother's, helping her with the yard. I keep telling her it's too early to put annuals out, but she's there in the dark trying to get the rest of the petunias in. She wants everything to look perfect for your shower. Have you come up with some dates yet?"

"Um…actually that's why I'm calling."

"Okay, shoot me some dates. I'll have to make sure it's a night Geoff can watch the boys, but at least we can get some possibilities on our calendars."

"Annie, I don't think…" She sighed. This whole shower thing was going to be beyond awkward.

"Evette? Is everything okay there?"

"I guess…"

"Anything else happen with the situation with… Judd's daughter?"

"We're adjusting. She's a sweet girl. If you'd told me a month ago I'd be saying this, Annie, I'd have told you you were crazy, but I'm actually enjoying having her. And…well, I have a feeling it's for the long haul." She wanted to take that phrase back as soon as it was out of her mouth. Her words made it sound like caring for Jolie was a burden. The truth was, Jolie had become a bright spot in their lives.

Not that Evette wouldn't have changed the circumstances by which Jolie had come to them, given a choice. But they were adjusting, and she felt more hopeful than she'd ever dreamed she could about the future. "We're anxious for you to meet Jolie. I'm just a little—" She lowered her voice. "Is Mom right there?"

"She's in the side garden. You can talk."

"I'm just worried how she'll behave with Jolie." There was something ridiculous about a grown woman having to worry about her mother's behavior.

"You're bringing Jolie here?"

"To the shower, you mean? Yes. I thought Mother said you wanted to wait and have the shower after basketball was over so Judd could be there."

"We did, but…you're bringing her, too?"

"Well, what did you expect us to do with her?"

There was silence on Annie's end. A silence that went on too long.

"Annie, are you hesitating because of Mother and Daddy, or because of Annie?"

"It's just that— Well, how are you going to explain her to the guests? I mean, it's not exactly something we can put in the invitations. And I don't think you want us making an announcement before the shower to explain your situation to everyone. It will just be…very awkward if she's here."

"Well, then it will just have to be awkward."

Her sister's slow exhalation said more than words. "Mother is going to have a fit. I'll try to smooth things over, but she's not going to like this, Evette. She thinks this will blow over, or that you'll come to your senses… Her words, not mine," Annie added quickly.

Evette echoed her sister's labored sigh. "I *have* come to my senses, but I don't think it's what Mother has in mind. You know, Annie…" She grabbed a pen from the mug on the counter and scratched a random series of stars on a notepad. "Maybe we should just wait until after the baby is born. I don't really need anything. I have drawers overflowing with stuff from…the first time." She'd stocked up on baby things during her first pregnancy, before it had ended in a miscarriage. The nursery was full of exactly the sort of things she'd get at a baby shower.

"You know, I think that might be the best thing. To cancel… I mean reschedule, of course. After things get back to normal for you guys." The relief in Annie's voice told Evette she'd been hoping for just such a suggestion.

But she wasn't going to let Annie off so easy. "I think 'normal' for us is probably going to mean having Jolie. She's part of our family now, Annie, and everybody is just going to have to get used to that." Saying those words filled her with pride. She'd come a long way since that trip home from her parents'—was it only three weeks ago? It seemed like a lifetime.

"Evette? Are you sure…are you sure you're not just caving in to Judd? He's asking a lot of you. I know if Geoffrey ever asked me to take in his child with… another woman, I think that would be the end of it for us. You don't have to do this, you know."

"No. I don't have to. But I know it's the right thing to do. I know it's what God wants me to do."

"All I can say is, you're a better woman than I am."

"Well, that's a first." She gave a wry laugh. "Be sure you tell Mother and Daddy."

"Tell them you're a better woman? Ha!" Annie scoffed. "Like they need another reason to make your pedestal taller."

"What are you talking about? You're the one who hung the moon, remember?"

"Well, I must have hung it crooked and you set it

straight because all I ever hear about is how perfect you are. You and Judd."

Evette could hardly believe what was coming from her sister's mouth. "You're kidding, right?"

"Would I kid about something like that?"

"If you're not, I'm guessing this whole thing with Jolie took me down a peg or two."

Annie's laugh answered her question.

"But don't worry," her sister said. "It's still a far stretch from my pedestal to yours. We both need some serious psychological help, sis."

Evette laughed, but quickly realized it wasn't exactly funny. "I think it's spiritual help we need," she said, sobering. "I know you don't put a lot of stock in that kind of thing, but God has really been showing me things in a different light since Jolie came to be with us. We… I have a lot of prejudices I didn't realize I held. I don't mean to blame Mother and Daddy. It's the way they were raised, right or wrong. But I've really been praying that I don't pass those attitudes down to my kids. I don't want them to grow up with the same—"

"Oh, sorry, Evette… Mother's calling me. I'd better see what she wants and break the news about the shower to her. Gee, thanks! I'll let you know how it goes, though. Gotta run!" The phone went dead.

It figured. No matter how careful Evette was not to preach, Annie always changed the subject when the conversation skirted too close to "religion," as she called anything that involved God or an acknowledgment that Evette talked to Him.

She put the phone on its charger and went down the hall to check on Jolie. She had a feeling her mother would be as relieved about canceling the shower as she was. She also had a feeling she wouldn't be needing that guest room for her family as long as Jolie was here.

Sadness swept over her. She loved her family. It hurt her to think that they would cut ties with her because of Judd's confession, because of Jolie. If she were honest with herself about their motives, it all boiled down to the color of Jolie's skin.

She hated that with all her being.

Chapter Thirty

Judd pushed away from his desk and rubbed his eyes. Whatever made him think he would enjoy being an accountant? Especially when, if not for a few points in a lousy sectionals game, he could have been coaching a state championship team right now.

He shook his head, angry with himself for obsessing over that stupid game. But he couldn't help it. They should have won. The more he rehashed it, the more he second-guessed the way he'd coached that game. He'd dissected every play with Evette and with Randall Hazen till he was blue in the face and they were both glassy-eyed. And they'd both told Judd, in so many words, to let it go.

But he couldn't seem to do that.

His computer screen went black and Judd clicked the mouse, bringing up the tax forms that awaited him. Three more days. He had to get through April fifteenth, and then he would meet with the team—make sure uniforms were turned in, do a little confidence building toward next year and get a feel for how the guys were taking things.

He'd half expected to have Tom Clairmont in the accounting office Monday morning. But he hadn't heard a word from any of the parents. Not a dressing-down, but neither a word of thanks. Maybe people knew he was swamped at the firm and were just waiting until after tax day to descend on his office.

Time would tell. For now, he needed to keep his nose to the grindstone and prove to Karl Jantzi that he could do both of his jobs justice. Prove it to himself, for that matter.

He heard Cindy, the receptionist, laughing in the front, and a woman's voice…familiar, but he couldn't quite place it.

He adjusted his keyboard and went back to the forms he was working on, but a minute later a knock on his office door made him look up. Karen Clairmont stood there, smiling, and he realized hers was the voice he couldn't place.

"Hi, Coach."

He rolled his chair back and rose. "Karen, come on in." Funny that Rafe's mom should show up just when he'd been thinking about the team. Of course, when wasn't he thinking about the team lately?

"Are you going through withdrawal?" She laughed. "From basketball, I mean?"

"Oh, a little bit, I suppose. Here—" He motioned toward two chairs in front of his desk. "Have a seat. The truth is, I'm so swamped here I haven't had much time to think about it." Well, that was a big fat lie…and he'd gone to a lot of trouble to label it as truth. Watch it, McGlin. "But yes, I wasn't ready for the season to be over. I don't think anybody was."

Karen stayed in the doorway. She shifted her purse from one shoulder to the other.

"Sit down," Judd said again.

She waved him off. "You're busy. I can't stay. I just…" She took an intense interest in the carpet beneath her feet. Finally, she looked up. "I just wanted you to know that I don't agree with the stuff that's being said…about you."

Uh-oh. This wasn't good. "I guess…I'm not sure what *is* being said about me."

She held his gaze for a long minute, as if trying to decide whether she believed him.

Finally, uncomfortable, he looked away. "Maybe I don't want to know…"

"It's just—some of the parents are still upset about us losing to Lindmayer."

"Can't blame them for that."

"The thing is, they're blaming it on you."

"Well, join the club. Any coach worth his salt takes responsibility for the game."

"Well, I just didn't want you to think I was in on any of this. I know you had a lot on your mind and—" She worried a hangnail. "I know you did the best you could in spite of everything that happened with…your little girl and all…"

He didn't really want to have this discussion, but his curiosity got the best of him. "Is there something I'm not aware of?"

"Tom and some of the other parents are going to the board. They think we lost the game because you had—have—too much on your plate. They think you've been preoccupied with the whole scandal with your marriage and your—"

"Wait a minute. Wait just a minute…my marriage? What are you talking about?"

"Well, I just mean…with your daughter showing up and all. I'm sure that's taken a toll on—"

"My marriage is fine, Mrs. Clairmont. My daughter has absolutely nothing to do with my coaching abilities. It may be my fault that we lost the game, but for anyone to imply that it had anything at all to do with Jolie or with my marriage…that's just ludicrous." He sat down hard in his chair and rolled it up to his desk, not caring that she remained standing. He pulled a pen from his shirt pocket and clicked it off and on, a poor substitute for punching someone's lights out.

She threw him a coy smile. "Hey, don't shoot the messenger. I'm just telling you what I know…in case you were in the dark. I thought you should know, that's all."

"I'm sorry. I didn't mean to snap at you." Something told him he needed to end this conversation, but he sure wasn't going to thank her for coming. Or tell her he appreciated it. He didn't. "I probably should get back to work." He repositioned his keyboard, hoping she'd take the hint.

Instead, she came to his desk, deposited her purse on the seat of a chair and rested her palms flat on the desktop. Looking down at him, she bit her bottom lip. "I was only trying to help. But now…well, the gentleman doth protest too much, methinks."

Then Karen Clairmont snatched her purse off the chair, lifted her chin and sashayed from his office.

"So, are you going to the board meeting?" Evette studied him across the kitchen table. It struck her that ever since the phone call from Carla, they'd avoided having discussions in Judd's study. The kitchen table was their new family council location. Jolie was in bed for the night and Judd had just told her about Karen Clairmont's visit to his office.

"What purpose would it serve? If Rafe's mother hadn't tattled, I'd never be the wiser. Unless John Severn asks me to come to that meeting, I see no reason to add credence to their accusations. I may not have coached the game perfectly, but I didn't do anything criminal."

"Of course not." Evette slipped from her chair and came around to put her hands on Judd's shoulders. She kneaded the taut muscles in silence until she felt the tension ease. "So what did you tell Gertrude?"

Judd threw a quizzical look over his shoulder. "Gertrude?"

"You know, Hamlet's mother…Shakespeare. 'Methinks…'"

"Ah…is that where that line came from?"

"Yes." She shook her head and resumed massaging his shoulders. "And methinks the lady came to your office to stir up trouble."

Judd tilted his head way back till their eyes met. "You think so?"

"Either that or she's got a thing for the coach."

"Oh, please."

She squeezed his shoulder blades tight.

"Ouch!"

"Why do men never get that?"

"What are you talking about?" He leaned forward in his chair, resting his head on his arms on the table, a hint that she should rub his back. But a way not to have to look at her, too, she suspected.

She obliged, making blades of the sides of her hands and pounding on him with a chop-chop motion. "You didn't see the hungry way she was looking at you that night of the basketball dinner?"

"Hungry? We were all hungry. It *was* a dinner."

His face was hidden from her sight, but she could picture his tongue tracing the inside of his cheek.

"Ha-ha, very funny." But his response told her he knew very well that Rafe's mother had been giving him the eye that night. Probably flirting with him after she and Jolie left, though she hadn't actually witnessed that. Judd was a good-looking guy and Evette was used to women noticing him. It had never bothered her because he never flirted back.

"I don't know why she came to see me." His voice was muffled through his shirtsleeves. "But I wish she hadn't told me. How am I supposed to act around people now? You know me…I can't pretend I don't know something when I do."

She smiled to herself, thinking about that day in the parking lot when he'd given her the booties and agreed to come to the ultrasound with her. "Just be glad you have an excuse to work late—and to stay away from the high school."

He went still beneath her hands. "That's not exactly what I wanted to hear."

"Oh, Judd…I'm sorry. That's not what I meant. I wish like crazy that you'd gone to State." She had said as much a hundred times since the night they'd lost to Lindmayer.

He straightened in his chair and reached behind him to pull her head down beside his. He pulled her around the chair and onto his lap. Her belly was pressed against his and she felt the baby roll and then kick against him.

He looked up, laughing. "Did you tell Bambino to do that?"

She joined his laughter. "No, but you probably did need a swift kick."

"Thanks, babe." His voice turned serious. "I don't know what I would have done without you these last few weeks. Months, really..." His voice trailed off.

With his arms around her and their cheeks pressed together, she felt at one with him. Whatever happened—with basketball, with Jolie, with her family—they were in this together. They'd been thrown some seemingly insurmountable challenges, but tonight she could truly believe they would make it through. Together and still in love.

Chapter Thirty-One

Evette hurried down the hallway of the nursing center, a cold can of Coke in each hand. Essie, Tabrina's roommate, was away at a doctor's appointment and she'd left Jolie alone in the room while she went to get them something to drink.

This was their fifth visit to Lebanon. Their weekly trips were starting to be routine. Spring was in full throttle, and it had been a pleasant drive with the dogwood blooming and everything turning lush and green.

She'd enjoyed the time with Jolie more than she could have imagined. They'd become friends. More than that; she'd stopped thinking of Jolie as "Judd's daughter" and sometimes had to remind herself that she wasn't Jolie's mother. These trips were good for that, too.

It worried her that Jolie sometimes, understandably, seemed down on the way home. She almost always snapped out of it by the time they reached the driveway— and if not, the minute Judd walked through the door to coax her into the backyard to shoot some hoops, she was her cheerful self again.

But Evette worried about the long-term effects on her, seeing her mother like this week after week, with no response whatsoever. She and Judd had talked to the counselor at the elementary school, and she agreed with them that as long as Jolie didn't remain depressed after a visit, it was probably best for her to stay in contact with her mother. And with Carla.

Since Judd's load at work had lessened, they'd been making their trips to see Tabrina on the weekend. Carla usually met them here. But she hadn't showed up last weekend, and they hadn't heard from her for almost two weeks. Evette made a mental note to ask the nurse about her on the way out.

She wished Judd were here. Now that tax season was over, he'd been able to be much more involved with Jolie. But he would start coaching a junior-high summer-league team soon, and after the baby came, they'd only have a few months before the school's basketball season kicked into high gear.

Judd had been making noises about teaching full-time and doing his accounting on the side. He loved working with kids, and he would make an incredible teacher, but there was no way they could live on a teacher's salary. She'd gotten used to the idea that the house they were in might be all they could afford for a while, but there was no way Judd could make good on the teaching threat now. Not unless he was willing to start looking for a house half the size. And as long as they had Jolie, that wasn't an option.

Once basketball started again, she would probably be on her own again taking Jolie to see Tabrina. She tried not to think about the logistics of continuing their trips to Lebanon after the baby came.

As she neared the door to Tabrina's room, she heard Jolie talking. She slowed her steps and stood outside the door, straining to hear what Jolie was saying.

"It's okay, Mama. You can tell me when you're ready. I know you can hear me. Grams and Dad and Evie all said you could. Did you like my braids? Evie took me to Maisie again and she washed my head and done 'em— *did* 'em all over again. Evie makes me talk right, too. But that's okay. I don't mind."

Evette smiled, feeling a sudden kinship with Tabrina, and proud that she'd honored one of Tabrina's desires for her daughter.

Feeling a bit guilty about eavesdropping, she slipped into the room, clearing her throat softly.

Jolie whirled around, her face brightening when she saw Evette. "Mama opened her eyes and looked at me."

"She did?" Evette studied Jolie's face, wondering if she was teasing.

"Uh-huh. She saw me."

"She opened her eyes? Really?" Evette had never seen Tabrina so much as blink.

"Uh-huh. And she saw me."

Once, when two nurse's aides were working with Tabrina, Evette had watched as one of them lifted Tabrina's eyelid to squeeze in some eyedrops. Strangely, it had startled her to see that there was actually a dark eyeball behind each lid. She patted Jolie's arm. "Well, maybe she did, honey."

"No. She *did*." Jolie's chin bobbed with conviction. "I bet she's gonna wake up today."

The eager certainty on Jolie's face broke Evette's heart. "Oh, honey, I wish she would. But…the doctors don't think that will probably happen."

"But we prayed. You and me and Dad. 'Member?"

"Yes, sweetie…I remember." She swallowed hard. "And we'll keep praying for your mama. But I don't want you to get your hopes up."

"What's that mean?"

"Get your hopes up? It means…well, just that your mama might not wake up, and we don't want to be too disappointed if she doesn't."

Jolie propped her fists on her tiny waist. "Then hows come we were prayin' to Jesus?"

"Well, we—" Goodness! This child caused her to think harder—about faith, about miracles, about what Evette McGlin really believed—than she'd ever had to think. *Father, give me an answer that will satisfy this little girl.* "I think, Jolie, that we pray because…we don't know what God might do. We don't know what's best. Only God knows that. And He wants us to trust Him to do the right thing. So we always want to pray that whatever He wants is what will happen. Does that make sense?"

"No." Jolie shook her head matter-of-factly.

Evette couldn't help but laugh. But her laughter quickly threatened to turn into tears. She loved this little girl. And if God answered Jolie's prayer—one she herself had once prayed for a very different reason—it would mean she might lose the privilege of having Jolie in their lives.

She slid into the chair beside Tabrina's bed and scooped Jolie into her lap. Her hair smelled of shampoo and fresh Pink oil and the other magical scents of Maisie's back room.

"Let's just tell God we trust Him and we know He'll take care of your mama better than anybody else ever could. Sound okay?"

Jolie nodded against Evette's chest.

* * *

Judd fluffed the pillows while Evette turned down the covers of Jolie's bed. "Come on, squirt. Hop in."

He opened the drawer of her nightstand and took out the bottle of lotion, as he and Evette began the nightly task of moisturizing Jolie's skin before they put her to bed. He'd been assigned feet to knees, Evette did back, arms and hands, and they were teaching Jolie to do the rest. He'd grown to enjoy the ritual, which usually included much giggling on the part of his two girls.

Jolie climbed into bed, singing to Barksey and stroking his curly fur, in her own little world of pretend. But when Judd squeezed a dollop of hand lotion into her hands for the nightly moisturizing routine, she scurried under the blanket and scooted almost to the foot of the bed. "No! I don't want any."

He held the bottle up. "But you like lotion."

"No, I don't want it no more."

"*Anymore*. But you need it, Jolie." Evette tickled her feet under the covers. "Come on…get up here. Remember how ashy your skin gets when you don't use it? Maisie will have a fit if she sees we didn't keep you greased."

Evette took the bottle of lotion from Judd and squirted some into her hands. "Hurry up, punkin. It's already past bedtime. Let's get this done."

"No! I don't want it." She grabbed for the quilt.

Losing patience, Judd made his voice stern. "Jolie, get up here right now. If we don't do this, your skin will turn all white like it did before."

She tugged on the quilt and pulled it up around her chin. "I *wanna* turn white."

Judd looked at Evette, then back to his daughter. "What do you mean, Jolie?"

"I wanna turn white. I don't want any lotion 'cause then I'll turn white." Her face brightened. "Just like you, Dad, right?"

He took a deep breath. "Who told you that?"

"Teacher."

"Mrs. Markham?"

Jolie nodded.

Evette sat down gently on the side of the bed. "I think you misunderstood, honey."

"You were there."

Judd looked at Evette, but her expression was blank. "You think Evie was there when Mrs. Markham said something."

She nodded vigorously. "Teacher said, 'If you don't put that lotion on, you'll turn white as her.'" She jabbed a finger at Evette.

"Ohh…" Something dawned in Evette's eyes. She turned to Judd. "Mrs. Markham did say that the day we enrolled." She squeezed Jolie's foot under the blanket. "You have a memory like an elephant, you little squirt. But, honey, Mrs. Markham didn't mean you'd really turn white."

"Uh-huh. That's what she said."

"But she didn't mean…not white skin like me and Dad. You're a beautiful, beautiful black girl, and we wouldn't want you to turn white. You wouldn't be our Jolie, you wouldn't be who God made you to be, if you woke up white tomorrow."

"Oh, sweetie…" Judd pulled Jolie onto his lap. "We love you just the way you are. Don't you change a thing." He looked around the cluttered room and winked at Evette. "Well, maybe you could start keeping your room picked up a little better…"

"Amen to that." Evette picked up Barksey and tickled Jolie with the pooch's nose until she giggled her sweet, musical giggle.

Judd marveled at the way his wife had grown into motherhood, until now it seemed as natural as if Jolie were her own. He wanted to kiss her. He *would* kiss her, first chance he got.

But first they had to keep their little girl from turning white. Winking at Evette, he held out his hand. She handed him the bottle and they went to work on this little girl God had placed in their lives.

It wasn't long before she was giggling again.

Chapter Thirty-Two

Judd stared at the clock, surprised that it was already noon. He'd planned to run by the school district office over his lunch hour and pick up the applications for the junior-high summer-league basketball team he was coaching. The schools had agreed to distribute and collect the forms for Judd.

He picked up the phone and dialed the office. It would be good to start the summer season. He'd even discovered a fund-raiser benefit tournament he could pick up right after school was out. It would be good practice time for the boys, and a chance for him to shake off the dust of the sectionals loss.

Judd told the district secretary what he was calling about.

"I have a few forms for you. And listen, John has been trying to get hold of you."

"John Severn?" What did the principal want?

"He couldn't get through on your cell phone and called here just a minute ago asking if we had your work number. If you'll hang on, I'll connect you."

Judd waited for a full minute before John Severn came on the line. "Hi, Judd. Janice said you were coming in to pick up those forms. Would you have time to stop by my office while you're over here?"

"Sure. I'll see you in ten minutes."

John was standing in his office waiting when he arrived. Judd shook the principal's hand and gave him a knowing smile. "You look stressed. The end of the school year must be as crazy around here as tax time is at our office."

John ignored his quip and indicated a chair in front of his desk. "Sit down, Judd."

Uh-oh. This didn't sound good. "Is everything all right?"

John went behind his desk, but he didn't sit down. He paced behind the desk, making Judd feel more nervous as the seconds ticked off on the clock above the window.

"I don't know if anyone has talked to you, but some of the parents—the basketball parents—are upset about the loss to Lindmayer."

Judd straightened in his chair, resisting the temptation to stand and put himself at eye level with John. "I've heard some rumblings…"

"I'm afraid it's more than rumblings. A…contingent, I guess you'd say, was in my office last Tuesday. They're calling for your resignation."

That did propel him from his chair. "What? My resignation? Because we lost a game? That's crazy!"

"It's not just the loss. They're claiming that you've neglected your job."

"Who's claiming that?"

"I don't know if it would be right for me to name names."

"Is this going to be public knowledge?"

"No. I wouldn't do that to you, Coach. I heard the complaints privately."

Judd felt somewhat comforted by that—and by John referring to him as "Coach," but still, the charge of neglect was ridiculous. "I know Tom Clairmont was at the heart of this. His wife warned me that he was upset. But—if you won't give me names, at least tell me how many people were there. Is this just a couple of people Tom rustled up?"

"There were four families represented...seven people here in all. I have to take that seriously, Judd. It represents a decent percentage of the team."

"How can they claim neglect? My boss at Jantzi could make that claim because of all the time I devoted to basketball during tax season. But I don't see how the team could possibly make such a claim. I missed one practice. That's it. How is that neglect?"

John dipped his head before making eye contact again. "They're saying you were preoccupied with this whole mess with your daughter. And you may as well know that Tom also accused you of making a pass at his wife."

Judd stopped in his tracks. "You have got to be kidding!"

John shook his head.

"Was his wife at the meeting?"

The principal hesitated before answering. "No. She wasn't there. I'm afraid that just gave credence to the accusation."

"That is an out-and-out lie, John. If I'm so preoccupied with my daughter's 'mess,'—" he deliberately used John's word "—then how in the world would I have time to make a pass at anyone's wife? Shoot, I've barely had time to make a pass at my own wife these last few months." He forced a laugh, regretting that last line. Mostly because it was too true. Things had grown steadily warmer between him and Evette, but the sheer busyness of their lives—between basketball, tax season and adjusting to life with Jolie—had definitely challenged their love life. Still, he regretted having implied as much to this man.

John held up a hand. "I'm just telling you what was said. And what was recommended."

"By whom?"

"It came from the parents. Mostly senior parents."

That told him a lot. "So…are you firing me?"

"No. But I have to tell you that the board may ultimately make that recommendation. It's on the agenda for the next meeting."

"In executive session, I hope?"

"That's my hope. But you realize, Judd, if we end up taking action, it will be public anyway."

"Action? Am I really going to lose my job over this?" He could not believe what he was hearing.

"I hope not. But Tom Clairmont is pretty worked up. He feels you not only killed Rafe's chances at a scholarship, but also humiliated him by sitting Rafe on the bench, and embarrassed him by hitting on his wife… Like I said, he was pretty hot under the collar. I'm not giving credence to any of that, but that's where he is right now. And he had other parents to back him up."

"To back him up that I hit on his wife?" *Unbelievable!*

"No, no…" John held up a hand. "I mean the neglect charge."

"Was there anybody there in my defense?" The phrase

"stabbed in the back" suddenly had new meaning for him. And it hurt.

"There were no parents representing the…other side, if that's what you mean. As I told Clairmont, the school is unaware of any complaints against you in the past. The board has to listen to all reasonable grievances, but we're not unhappy with your performance."

"Well…that's something, I guess."

"I hope this will die a quiet death. But…" He blew out a heavy breath. "You might want to go to Tom Clairmont and see if you can smooth things over. I think if he drops it, the others will."

The more John's words sank in, the faster Judd's temper simmered. He needed to get out of here. He moved toward the door. "Thanks for…letting me know." Thanks, but no thanks. He needed this like a hole in the head. He felt paralyzed. Maybe he should have given Karen's warning more heed. But never in his wildest dreams had he thought anything would come of any of this.

Had she gone home and told her husband he'd made a pass at her? Right there in his office at Jantzi and Associates? Good grief. It was completely absurd! This whole thing was.

"I need to get back to work." He turned and strode from the principal's office.

John's voice followed him. "Judd!"

He turned, anger almost blinding him.

The principal held out a sheaf of papers. "Don't forget the summer-league forms you came for."

He met John halfway and took the papers from him. "You don't have any complaints about me coaching summer league, do you?"

John's expression told him his snide comment hadn't helped matters. He should have quit while he was ahead.

"Maybe I should just resign."

"Oh, Judd." He looked so pale, Evette worried he was making himself sick over this whole thing. "You don't mean that."

"Well, think about it, Evette. When this gets out—and you know it will—what kind of authority will I have with the guys? I've already lost any witness I might have had—because of Jolie."

She came to put her arms around him. "Judd McGlin, stop that right now. You know that's not true. If anything, you've been an example to the guys of what can happen if…" She hesitated. "Well, you know. And you've shown them how to make an apology and how even something seemingly bad can turn out for good." She stopped, suddenly filled with gratitude. There had been so many lessons in this journey. Things she hadn't realized until this moment, enumerating them for her husband.

"Maybe the best thing is for me to quit. Karl's been pushing me to take on some new clients. That will mean extra hours, but probably not as many as I'm putting in coaching. And the extra money will be at least as good."

"Oh, Judd, but you love coaching. Could you even be happy if you weren't coaching?"

He rubbed his face hard. "I don't know. I just—" He met her gaze, an enigmatic expression on his face. "I'm starting to think this is all by God's design."

"What do you mean?"

"Think about it. If I wasn't coaching, I wouldn't be leaving the house at six in the morning. I'd be home every night for dinner. Our weekends would be free. It's bad enough with Jolie, but once the baby comes…" He moved his chair closer to hers. "I don't want to be an absentee dad. I want to be there for Jolie, for Bambino…" He put a hand on her belly. His features softened, and the tension seemed to drain from him.

"You've been a good dad. You've been more wonderful with Jolie than I ever dreamed. I can't wait to see you with our baby…." She didn't trust her voice to go on.

He stood and pulled her up into his arms. "I hate that this has happened, but maybe this is God trying to get my attention. It's not realistic to think that I can handle two jobs once we have two kids."

She nodded into his shoulder, trying to say without words that she knew what a sacrifice this was for him. And yet, if she were honest, she was thrilled with the thought of having him home more. And having help with the baby.

"If we get to have Jolie permanently in our lives, it's going to take a real effort to keep her connected to Tabrina and Carla. It's not fair to let that all fall on you." He leaned away and took her face in his hands. "I'm sorry I've done that up to now."

She shook her head. "It was where we were at the time, babe. You couldn't just drop your responsibilities. I understand that now. It was a blessing that I wasn't working and could do that. I…I'm sorry I resented it. And took it out on you."

He laughed softly. "We're quite a mess, aren't we?"

She joined his laughter. "Yes, but we're a moldable mess. I think we're shaping up quite nicely, don't you?"

He ran his hands down her sides, around to her belly, then kissed the tip of her nose. "One of us is shaping up nicer than the other."

Oh, she loved this man.

He pulled her close and echoed her thoughts in prayer. "Thank you, Lord, for being patient with us. For getting us through this far. Please show me what You want me to do about the coaching job. Just open our eyes to Your will for our lives. For whatever the future holds, we're Yours, Lord. Whatever that might mean..."

He let his voice trail off and Evette pressed close to him, feeling the warm shelter of his arms. Something told her their storm wasn't over yet.

Chapter Thirty-Three

Evette sat straight up in bed, wondering what had awakened her. She got her answer a second later when the phone rang, and she realized that it had already rung several times.

Beside her, Judd snored softly. She raised up on one elbow and squinted at the alarm clock on his nightstand. Five in the morning? Who could be calling at this hour?

She nudged Judd. "Wake up. Judd? Wake up…the phone's ringing."

He rolled over and groped at the nightstand. "Hello? Yes…what? Are you sure?"

Wide-awake now, Evette turned on the lamp, crawled out of bed and slipped into her robe, trying—from Judd's end of the conversation—to figure out what was going on. Had something happened to one of their parents? But it didn't sound like bad news, judging by Judd's comments. Still, people didn't call at this hour unless it was important.

He was out of bed now, pacing as far as the corded phone would allow. "So you haven't seen her yet? Okay. I understand. We'll wait for your call…you, too. We'll be praying."

He hung up and sat back down on the bed looking stunned.

"What is it? What's wrong, Judd?"

"That was Carla." Still looking dazed, he turned to her. "Tabrina…woke up last night."

"Woke up?" Evette sank back onto the bed, feeling as if he'd punched her dead center in the chest. She struggled to breathe, her mind whirling with all this might mean. "Oh, dear God. What…? How is she?"

"Carla didn't know anything except that she got a call from Lebanon saying that Tabrina had woken up in the middle of the night. They asked her to get there as quickly as possible. She was about to leave home and she wants us to meet her there as soon as we can."

"But what will we do about Jolie?"

Judd picked up a stack of bed pillows from the floor and tossed them against the headboard. "Carla wants us to bring her."

"Oh, Judd…do you think that's a good idea?"

"Carla is sure if Tabrina's awake she'll want—need— to see Jolie."

She nodded. "Of course."

Her mind raced with scenarios. What if Tabrina was well? Surely there'd be a period of rehab after being comatose for…what was it…three months now? But what if she recovered? What if she took Jolie back? Well, of course she would. She was Jolie's mother.

Evette wrapped her arms around herself, cradling her pregnant belly, as if she might lose the baby, too. *Oh, God, please. We can't lose her. Not now. I love her, Lord.* Her eyes stung with the truth of it.

Judd came around the bed and stepped into the walk-in closet. He stood in front of the racks of shirts and trousers, looking stunned himself.

It would kill Judd if Tabrina took Jolie back. Surely he could get visitation rights, but it wouldn't be the same. Nothing would ever be the same.

"Judd?"

He turned toward her voice, but his eyes were glazed, and she knew he was having the same thoughts she was.

"I'll go wake Jolie up."

He nodded, and she could see that he tried to smile. Then his face crumpled and he put a fist to his mouth. But it couldn't stanch the strangled sob that shook him.

The guttural cries emanating from Tabrina's room were otherworldly. Judd stopped in the hallway, looking to Evette for direction. With a little shake of her head, she gave it with certainty: *We are not taking Jolie in there.*

She cleared her throat and waved a hand at him, her eyes telegraphing another message. "Jolie, you haven't had breakfast. Let's go get something from the snack machine. You go on down, Judd…"

They hadn't told Jolie why they were making this unexpected early-morning trip. She'd slept most of the way here and her eyes were still droopy. She hadn't seemed to notice the noise, though it chilled Judd to recognize Tabrina's voice—if you could call it that.

Evette stretched to graze his cheek with a kiss, and whispered in his ear, "We'll be in the snack room. Come and get us if it's…" She didn't finish her sentence. And he couldn't have finished it for her. He had no idea what to expect.

He watched Evette and Jolie until they turned the corner down the hallway that led to the vending machines. He could hardly make his legs carry him toward Tabrina's room. He prayed Carla was already there.

The room was silent when he stuck his head around the corner. Carla was leaning over Tabrina's bed rail, her back to him. A nurse or an aide—he couldn't tell them apart—was working on Tabrina on the other side of the bed. Essie was asleep in her bed near the door. He cleared his throat quietly, not sure he should go in.

Carla turned and saw him. She quickly pulled the curtain halfway, hiding the head of the bed before she came to the doorway.

"How is she? What happened?"

Carla looked completely wrung out. "Oh, Judd…"

For the first time since this all began, he saw Tabrina's mother weep. He didn't know if he should offer a hankie or a shoulder.

But she sucked in a deep breath, straightened her sweater and motioned him out into the hall. "She's awake, but she's not…right. In the head. The doctor saw her this morning, but he wouldn't say anything yet. Not until after they do some evaluations. She's paralyzed. Completely, on one side. Maybe she'll get some movement back…" A spark of hope flared in her eyes and quickly went out again. "The nurse said not to get our hopes up."

He touched her arm gently. "They don't know what God can do. We'll pray. Do you think… Does she know you?"

"I don't know. She's so…agitated. I think she's trying to talk, and it just comes out gibberish." Carla started and looked past him, her eyes darting around the hallway and back into Tabrina's room. "Where's Jolie? You brought her, didn't you?"

He nodded. "Evette took her down the hall. We heard all the…the commotion. We didn't want her to be frightened."

"I want her to see Jolie. I tried to tell her Jolie was okay, but maybe she can't understand. Dr. Toliver said sometimes aphasia can affect understanding, not just speech. Maybe if she sees Jolie…"

"Okay. I'll go get her. But—" He shifted from one foot to the other. "Do you think I should talk to her first? It's been…a long time. I think I should be with Jolie when she goes in, but I don't want to surprise… I'm not sure how it would affect Tabrina to see me after all this time."

Carla put her hand on his elbow and pushed him toward the room. "Go see her. Maybe you can make her understand about Jolie."

"Did you tell her about me…that Jolie is with me? With us?"

Carla shook her head. "I haven't had a chance to say much of anything. She's been too upset."

Judd looked past her into the room. He heard the nurse murmuring to Tabrina, but she was quiet for now.

"I'll come with you." Carla took his arm.

Judd was grateful for someone to lean on.

"Can we see her?" Carla called to the nurse as they entered the room.

Essie stirred, but slept on.

"Come on." The young nurse came around the hospital bed and opened the curtain again. "I gave her something to calm her down. She might act drowsy, but she's still awake. It's amazing…"

He followed Carla to the side of the bed. Tabrina

looked awful—her hair was a frowsy, matted mess and her skin was splotchy. They had her propped up with half a dozen pillows, and there were towels rolled up and tucked between her limbs.

Carla leaned in close to her head. "Tabrina? Hey, girl…wake up. There's someone here to see you. Judd's here."

Judd could see the muscles in her eyelids twitching as if she was trying to open her eyes but couldn't. At Carla's signal, he traded places with her and moved near the head of the bed.

His throat felt thick. "Tabrina, it's Judd. Welcome back. You…you gave us a scare. Jolie's here. Do you want to see her?" With every word he spoke, he felt he was digging himself into a deeper pit. He didn't know how much Tabrina could understand, but if she was coherent, she might think he was trying to come back into her life.

Eyes still closed, she arched her neck. Her head lolled to one side. He wanted someone to help position her head, but it couldn't be him. It just couldn't.

He held on to the rail and knelt at the side of the bed so he could be at eye level with her. "Tabrina? Do you want to see Jolie? She's been coming to see you. Every week. She'll be so happy to know you're awake." He waited for some kind of a response. "Can you open your eyes?"

She moaned and her lashes fluttered against her cheek. Carla knelt beside Judd, peering through the rail. "Come on, girl. Open those eyes. You been sleeping long enough."

She stood and, to Judd's relief, repositioned Tabrina's head on the pillow. She patted her cheeks gently. "Wake up, baby."

Tabrina's eyes flew open, then closed just as quickly.

Carla kept patting. "Come on, baby. Wake up. You can do it. Jolie's here. Judd brought Jolie to see you."

The eyes came open again, this time focusing on Judd. What he saw in her eyes made his breath catch. On some level, she recognized him, but she was changed. The woman in this hospital bed was not the woman he'd loved, not even the woman Jolie had called "Mama."

And he saw in that dull sheen of her eyes that it would be a miracle if anyone ever saw that woman again.

Chapter Thirty-Four

Judd hurried down the hall, panning the vending area and the adjacent sitting room for Evette and Jolie. He spotted them—Jolie curled up on Evette's lap in a large vinyl chair. Both of them with eyes closed. Something plucked at his heart at the sight of them together.

Evette must have heard his footsteps, for her eyes fluttered open. She started and straightened, shifting Jolie in her lap. Judd felt a strange relief to see the vitality, the wit that sparked behind her blue eyes.

"What? How is she?" she whispered.

Judd kept his voice low. "They gave her something to calm her. She's awake, but she's—" He shook his head and pawed at the carpet with the toe of his shoe. "It's not good."

"Do you think…?" She pointed to Jolie. "Should we take her down there?"

"Carla wants her to. She thinks it might help."

"Maybe I should stay here. This time."

He nodded. "Thanks, Evie. That might be best. I think she's having trouble putting everything together in her mind."

"Did she—do you think she knew you?"

He shrugged. "Maybe. It's…hard to tell."

Evette nudged Jolie from her lap and stood, bending over the dark head. "Hey, sweetie. Wake up. Your mama… You need to go with Daddy to see your mama."

Jolie rubbed her eyes and hung onto Evette's hand. "How come you're not comin', Evie?"

"I might later. Right now you just go with Daddy, okay?"

She took Judd's hand.

Pray, he mouthed over his shoulder to Evette.

She placed a hand over her heart. *I will,* she mouthed back.

Jolie darted out the door and started down the hall to her mother's room as she always did. Judd ran to catch up with her and put a hand on her shoulder to stop her.

"Wait a minute, sweetie. Come here." He knelt beside her, praying for the right words. "Daddy needs to tell you something."

Jolie tilted her head to one side, obviously seeing something on his face she wasn't accustomed to.

When he squatted at her eye level, he had her full attention. "Your mama woke up last night. She's still not doing too well. She can't walk or take care of herself. And she can't talk very well. But she can open her eyes, and she can hear you. You can talk to her…just like you have been."

Jolie looked over her shoulder to where Evette was standing in the doorway of the snack room, as if asking permission. Evette nodded.

Judd rose from his haunches. "Let's go."

Evette blew him a kiss and folded her hands, her way of telling him she'd be praying for them.

* * *

After greeting Carla in the hallway, Judd took Jolie's hand. She poked her little head in warily, to check Essie's bed, he knew. Seeing that the woman was asleep, Jolie approached the side of Tabrina's bed. Tabrina's head had lolled to one side again. This time, Judd gently put a hand to one side of her cheek and turned her head toward Jolie.

"Tabrina," he coaxed. "Wake up. Jolie is here. She's been waiting to talk to you." He nodded at Jolie, taking his hand off Tabrina's cheek and drawing his daughter to his side. "Talk to your mama…"

"Hi, Mama." She looked up at Judd, a question on her face. "I thought you said she was awake."

"She is…it's just hard for her to keep her eyes open. Keep talking to her. She'll like hearing your voice."

"What do I say?"

"Tell her about what you and Ev—" He stopped short. Tabrina didn't have a clue who Evie was. This was going to be tricky. "Tell her about Mrs. Markham and what she said about your reading."

"I don't remember."

"Yes, you do. Remember how she said you were reading as well as a fifth grader?"

Jolie shrugged and looked to the bed, where her mother stirred.

Judd touched Tabrina's cool hand. "Tabrina? Wake up."

She moaned and her eyes opened. At first she stared straight ahead, but then her eyes found Jolie and widened.

Jolie gave a happy little gasp. "She did wake up!" She looked up to Judd as if she needed him to confirm that she wasn't just seeing things. "She's awake, isn't she, Daddy?"

"See, I told you." He lifted Jolie up between him and Tabrina, letting her rest her feet on the bottom of the bed rail.

Jolie leaned down and traced her mother's forehead with one finger. "Hi, Mama. It's me."

Tabrina's eyes grew even wider and she opened her mouth. The guttural moan that started grew quickly into the eerie sound he and Evette had heard when they arrived this morning. Only now they didn't have the benefit of one hundred feet of hallway to filter it.

Carla came in and hurried to the other side of the bed. She tried to calm Tabrina, but Jolie pushed off the bed rail with her feet, lunging back against Judd. He almost lost his balance, but quickly recovered and pulled Jolie into his arms. "It's okay, honey. Your mom is just happy to see you. The stroke makes it hard for her talk, or even laugh."

Looking at Tabrina's face, he realized that in spite of the mournful sound of her keening, she was struggling to express surprise and joy and love all at once…and probably confusion about what had happened to her and why she couldn't make her limbs or her voice work the way her brain told them to.

But Jolie was distraught. Her breath came in short, panicked gasps, and she kicked against Judd. "Go away… go away!" He somehow knew she wasn't screaming for Tabrina to go away, but was asking him to take *her* away from the frightening situation.

"Shh…" He put his hand on the top of her head and touched his forehead to hers. "Shush now…it's okay, Jolie. Your mama is just happy to see you."

But Jolie's screams rose to match Tabrina's. "That's not my mama! No! I want my mama back!" She sobbed inconsolably.

"Judd?"

He whirled at the sound of Evette's voice in the doorway. He took Jolie to her.

"Evie! Evie!" She lunged into Evette's arms.

"Take her out," he whispered. Somewhere behind the horror of the moment, he took comfort in the way Jolie had gone to Evette…the way any child sought a mother's arms in a moment of terror. But even as he pondered that truth, his eyes met Carla's and he saw the same realization on her face. Only for her it brought anguish. And one more loss.

He shrugged a meek apology to Carla and started to go to her, but she waved him off and bent to tend to Tabrina.

He dropped his head, praying for words that could undo what had just happened.

There were none.

Chapter Thirty-Five

Judd caught up with Evette and Jolie in the hallway. Evette had never been more grateful for his strength. Tabrina's wails and Carla's ever more strident pleas, trying to calm her, wafted along the hallway, and Evette let Judd guide her and Jolie on out to the parking lot.

There were benches under an awning at the entrance and they sat down there. The sun was just coming up, pink and bright.

Judd tried to take Jolie from her, but she clung to Evette's neck like an empty cicada shell to the bark of a tree.

Judd scooted close and rubbed Jolie's back. "I'm sorry, sweetie. I know it's hard to understand why your mama was acting like that. But it's not her fault. It's the stroke. The sickness."

Jolie didn't respond, but after a few minutes, she quieted, sucking her thumb.

Evette exchanged looks with Judd, trying to figure out what he wanted to do. They couldn't go back in there. It was too traumatic for Jolie. But they couldn't avoid

Tabrina forever. Maybe she would regain control of her body and emotions with time, and they'd be able to resume visits with Jolie. Her mind spun with questions.

Evette's back ached with the weight of Jolie pressing against her belly, and the baby within kicked in protest. *Can you take her?* she mouthed to Judd over Jolie's head.

He nodded and reached to peel Jolie off Evette's lap.

She didn't protest and after a minute of leaning her head against Judd's chest, she sat up and turned to face Evette. "Mama hates me." She said it the way she might have said, *There's a cloud in the sky.*

Evette gasped. "Jolie! Honey…why would you say something like that? Your mama loves you very much."

Jolie shook her head. "No, she doesn't."

Evette slid from the bench and bent down on her knee in front of Judd and Jolie. "Why do you think she doesn't love you?"

"'Cause she won't talk to me no more."

Evette dropped her head. "Oh, honey…of course she loves you. But the stroke hurt your mama really bad. She can't talk to anybody. Not just you. So even though she wants to tell you how much she loves you, she just can't. But I know she still feels that love—" Evette placed her hand over her heart, then took Jolie's hand and placed it over her heart. "Right in here."

Jolie took a stuttered breath. "Then hows come she was yellin' at me?"

"Oh, sweetie…" Evette swallowed past the lump in her throat. She pulled Jolie's jacket around her, hugging her between her and Judd. "She wasn't yelling at you. She was just…she was frustrated because she can't make her body—or her voice—do what she wants it to do."

"I think your mom was actually happy," Judd said. He caught Evette's eye and she knew what he was about to say was for her as much as for Jolie. "I…I saw her face when she saw you, Jolie, and she…she knew it was you. But when she tried to laugh and tell you how glad she was to see you, her voice wouldn't work right."

"But she was screamin'," Jolie sobbed.

"It probably scared her that she couldn't talk right… that her voice wouldn't work."

Evette tried to absorb what Judd had said. Tabrina recognized Jolie. She was coherent. It was more important now than ever that they nurture the connection between Jolie and her mother.

Judd put a finger under Jolie's chin and lifted it until she met his eyes. "I happen to know," he said, "that your mother loves you more than anything in the whole wide world. It's just that the accident, the stroke, won't let her be a mommy to you the way she'd like to be."

Evette put her hands over her swollen belly. "I think your mama was upset that she couldn't make the words come out like she wanted today. I just know she was trying to tell you how much she loved you. That she loves you more than you can even imagine." With those words, Evette found herself feeling a fresh compassion for Tabrina. Just thinking about not being able to express her love for this baby in her womb brought a huge lump to her throat.

"But I love Mama more," Jolie insisted.

"More than she loves you?"

She nodded solemnly.

"I don't think so, Jolie." She pulled the little girl onto her lap and rested her chin on top of the nest of fragrant braids. "I have a feeling your mama loves you more than any mama ever loved her little girl."

But Jolie shook her head. "But I still love Mama more."

Over Jolie's head, Judd looked at Evette with a question in his eyes.

"I still love her more," Jolie said again, punctuating her words with a bob of her head.

Evette shook her head, playing the game but determined to convince her. "Not more than she loves you. Maybe it's a tie, you think?"

"Uh-uh," she said again. "Mama has only loved me for part of her life, but I been lovin' her my whole, whole, whole life."

Evette's breath caught. How did words so profound come from the mouth of a six-year-old?

She hugged her tighter, glad Jolie couldn't see her face. She closed her eyes, but the tears seeped out anyway, and in that moment, Evette knew that if this little girl were her own flesh and blood she could not possibly love her more. But more than that, she loved Jolie exactly the way she was. Loved every inch of her, from her Pink-oiled scalp to her pudgy toes.

Chapter Thirty-Six

Judd and Evette sat in the car and watched as Jolie slogged up the walk to the school, shoulders hunched and head down. He fought tears, seeing his little girl like this.

When Jolie disappeared into the school, Evette turned in her seat to face him. "Oh, Judd...do we dare leave her like this?"

"She'll be okay. We'll be home before school's out. We need to get some things settled." But he sat with the engine idling, watching the door, half expecting Jolie to come running back to the car.

Two weeks had gone by since Tabrina had awakened from her coma. Since then, a cloud of melancholy had settled over the McGlin household. The cheerful little soul who'd filled their home with giggles and chattering had been replaced by a sullen girl who retreated to her room after school and sulked through mealtimes. He and Evette had tried everything they could think of to cheer her up, to reassure her that Tabrina loved her and that she was in good hands. But Jolie remained unconvinced.

He and Evette were depressed for a different reason. Carla had started talking about bringing Tabrina home to Charlack—and taking Jolie with her as soon as school was out.

That was three days away. He could hardly bear to think about it, let alone talk about it. Every time Evette broached the topic with him, saying, "What are we going to do, Judd?" he shushed her and changed the subject.

But they had to talk about it sometime, or they might lose their little girl—*his* little girl. It took him aback to realize that he'd begun to think of Jolie as *theirs*—his and Evette's together. He had a feeling Evette felt the same way.

A horn tooted behind him and Evette's voice broke into his troubled reverie. "Judd?"

"Sorry…" He put the car in gear and eased away from the curb, rolling through the drop-off zone.

Once back on the street, he turned to Evette. "It's only going to make things easier now that school's almost out."

"Easier?"

He rubbed the bridge of his nose. He hadn't meant to speak the words aloud, but they had to talk about it sometime. He sighed. "I'm afraid Carla will use school being out as an excuse to…to take Jolie back."

Evette bit the bottom of her lip. "How can she think it would be healthy to have Jolie living under those circumstances?"

"They love her, too, Evette."

She drew back as if he'd struck her, and only then did he realize that he'd snapped at her.

"I'm sorry. I didn't mean for it to come out that way. I'm just… It kills me to think of losing her, Evie. I can't even imagine."

She shook her head. "I know."

They drove for a while, headed to Lebanon at Carla's request. Evette's soft laughter made him start. "What's funny?" What could possibly be funny in this whole mess?

She gave him a sad smile. "I was just thinking…if you'd told me last winter how this…how it would all end up, I would never have believed you."

"She's changed us, hasn't she?"

Evette's eyes filled. "She's changed everything. I can't even imagine life without her, Judd."

"I know."

"But what will happen to her if she has to go with Carla? It will kill her, Judd. She's still…traumatized by that."

They had taken Jolie to talk to Pastor Mike last night. He'd been so sweet and gentle with her, with all of them. And already this morning, a prayer request had popped up in the all-church e-mail list they were on, asking the congregation to pray for Jolie, for Tabrina's health, and for "difficult decisions that must be made by the family." It sounded so innocuous on the computer screen. Not so much when they were living it. "Difficult" didn't begin to describe the anguish they felt.

Jolie had actually seemed better when they put her to bed after coming home from the pastor's office. She even laughed a little when Judd tickled her as he tucked her in. But the frown had been back this morning, and she'd barely eaten a bite at breakfast. In just two weeks, she'd grown frighteningly thin.

"What is Carla thinking?" Evette's voice broke. "She'll be consumed with taking care of Tabrina. Jolie will just get…she'll get lost." She put her face in her hands and wept.

He patted her leg, trying to comfort her. What he wanted to do was drive out into the country and wail at the top of his lungs.

And yet, he couldn't ignore the silver lining in this very dark cloud. He'd never dared to believe there might be a day when Evette would mourn with him at the prospect of losing Jolie. As she'd said, a short while ago, she might have seen this as an answer to her prayers.

Jolie's presence in their lives had somehow healed things between them—things they'd never actually acknowledged were wrong. And even if they ultimately lost Jolie to Carla—a possibility that he almost couldn't put into words—Judd knew he would never lose the newfound love he felt for his wife.

Evette straightened in her seat, blew her nose and wiped her eyes. "We have to talk some sense into Carla, Judd. We have to!" she said again, sounding on the edge of hysteria.

"She loves Jolie, too, Evette. We can't forget that."

"But she can't take care of her! It will be horrible—just horrible—for Jolie to have to live with that…the way Tabrina is. That's no way for a little girl to live. What is Carla thinking?"

Judd merged onto I-44, heading west toward Lebanon. "Maybe seeing Tabrina so…diminished made Carla realize that she won't ever be the same…won't ever be able to care for herself, or even express herself. It's easy to see how she could lose hope. Jolie—she represents hope. I guess that's not so hard to understand."

"Oh, but, Judd…" The tears started again. "It's not fair to Jolie. And when will we ever see her? And summer is the worst time for her to go. What will she do all day?"

"If the worst happens, Evie, we'll make sure we see her." He shook his head and set his jaw. "We have the right to visitation. We can arrange to have her every other weekend at least."

Evette shook her head. "You don't know how much I've fantasized about just running away with her." She gave a nervous laugh and looked up at him beneath damp lashes.

"Oh, man. I'm right there with you. I can't…I can't even imagine not having her. All the time. Not just a few lousy weekends." He reached over and put his hand on Evette's belly.

This poor baby had gotten lost in the shuffle. They were less than ten weeks from welcoming their child into their home, and the whole ordeal with Jolie—and now with Tabrina—had consumed them.

But a new baby would be a blessing. If the worst happened and they had to give up the right to raise Jolie, this child would be a slice of joy in the midst of their grief. And it would be grief, genuine grief, if they lost her. The very thought made his gut churn.

His hand stilled, fingers splayed over Evette's stomach. He'd so looked forward to seeing Jolie in the role of big sister.

"Judd…" Evette looked up at him, anguish on her face, her voice strangled. "I don't know if I can do this. What if we lose her?"

We. What if *we* lose her? If she only knew how, in the midst of their sorrow, that simple word warmed his heart.

Chapter Thirty-Seven

Evette walked—waddled was more like it—to the refrigerator and rearranged the shelves to make room for the leftovers from dinner. Down the hall, she heard Judd reading a bedtime story to Jolie.

Another month had gone by and as June faded into July, Evette felt as if they were living under multiple death sentences. The ugly rumors surrounding Judd's coaching position still hung over their heads, though no action had been taken against him. The whole thing had caused Judd to reconsider whether he should coach the team next year. As much as Evette would have welcomed having him home more—especially after the baby came—she wasn't sure her husband could truly be happy without a team to coach. Besides, if she was going to stay home with Jolie and the baby, they would need every extra penny.

But money was a minor issue compared to the question of Jolie. Carla continued to make noises about bringing Jolie to Charlack to live with her and Walt, the plan being to move Tabrina to a nursing home close by. But no date had been set.

It drove Evette crazy to have so many issues unsettled, but Judd was of the mind that if they didn't make waves, maybe things could just go on as they were. For the same reason—and because Judd was, after all, Jolie's birth father—he and Evette hadn't taken steps to legalize their guardianship of her. "I'm her dad, what else do they need to know?" Judd had barked one night when Evette was filling out a permission slip for Jolie to ride with her T-ball team to an out-of-town game.

Evette feared their lack of diligence in the matter would backfire on them. Even if they'd had the financial means to seek custody of Jolie, she doubted they'd win— and when she searched her heart, she wasn't sure it would be in Jolie's best interests.

But neither could it be in her best interests to be exposed to Tabrina's situation on a daily basis, nor to have as a caretaker a grandmother who was preoccupied with Tabrina's well-being. Oh, how she wanted things to be settled with Jolie before the baby came. And yet, like Judd, she was afraid if they pushed for some sort of ultimatum, it would go against them. Still, she didn't want to risk getting bad news before she went into labor. Or worse, after the baby came and they were celebrating a new life.

She was growing big as a house. The baby had taken to being active late at night, kicking and somersaulting and keeping Evette awake. But all was quiet in her womb right now. Jolie had taken a strong interest in the whole birth process and drove Evette batty asking questions and snuggling up to her belly to talk to the baby.

She and Judd had managed to keep from revealing the baby's gender, and she treasured having that secret with him. They'd finally decided on a name, but she and

Judd—and Jolie, too—still called the baby "Little Bambino." They'd spent many an evening in the nursery dreaming about what life would be like with a baby in the house. *Oh, Lord, please let Jolie get a chance to be a big sister. Please, Father…*

The doorbell rang and Evette hollered down the hall. "Judd? Can you get that?"

He apparently didn't hear. She stuffed a foil-wrapped casserole dish on top of a package of rolls and went to the entryway.

It was almost dark outside, so she flipped on the porch light before she opened the door.

"Carla? Is everything all right? Come in." Had something happened to Tabrina? In spite of their invitations, Carla had never come to see Jolie here. Jolie's visits with her had always taken place wherever Tabrina was.

Evette opened the door wider and Carla stepped through. "Come on in. Judd was just putting Jolie to bed, but I don't think she's asleep yet."

Carla looked around the room and down the foyer, as if appraising the place.

"How is Tabrina? Is everything all right?"

"We're moving her. There's an opening at a place in St. Louis. It's cheaper and a lot closer."

"Oh? Good. I'm glad. Come on back to her room. Jolie will be happy to see you. We've been saying we needed to have you over…so you could see where Jolie—" She cleared her throat, swallowing the rest of the sentence. She'd almost said, *so you could see where Jolie lives.*

"Follow me. They're back here. You can probably hear Jolie giggling." She knew she was chattering like a monkey, but she couldn't seem to help herself. Why had Carla come?

"Judd? Jolie? Look who's here…" Evette entered the room then stepped aside to reveal Carla.

Judd jumped up from the bed where he'd been reading to Jolie. "Carla. Hello."

Jolie sat up in bed, her brow crinkled in a question mark. "Hi, Grams. How come you're here?"

Carla swept into the room. "You need to get your things together, Jolie."

"What?" Judd stepped between Carla and Jolie's bed.

"I told her—" Carla angled her head toward Evette. "We've moved Tabrina to a place closer to home. It's affordable and they can help with her therapy. We're ready to bring Jolie back home. Get your stuff, baby girl. Come on." She stood with arms folded over her chest.

Evette stood, unable to speak. Surely Carla didn't intend to take Jolie right now—out of her bed!

"Carla…" Judd's voice sounded uncertain. "Let's go out into the living room. We need to talk this over."

"There's nothing to talk about."

Judd took a step toward her. "Well, yes, there is. But we're not going to talk about it right here." His eyes swept to Jolie, who sat wide-eyed on the bed.

Evette went and perched on the edge of the bed, pulling the covers up around Jolie's chin. "Night-night, sweetie. We're going to go sit in the living room and talk."

"Night-night, Evie. Don't let the bedbugs bite?" Jolie echoed. But her good night came out more like a question.

Willing her voice to sound confident, Evette bent to kiss her. "That's right. Don't let the bedbugs bite." She took a risk. "See you in the morning."

That seemed to calm Jolie.

Judd had persuaded Carla as far as the hallway and Evette turned out the light, pulled Jolie's door to within an inch of closed and went to join them.

Judd was seething, practically hissing at Carla. "This is my daughter, and you're not going to march in here unannounced and haul her away before we've even had a chance to discuss what should happen."

"There is nothing to discuss. You don't have custody. You don't—"

Evette put a hand on each of their backs. "Please," she whispered. "Let's go talk in the living room."

They let her usher them into the dim room. Evette switched on a couple of table lamps.

Judd paced while Carla sat on the edge of the sofa. "You don't have any rights to Jolie," she said. "You gave those up when you walked out on my daughter. And don't you dare try to pull the concerned-father routine now."

Evette rubbed her temples. "Carla, please. You can't just take her away from everything familiar and move her like this. She is just finally getting over the trauma of seeing Tabrina like…she was. And who's going to take care of her all day while you're working?"

"Walt's retired. He's home all day."

"You said yourself that he doesn't like kids," Judd growled.

"He likes kids fine."

Evette started to tremble. Carla seemed determined. What could they do to stop her? They didn't have any rights to Jolie. Not really. Not immediately anyway. She'd seen too many custody battles portrayed on television. It was always a long, drawn-out process. Nobody ever won, and the children always lost.

Evette went to sit beside Carla on the sofa. She angled her body toward her, clasping her hands together so Carla wouldn't see how badly they were shaking. "Carla. Don't take her tonight. Please. We can drive up to Charlack, bring her to you…as soon as you have Tabrina settled in." She pointed down the hall where all was silent. "She's probably already asleep. It will take her some time to get used to the idea of adjusting to a new place all over again."

Judd joined Evette's plea. "Please, just let us talk to her about it first. The last thing she needs is to be wrenched out of her bed without any warning."

'No!" Carla whirled to face him and jabbed a slender finger at his chest. "The last thing she needs is to live in this lily-white town a hundred miles from the people who love her most, the people who raised her from a tiny baby." Her voice rose to a screech. "I will not lose her and Tabrina both!"

Carla started pacing, and Judd slumped onto the sofa where she'd been sitting, exchanging worried frowns with Evette.

Evette broke the silence. "I'm so sorry about Tabrina, Carla. We've been praying for her. That she'll continue to improve…"

"She needs to see Jolie. She can't get well if she doesn't remember what she's fighting for."

"We'll bring her, Carla. Every week, twice a week if you want." Judd's tone had reached desperation.

"Twice a week isn't enough. Tabrina needs to see her daughter every day. She needs to know that when she's not by her side, she's just up the street in Charlack. My girl needs a reason to get better!"

Judd's shoulders rose with a deep intake of breath,

and Evette knew he was forcing himself to stay calm. He cleared his throat. "How will you manage taking care of Tabrina and Jolie both, Carla?"

"Why do you think we moved her closer? Don't think I haven't thought this through. Don't think I've thought of anything else these last weeks." Carla glared at him.

Judd rose and went to Carla, touched her arm.

But she shook him off, wagging her head. "I'm not losing Jolie, too, Judd," she said again. "I'm not."

"Carla?" Evette made her voice soft. "Please, let's wait till morning. We're all tired right now. Jolie's in bed. It's not fair to wake her."

Carla's shoulders sagged.

Judd took another tentative step toward her. "We can call and find you a place to stay tonight. Here in the Falls…so you don't have to drive back so late. We can talk it over tomorrow. Talk to Jolie…"

Carla waved him off. "You don't need to be getting me a place to stay. I'm not an invalid—"

"No…no, of course not. I just thought…" Judd let his voice trail off, waiting.

Carla's gaze darted around the room, as if she'd find what her next move should be written on one of the walls. Finally, she sighed and hiked her purse up over her shoulder. "I'm going. I won't disturb Jolie's sleep. But I'll be back in the morning. Have her things packed."

She left without another word.

Evette stood in the doorway, watching her walk down the driveway to her car. Judd came and stood beside her, putting his arm around her.

Neither of them spoke, but Evette's mind raced.

They might have staved her off for tonight, but this woman was not going to back down. Not ever.

Chapter Thirty-Eight

Judd lay on the bed in the master bedroom, staring at the ceiling fan. In the dim glow of the night-light, he could just make out the blades turning lazily overhead. Evette's head was heavy on his bare shoulder. They'd managed to dissuade Carla for tonight, but she'd promised to come back first thing in the morning for Jolie. For his daughter.

"Oh, Judd. What are we going to do?"

He stroked Evette's hair and brushed the tears from her cheeks. "We're going to wait until morning and take one day at a time…one minute at a time. No matter what happens, we'll still get to see her, Evie. Carla won't deny us that. I know she won't."

"But it won't be the same."

"No. It won't."

Nothing would ever be the same. He closed his eyes and prayed as he'd never prayed before. Surely God hadn't brought Jolie into their lives only to rip her from their arms. Not when Evette had just grown to love her.

Please, Lord…don't let this happen. I don't know

*what's right. I don't know what You have planned for
Jolie…for any of us. But, God, please, don't let Evie be
hurt in this. Please comfort her. Let her know Your
perfect peace—no matter what happens.*

And even as he prayed, he realized that God had
already answered that prayer. He tightened his arms
around her and felt her slow, even breaths against his
chest…this woman he loved more than his own life.

Carla called around eight to say that she'd be there
within the hour. With a heavy heart, Evette called Judd at
work to tell him to come home as she went to wake up
Jolie.

Her little pink-bottomed toes stuck out from the end
of the rumpled quilts and Evette's knees went weak. She
couldn't do this. She could not let this child go.

But she had no choice. And she couldn't let Jolie see
her emotion. Jolie had been through the wringer since
Tabrina had awakened.

She sat on the side of the bed and patted Jolie's arm.
"Wake up, sweetie. It's time to get up."

Jolie popped up in the bed with her usual cheery smile.
"Hows come I hafta wake up? It's not school time."

Evette forced a smile. "No. Not school. But Grams is
coming to get you today."

Jolie's smile faded. "I wanna see Grams. But do I
hafta stay all night at her house?"

"Yes, sweetie."

"How many nights?"

Evette swallowed hard. "I don't know, punkin. We'll
just have to see." She pulled the quilts off and lifted Jolie
to the floor. When had she gotten so heavy? "You go
wash up and I'll pack your things."

Jolie did as she was told.

Evette went to the closet and dug out the little lime-colored suitcase. She slid open Jolie's dresser drawer and started putting things inside the case. The reality hit her then. This room would be empty tonight. The house would be silent. Their hearts broken. They were losing this precious little girl.

Evette buried her face in her hands and wept.

The smell of singed hair, perm solution and hair spray met Evette's nostrils as she walked through the salon and back to Maisie's "office." It felt strange being here without Jolie, but when Evette had picked up the phone this morning to call and cancel Jolie's braid appointment, she'd felt drawn instead to come and talk to Maisie in person.

The hairdresser was bent over a large sink in the back room, scrubbing something furiously in the depths beneath the suds. And she was singing softly to herself.

"Maisie?" Evette knocked on the doorjamb.

The woman stopped singing and turned. "Evette McGlin." She looked behind Evette, then panned the room with her gaze. "Where's that Miss Jolie?"

"Oh, Maisie…"

The woman's eyes grew big. "Don't tell me something terrible happened to that girl? Don't you tell me that."

The dam broke and Evette stood in the middle of the room, sobbing until her shoulders ached. Maisie closed the gap between them in two broad steps, putting her damp, soapy arms around her.

Finally, Evette managed to shake her head, reassure Maisie. "She's okay. Jolie's okay. But…her grandmother came and got her this morning. Took her away. I'm afraid we've lost her, Maisie."

The whole story poured out and she wept for the tenth time that day in Maisie's ample arms, comforted somehow by the rhythm of the woman's musical "uh-huh, uh-huh."

"I don't know what's right. I don't know how to pray. I can truly understand why we *all* want her. Why we each think it's best if Jolie lives with us."

Maisie waited, arms akimbo, letting her talk.

"Jolie…she needs her mother and her grandmother, but she needs us, too. Her dad, especially. Oh, Maisie, this is killing my husband."

Maisie let her cry, then looked her full in the face. "So what do you think is right? In here…" She made a fist and laid it over her heart.

"I don't know. Carla has a point. Jolie will be in the minority in The Falls. What is that like for you? For your daughter? Do you regret raising Betsy here?"

"I got no complaints. Betsy, she *sure* got no complaints."

Evette smiled. Betsy had a boy she was sweet on. Maisie had regaled her and Jolie with the story last time they'd been in to have Jolie's hair done. Maisie turned serious. "But then she ain't known any different, my Betsy. She was just a baby when Ronald took his job, moved us out to the country." A faraway look came to her eyes. "Oh, child…there might be some tough times, raisin' your girl here. But there'd be some tough times no matter where she was."

"We promised Carla…if Jolie stayed with us, we'd make sure she had time with her Grams and her mother. But she wouldn't listen."

"Maybe she listen, but she just don't like what she hear?"

Evette leaned away from Maisie and wiped her tears with the back of her hands. "I don't know, Maisie. Maybe I just…maybe I just love Jolie so much I can't see what's truly best for her."

"What matters…what's most important is love." Maisie smoothed a hand across the vinyl of the sofa. Back and forth, back and forth. "As long as she grows up with love, she'll be all right. Can't me or anybody else tell you what's right for your Jolie. That's somethin' only God can figure out. But if you all decide together, with love, I have a feelin' it will all work out just about right."

Hearing the peace in Maisie's voice, Evette could almost believe she was right.

Evette put the lid on the slow cooker and turned it on high. If they ended up going to Charlack today, she wouldn't have time to fix dinner, so she'd put some chicken on to stew. But there was no joy in cooking anymore. They'd been without Jolie for two weeks now and the house fairly boomed with the quiet. If not for the coming baby, she wasn't sure how she would go on.

Carla hadn't balked when they wanted to come and get Jolie for an overnight at their house, but it wasn't the same. Jolie had turned glum again, the way she had after that awful day in the nursing home. It broke Evette's heart to see the lights go out in the sunny girl's eyes.

According to Carla, things hadn't changed much with Tabrina. "If anything, the move was a setback for her," Carla had said. "But she'll come around. She'll come around. She has to." Evette hoped she was right. For Jolie's sake.

They hadn't talked to Tabrina's doctors about her

prognosis. She'd encouraged Judd to try to find out what the doctors expected Tabrina's quality of life to be. If she knew Tabrina would get better, that she could ever be a mother to Jolie, maybe she could get over this sadness that seemed to follow her everywhere.

She turned to open the refrigerator and felt something give way inside her. She inhaled a sharp breath, then felt a liquid warmth that could only mean one thing. Her water had broken.

"Judd!" The room spun. She squeaked out his name. "Judd!"

He appeared in the doorway to the family room. "Did you call me?" His face went pale when he saw her clinging to the counter, holding her belly. "Evette! What is it? What's wrong?"

She forced a smile as a contraction rolled over her like an ocean breaker. "Nothing's wrong. I think…I think we're about to meet our Little Bambino."

Chapter Thirty-Nine

"You're doing great, Evie. You're doing great. Here comes another one. You can do this..." Judd willed his hands not to tremble as he swabbed Evette's forehead with a damp cloth and looked over at the monitors. The nurses were calm and everything seemed to be proceeding the way they expected, but he sensed Evette was at the end of her strength. She'd been pushing for more than two hours and still no baby.

The contraction peaked and Evette bore down, her face beet-red, and her entire body wracked by tremors.

Something seemed different about this push, though. He saw a new spark in Evette's eyes. He shot up his thousandth prayer of the day.

The next contraction began almost before the last was finished and suddenly everything was happening at once. The doctor and two nurses materialized at Evette's side and the next thing he knew, a lusty wail filled the room and joined with Evette's whimpers.

She tried to rise up in the bed. "Oh! Oh!" Her voice wavered, whether with exhaustion or emotion, Judd couldn't tell. "Is she okay? Is the baby okay, Judd?"

Looking at the angry, purplish creature the doctor had drawn from her body, he wasn't sure how to answer.

But Dr. Benson laughed out loud and held the screaming little girl up for them to see. "She's just fine. Not too happy about us making her stay in there so long, but she looks like a healthy, strong little girl."

Clara, the nurse who'd remained here past her shift to stay with Evette, came to the head of the bed and patted Evette's shoulder. "Good job, Mama. Do you have a name picked out for her?"

Evette's eyes had been glued to the baby since her first cries of life, but now she stole a glance at Judd, a question in her eyes.

He nodded, feeling his relief grow into a wide smile. It was all over, and his wife and daughter were safe and well. *Thank you, God.*

Evette cleared her throat. "Her name is Kirstie Jolie McGlin."

Judd held his baby daughter in his arms and let the tears fall. Evette was asleep, breathing deeply in the bed beside him, and he was counting his blessings. But his heart ached that Jolie wasn't here. They would see her tomorrow night. Carla had promised to bring her to the house to meet the baby. But he wanted her in the guest room down the hall. He wanted to help Evette rub lotion on her little brown toes and listen to the beads on the tips of her braids clack as she ran down the hall or tossed him the basketball on the driveway. Like this infant on his lap, Jolie was flesh of his flesh, and he wanted to be a part of her everyday life.

And that wasn't going to happen.

The baby stretched and moved her rosebud mouth. Judd inhaled the innocent powdery scent of her. He would have made any sacrifice so that his two daughters could grow up together. But God hadn't provided the avenue for that to happen, and he—they—would have to learn to live with that.

When the ultrasound had revealed that they were having a girl, he and Evette had easily agreed on Kirstie for her name. It was a Scottish name that meant "follower of Christ." That was their desire for their daughter. They'd had a different middle name picked out—Erin. But that night after Carla came and took Jolie away, Evette had laid her head on his shoulder, weeping. "I want to give our daughter Jolie's name—as a middle name. If they can't grow up together, as sisters, at least maybe that will show Jolie how much we love her, how much we miss her."

Judd had been moved too deeply to speak. It was the first of many times they'd wept together over Jolie since then. But in the days since, as the edge of his grief dulled, he'd begun to wonder if perhaps Jolie's time with them had been exactly as long as God intended from the beginning.

Her presence in their home had ultimately brought healing. Healing to Evette's way of thinking, healing to their marriage. Perhaps it had even changed the kind of mother Evette would be to this precious baby in his arms. He would never say that to Evette, of course, but he had seen a new softness in his wife that had warmed his heart toward her and melded their love into something he hadn't dared to hope for.

Life hurt…oh, how it hurt sometimes. But God was good, and Judd bowed his head and gave thanks once again.

"Who do you think she looks like?" From her hospital bed, Evette watched her mother beam down at Kirstie.

"Oh, I couldn't say. She has your father's ears, but—"

"His ears?" Evette laughed. "Well, Daddy, that's quite a legacy to leave. Your ears?"

Her father preened and stretched his neck, presenting his ears and they all laughed. It felt good to be with her family this way again.

Her mother smoothed a veined hand over the baby's ears as if she could pin them closer to her head. "I think she has Judd's mouth. Certainly she got his fingers and toes." She unwrapped the pink receiving blanket to reveal a tiny hand.

The declarations made Evette smile to herself. Jolie had Judd's mouth, and his long, tapered fingers. It would make her happy if the sisters shared his features. How she hoped they could be friends—Judd's two daughters—in spite of the distance that separated them.

"You look sleepy, dear." Her mother patted her arm.

"Not sleepy, just…thoughtful."

"Well, everything turned out well." She tucked a graying strand of hair behind one ear and looked down at the baby. "Now, thank goodness, the three of you can get on with your lives together."

Anger started to simmer. Why did she have to ruin everything? Evette sent up a prayer for patience and forced her voice to remain steady. "Yes…I'm eager to do that, Mother. And I can't wait for Jolie to meet Kirstie. And for you and Daddy to meet Jolie. Carla's bringing her over tomorrow night to meet the baby. You and Daddy will stay long enough to meet her, won't you?"

"Oh, well, I…" Tessa Bryant sputtered and coughed. "I suspect your father will want to get back to the city before that."

"Mother, please. We'd really like you to know her." She felt a little underhanded setting her mother up this way, but she'd made it her mission to give Jolie a chance to win Mother over the way she'd won Evette's heart.

Daddy was already coming around. When he'd held the baby for the first time this morning, he'd declared, "She's an answer to prayer, this one." But then her father leaned in and whispered to her. "Did you ever think, Evie, that Judd's girl might be an answer to your prayers, too? I've been thinking on it and that's what I keep coming up with."

His words still stunned her every time she thought about them. And if anyone could bring her mother around, it was Daddy.

Annie appeared in the doorway. "My turn!"

Her mother held the baby out and Annie stepped in and took the bundle.

"Why don't you and Daddy go down and get some lunch? Judd won't be here for another hour or so."

Her father patted his midsection. "Maybe we'll do that. Give you girls a chance to talk. Come on, Tessa. This old man's hungry."

"Oh, Bert, you can't be hungry. You ate enough breakfast to feed an army." But she rose and followed him to the door. "Don't wear that baby out, now. She's going to want to spend some quality time with her grandmother." She gave Annie a stern look. "I have dibs when we get back."

"Don't you worry, Mother. She'll still be here."

As they left the room, Annie rolled her eyes for Evette's benefit and they giggled together. She held Kirstie for a few minutes before tucking her back into the hospital bassinet.

She slid her chair closer to Evette's bed and plopped down. A wistful smile shadowed her face. "Well, you got your girl. I'm a little jealous, you know."

She laughed. "Hey, talk to Geoff…I'm sure he can arrange something."

Annie reached up to touch the baby's hand in the bassinet. "She's so beautiful."

"I loved her instantly, Annie." She swallowed the lump in her throat. "And suddenly I could understand how Judd could have loved Jolie so quickly and completely. I didn't get it then, but I do now. And—" She teared up. "That makes it all the harder to have lost her."

Annie nodded, but Evette could see in her eyes that she still didn't understand. Not really. Evette curbed a sigh. Had *she* harbored that vacant look before she'd finally understood where her treasures lay?

"So…" Annie's carefully penciled brows went up. "Were the labor and delivery too awful? Judd said you didn't even have an epidural. You're making the rest of us look bad, you know."

Evette cringed at the memory of the pain. "It was… worth it," she said, looking over at the baby. "It was worth it, but it's the hardest thing I've ever done." As soon as the words left her lips, she stopped, knowing what she'd said wasn't true. The hardest thing she'd ever done was learning to love Jolie…and then losing her. And that, too, was ultimately worth it. She believed that. What Jolie had given them in her innocence, her unconditional love, her joy in living, was worth all the pain and doubts and broken hearts.

She didn't think Annie was ready to hear that yet. But someday. Someday, with God's help, she would help her understand.

Chapter Forty

Kirstie's wails finally quieted and Evette risked carrying her to the crib to try and put her down. She lowered the baby to the mattress and, keeping one hand on her tummy, hummed a made-up lullaby. The tiny pursed lips puckered in a sucking motion, and she took in a shuddered breath, but she didn't wake up.

Evette watched her sleep for a while, still amazed by the miracle of her daughter. *Their* daughter. They'd had Kirstie home for ten days now, and she wasn't sleeping those twenty-plus hours all the baby books said she would. Evening seemed to be her fussy time, but most of the day she was content when she was awake.

"Are you ever coming out of there?" Judd's voice, though only a whisper, startled her.

She smiled. She had never loved Judd more than she had these past days. She knew already that this tiny person had bonded them together in a profound way. She felt so blessed and deeply happy to have the child she'd longed for since she and Judd had first married.

But despite all the joy the baby had brought, there was

a pall over the house. She and Judd hadn't spoken of it exactly, but she knew—by the faraway look that so often came to his eyes and by the hunch of his shoulders, as though he carried an invisible burden—he was grieving Jolie. They both were.

"Is she asleep?" Judd leaned his back against the doorjamb, watching Evette.

She nodded. "Finally. I hope she doesn't sleep too long. Jolie will be disappointed if she sleeps the whole time they're here."

It had been over a week since they'd last seen Jolie, but Carla was taking off work early and bringing her again tonight. Evette was looking forward to it…and dreading it at the same time. She felt a physical ache in her chest when she thought of sending Jolie home again with Carla tonight. Like opening an old wound. The room down the hall was unbearably empty without Jolie in it.

Judd held his watch to catch the light from the hallway. "She'll be here in less than an hour." The anticipation in his tone made him sound like a boy.

She nodded. It had been so hard to watch Jolie leave with Carla last time, so hard to watch Judd tell her goodbye. It broke her heart to think about that scene being replayed again tonight. But surely it would get easier as time went on. Surely they'd grow accustomed to the goodbyes.

She checked on the baby one last time and joined Judd in the doorway.

He took her in his arms and cradled her head against his shoulder. "This…this phrase keeps going through my head over and over."

She pulled away and looked up at him. "Phrase?"

He nodded, biting his bottom lip. "'The Lord giveth, and the Lord taketh away…'"

She looked up at him, put her hand on his cheek, tears burning her eyes. "Blessed be the name of the Lord," she whispered. "I miss her so much."

"Me, too. I just keep thinking about everything she's exposed to. In that nursing home, even in Carla's house. She told me back when she first called about Tabrina, that Walt didn't want Jolie. What if he ignores her? Or mistreats her? She was happy here. She was so happy with us."

"I know…" This wasn't the first time Judd had worried aloud to her. But what could they do? "It will be better for her once school starts. Then she'll have friends…and a teacher to keep an eye on her."

He shook his head. "I don't know, Evie. I just…I don't have a good feeling about it."

She ran a hand down his arm, took his hand in hers. "Come on. Let's go eat something. We'll feel better after we've seen her tonight, talked to her."

He followed her down the hall to the kitchen and they put together a light supper. Evette reheated a casserole a family from church had brought. Someone from church had delivered dinner every night for a week after Evette and the baby came home, and they had enough leftovers in the freezer for at least another week. She was touched by the way the church had reached out to them.

Judd did the dishes while she straightened the living room. "Why don't you try to find something for her to play with?" she hollered. They'd sent all Jolie's toys with her the morning Carla came to get her.

He appeared in the kitchen doorway. "I think Kirstie will probably provide all the entertainment."

"Good point." She smiled, remembering how Jolie had cradled the baby that first night, cooing to her and examining each tiny finger and toe.

Carla had said they'd be there by six-thirty, but seven came and went and they still hadn't showed up. Or called. Kirstie woke up and Evette went to nurse her.

By seven-thirty, Judd was pacing and fuming. "The least she could do is call."

"Why don't you call her?"

"I tried," he said. "She's not answering her phone."

Evette finished feeding the baby and changed her diaper and outfit. By the time they got here it would be Jolie's bedtime.

By eight-fifteen she was worried. Judd dialed their home number again when Carla didn't answer her cell phone. Judd put the speakerphone on after Walt answered and Evette listened in over the background noise of some shoot-'em-up TV show.

"They're not coming after all," Walt said.

"What do you mean they're not coming?"

"Just what I said. The girl's not cooperating, so we had to lay down the law."

Sitting across from each other in the living room, Judd and Evette exchanged incredulous looks and Judd sputtered into the phone. "Why didn't someone call us? We've been waiting for over two hours. For all we knew, they'd been in an accident or something."

"No accident. They're fine. Just a little necessary discipline." Television gunfire punctuated his words.

Judd raised his voice over the din. "May I speak to Carla, please?" He looked at Evette, shaking his head and rolling his eyes.

"She's not here. I think she's at the home."

"Is Jolie there? Is she still awake?"

"She's in bed, but I hear her. Hang on." A commotion, and then he bellowed Jolie's name.

A few seconds later Jolie's voice came on the line. She sounded timid and groggy. "Hello?"

"Hey, sweetie. It's Dad."

"Hi, Daddy. I couldn't come see you tonight." She sounded near tears.

"I heard." Judd kept his eyes on Evette as he spoke, as if she might give him the right words. "What happened?"

"I dunno." Her voice dropped to a whisper. "Walt got mad and he wouldn't let Carla go."

Evette gave Judd a look. Surely Walt hadn't meant he was disciplining Carla? Oh, my.

"I'm sorry, honey," Judd said. "Maybe we can see you tomorrow."

"Can you come and get me now?"

Judd sighed, and Evette was afraid he was going to cry on the phone. "Not tonight, sweetie. But we'll see you soon, okay?"

"Is my sister there?"

"Yes, she's sleeping."

"Oh. I wish she was awake." Jolie's voice sounded lifeless.

"She will be next time you come. If she's not, you can wake her up. You'd better get back to bed now, okay?"

"Can I talk to Evie?"

"She's right here. We have you on speakerphone."

"Hi, sweetie," Evette said, forcing a cheer she didn't feel into her voice.

"I miss you."

Evette's throat filled and she waved for Judd to cover for her until she could speak again.

"We miss you, too, Jolie," he said. But he was almost as choked up as she was.

"I love you, Jolie. Miss you, too…" Evette managed to choke the words out before she broke down.

"Bye, Daddy."

"See you soon, sweetie."

Judd clicked the phone off, but they sat in the living room together for several minutes, not talking, a little stunned by the exchange.

"She doesn't sound good," Judd finally said. "She sounds…I don't know—blah."

Evette nodded. "I don't like this. And if we're going to always have to wonder if she'll make it for visits or not…"

Judd shook his head, a disgusted look on his face. "I should have just told Carla I'd come and get her."

"But she offered…because of the baby."

"I don't care. She should have called." His jaw worked.

"We'll see her soon, babe." Evette tried to force optimism into her words, but she could tell by Judd's glum expression that she'd failed.

Chapter Forty-One

Brittle leaves skittered across the driveway and Judd pulled up the hood of his sweatshirt against the nip in the air. Someone in their neighborhood had lit a fireplace and the scent of wood smoke teased his nostrils pleasantly.

It was almost dark. He should go in. Evette would be worrying about him, knowing that since they'd lost Jolie, he only came out here when he was in the dumps.

He pumped the basketball and put up a shot. The ball hit the backboard with a clunk and dropped through the net. He shot a couple more from an imaginary free-throw line, then tucked the ball under his arm and started for the house.

Behind him he heard a car on the street slow. He turned to see a silver sedan pulling into their driveway. Carla. He shaded his eyes and tried to see through the windows. He didn't see Jolie. A frisson of fear went through him. Why was Carla here?

Clutching the basketball under one arm, he went to greet Carla as she got out of the car. Relief washed over him when Carla opened the back door and Jolie climbed out. She ran to Judd and hugged his knees.

He dropped the basketball on the driveway and lifted her into his arms, kissing her neck and reveling in her giggles. "What are you doing here, squirt?"

He took a step toward the car. "Hi, Carla. Is everything okay?"

She stood there, watching him with Jolie in his arms, a pensive expression shadowing her features. After a minute, she went to the door Jolie had just exited and drew something out. When she closed the door, Judd saw that it was Jolie's little lime-green suitcase.

Carla bowed her head and set the bag on the pavement beside her. When she looked up again, her eyes were moist. "Jolie, you go on in and see the baby now."

Judd's heart sped up. What did that little suitcase mean? He wanted to pick it up and carry it into the house before Carla could change her mind, but something made him refrain.

He set Jolie down and whispered in her ear, "We'll be in in a minute. You go see Kirstie." Oh, how he wished he could go with her to see the look on Evette's face when the doorbell rang and Jolie was standing on the other side.

When she was out of earshot, Carla folded her arms over her breast and frowned. "I can't do it."

Judd waited for her to explain, afraid to take a breath.

Carla ran a hand over her close-shorn hair. "I can't be a mama to her and my own daughter both." Her voice was throaty.

Judd dared to voice his deepest hope. "Are you letting her stay?"

"I have no choice, Judd. I thought I could do it, but

it's not right for her to be at the nursing home every night. That's no way to grow up. I...I remember Tabrina with her daddy and—I want Jolie to have that, too. Walt...he can't be that for her. It's just not in him." Her voice broke and she put her face in her hands.

Judd closed the distance between them and put his arms around Carla. He half expected her to shrug him off, but she let him hold her while she wept. "You've done everything you could do for Tabrina, Carla. I know she knows that...as far as a six-year-old is capable of knowing. You've been a good mother." For the recent past, it was true.

Carla pushed away from him, swabbed her damp cheeks with the sleeve of her jacket. "I know in my heart that Tabrina would want Jolie to be here. She's happy with you. Evette's been good to her."

Judd nodded. "Evette loves her." That, too, was true.

"I see she does."

"We'll do everything we can to make sure Jolie gets to see you—and Tabrina."

"I know you will. Thank you, Judd."

He put a hand at the small of Carla's back. "Come on in. Have you had dinner?"

She waved him off and started for the car. "I'll grab something on the way home."

"Nonsense. Come in, Carla." Surely she didn't intend to just drive away. Had she even told Jolie that she was staying? "Evette put leftovers in the fridge a few minutes ago. Some sort of Mexican dish. It's probably still warm. And it was good."

She took another step toward the car, her shoulders shaking. His heart went out to her.

"Carla, don't go without saying goodbye. We...we

can talk about this. Figure out the arrangements. Help Jolie understand what's happening." When she didn't respond, he risked asking, "Does she know…that you're leaving her with us?"

"I told her she was…" Carla gazed into the now-dark street. "I told her she was staying overnight. You should have heard her whoop. She's happy here. She never was happy with me."

"She loves you, Carla. She just—she's lost a lot for a six-year-old."

Carla reached for the car door, but her hand dropped and she turned and looked him up and down, then past him to the house where lights glowed warmly in every window. She offered a wavering smile. "She's found a lot, too."

He watched until her car disappeared into the night. Then he lifted up the little suitcase and walked up the driveway.

"There. All done. See if that works."

Evette smiled at the obvious pride in Judd's eyes as he stood back and eyed the youth bed he'd just finished putting together—an all-morning project.

Jolie dived onto the bed and rolled around on the naked mattress. "I like it! Can we put my new sheets on now, Evie?"

"Not till the dryer buzzes."

Across the room, Kirstie lay on her tummy in the crib, rooting around on the mattress, her tiny eyebrows just bobbing above the crib bumpers as she worked to raise her head. Even tiny as she was, she seemed to want in on this family event.

Evette sighed. The nursery would be crowded with Jolie's bed and all the baby equipment, but the baby didn't seem to notice, and Jolie was ecstatic to be sharing a room with her sister. More importantly, the guest room had been restored to its pre-Jolie status, and stood ready to welcome Carla whenever they could talk her into coming for a visit.

If anyone had told her months ago that she'd actually be excited about this arrangement, Evette would have told them they were crazy. She cringed to think how selfish she'd been then. How consumed she'd been with things that didn't matter one iota.

Oh, how she wished sometimes that she could go back and walk through this incredible journey with her newfound maturity, her grown-up faith. She had so many regrets about the way she'd responded to the challenge God had placed before them that long-ago February day.

And yet, she'd "grown up" just enough to know that she still had growing to do. She was imperfect—they all were—and God had known from the beginning that it would be so. And in His infinite wisdom, He'd provided a way to redeem it all. To redeem *them* all.

Romans 8:28 had become her favorite Scripture in the Bible. "And we know that all things work together for good to those who love God and are called according to his purposes." Time and time again, she'd seen Him take the mistakes and trials and sin in their lives, and not merely forgive, but turn it all into something beautiful—something only He could have made beautiful.

It was more than she could fathom, and when she thought about it, she could only sink to her knees and be grateful *she* wasn't the one running the universe.

Evette's camera flashed again, then again. Judd laughed, and adjusted his two girls on his knee, his heart swelling at her pride in the girls. "Good grief, Evie, you're going to blind us all!"

Some days life seemed terribly precarious and uncertain. This was one of them. But for today, they'd determined to put aside their fears about the future and to simply celebrate God's gift of this little girl.

"Uh-oh!" Jolie pointed at the baby. "She spitted up!"

"Oh, hand me that burp rag, would you, sweetie?"

Jolie ran for the rag and helped Judd wipe up the mess. Kirstie started to fuss and before long her fussing turned to wails.

Jolie laughed and covered her ears with her hands.

Evette put the baby over her shoulder. "I think she's hungry."

"Again?" Judd shook his head. "Do all babies eat every two hours?"

"What are you talking about? *You* eat every two hours," she teased.

"Do you need us for anything?"

"No, I think I'm going to take the baby and lie down for a while."

"Okay if Jolie and I go shoot some hoops?"

"Break a leg. In fact—" Evette hitched the baby up on her shoulder and grabbed a clean burp rag "—on second thought, we'll come with you. We could use some fresh air."

He leaned in for the kiss she offered.

"Come on, squirt. Let's go work on your shot."

"I don't have a shot."

"Not yet. But you will."

Evette laughed and stole another kiss from him as he held the door for her. A crisp autumn breeze sent maple leaves parachuting from the trees.

Judd snagged a basketball from a bushel basket by the door and tossed it at Jolie. "First one to make three baskets in a row is the winner."

She caught it easily. "No fair, Dad! You're tall."

"How about when it's your turn—" he lofted Jolie over his shoulder like a sack of flour "—I give you a lift."

"Yeah!" She squealed with glee and sank her first shot.

Things were working out better than he could have ever orchestrated himself.

Evette had cheerfully taken on the task of liaison between Carla, Tabrina and Jolie. He marveled at her ability to multitask. And she told him again and again that she was just grateful she was free—that she didn't have to take a job outside of their home—so she could make it all work.

"Watch this, Evie..." From his shoulders Jolie dunked a shot.

From the front steps Evette clapped and cheered, then took Kirstie's hands and helped the baby clap.

"She spitted up again, Evie!" Jolie hollered across the driveway.

"Oops! Thanks, sweetie. I'm on it."

Jolie had proved to be such a big help with the baby that, with Evette's blessing, Judd had decided to coach for another year. "You're such a good influence on the players, Judd," she said. "They look up to you—and for good reason." His chest had puffed out a little at that.

She laughed at him then. "Well, it doesn't take a rocket surgeon to see that you'd shrivel up and die without your basketball fix. Just remember," she said, turning serious. "It's only for a season. When the girls get older, we'll probably have to regroup. I don't want to be a basketball widow."

"I know, I know. Only for a season. Got it."

And wasn't everything in life only for a season? But he was going to enjoy this season of their lives. Every single minute of it.

He and Jolie took turns tossing the basketball at the hoop, and Judd remembered the times his own dad had shot hoops with him.

He'd called his parents from the hospital to tell them about the baby. They offered warm congratulations, but they hadn't asked about Jolie and he hadn't offered. Mom had sent a flowery baby card with a generous check inside. Judd would have paid twice the amount of that check just to have his parents hop on an airplane and come to meet his daughters—their beautiful granddaughters.

He prayed—with confidence—that someday Mom and Dad would come around.

He looked across the driveway where Evette was giggling at something Jolie had said.

After all, he'd seen miracles happen before.

Epilogue

One year later…

"Evie!"

Evette heard Jolie's cry from the family room and dropped the load of laundry she'd just taken from the dryer. Heart thudding, she raced through the kitchen and into the family room. "What's wrong?"

"Look! She's walkin'!"

Kirstie stood in the middle of the room, her chubby legs wide apart, grinning from ear to ear. Jolie sat on her haunches in front of the baby, with her hands spread out. "Come on, Kirstie baby! Show Mama how you can walk."

Jolie beamed up at Evette. "I taught her to walk, Evie!"

"Oh, my goodness! You sure did. Look at you, Kirstie!" Evette clapped her hands with glee, holding her breath as the baby looked up at her, then back at the floor. The one-year-old seemed to realize at that moment that she wasn't hanging on to anything, and she plopped down on the carpet.

Evette went to kneel beside Jolie. "Get her to do it again. How'd you do that?"

Jolie crawled over to where Kirstie sat and lifted her to a standing position. "Walk to Mama. You can do it. Show Mama how you can walk. Come on, Kirstie."

Evette held out her hands and Kirstie tottered toward her, falling forward into Evette's arms.

"Wait till we show Dad, huh, Evie?"

"Oh! He'll be so surprised!"

They giggled together at the prospect. But Evette kept a secret from all of them. After they "performed" for Judd tonight, she would present him with two little packages—gifts he'd first given to her once upon a time.

Oh, if she could have seen this day played out before her a year ago, how much pain they could have been spared. If only she'd trusted God to work things out...

But she wasn't going to dwell on her mistakes today. This was a day to celebrate—a baby's first steps, a precious big sister...and two babies on the way! She bit her lip, a little worried how Judd might take the news that she was expecting twins.

That day in the parking lot when he'd presented her with two pairs of booties seemed far away now. But he would remember. And his smile would light up the room.

She captured her two girls—one in each arm—and hugged them tight. "Let's go get our jackets on. Your mama is going to wonder where we are."

"Can I show her the picture I colored?"

"Sure you can." Tabrina would smile her crooked smile and wag her head in her awkward way. And Evette would pray that on some level she would know it was her daughter who'd presented her with this gift. And that she was happy.

Jolie started jumping up and down. "Can I show Mama how Kirstie can walk? Can I, Evie?"

"Of course. But you can't show her anything until you get your jacket on. Now scoot."

They were a family now. She and Judd and the girls—with an extended family that was nothing like they had planned. Certainly not the perfect storybook portrait Evette had once envisioned.

She would never be Jolie's mother, but God had put them all together, a family glued together with love as only He could.

"I'm a good big sister, huh, Evie?"

"Yes, you are, sweetie."

Evette pulled her in for a hug. The way she said "Evie" it almost sounded like "Mom."

* * * * *

Dear Reader,

As always, I come to the close of writing a book with a deep appreciation for the many people who make it possible for this story to come to life. It's always a little scary to start making a list, since literally hundreds of people helped in the research and writing of this book, and touched my life in ways that shaped this story into the finished whole.

These are the people who went the extra mile and gave of their time, their knowledge and from the depths of their kindness. Thank you from the bottom of my heart to: Tamera Alexander, Beverly Bishop, Colleen Coble, Galen and Debbie Dreier, Till Fell, Sharon Foster, Rene Gutteridge, Mel and Cheryl Hodde, Tobi and Ryan Layton, Judy Miller, Nancy Moser, Terry Stucky, Max and Winnie Teeter, Courtney Walsh and Steph Whitson.

My agent, Steve Laube, deserves so much credit and appreciation, as do my editors at Steeple Hill—Krista Stroever, Tina Colombo and Joan Marlow Golan.

Finally, thank you to my family—my greatest blessing from God—for exploring with me this question of racial social prejudice. Writing this novel was a lesson in humility and caused me to search deep inside for the places where my own prejudice and unkindness sometimes rear their ugly heads. I pray the insight I gained and portrayed through my characters might be a small drop of healing water in the river that flows toward unity in this country and around the world.

Deborah Raney
www.deborahraney.com

QUESTIONS FOR READERS

1. How do you think you would react if your spouse got the news that he/she had a child you didn't know about? Would you be able to be supportive as your spouse dealt with the news? How would things change if you learned the child was of mixed race?

2. How do you feel about Tabrina keeping Jolie a secret from Judd? What do you think her reasons might have been?

3. In light of Tabrina's decision to keep Jolie's existence a secret, and her subsequent incapacitation, what do think Judd's responsibility should have been—financially, relationally and spiritually—toward Tabrina and Jolie?

4. Do you see yourself as a fair and nonjudgmental person? Have you ever been surprised when feelings of prejudice rose up inside you? How did those emotions affect you? How did you handle those feelings?

5. Discuss the different ways Judd, Evette and Carla handled the situation with Tabrina and Jolie. With whom could you most identify?

6. From hair care to skin care to dialect, Evette faced many challenges in trying to care for Jolie. Thinking into the future of these characters, what other issues

stemming from racial differences might Judd and Evette face as Jolie grows up?

7. Jolie referred to Judd as "Dad" right away, but because she already had a mother in Tabrina, it didn't seem right for Jolie to call Evette "Mom." What are some solutions the McGlins might have come up with to address this issue? What did they do instead?

8. How do you feel about the way Judd handled the issues with the boys on the basketball team he coached? Do you think the boys' reactions and responses were realistic? How would you have responded to their prejudiced comments and attitudes?

9. Evette struggled with her parents' attitude toward Jolie, realizing that many of her own views and perceptions had been formed at an early age by listening to and watching her parents. Have you "absorbed" prejudices from people who were influential in your childhood? How aware of those mind-sets have you been as an adult? Were you raised to be compassionate and nonjudgmental, or have you had to fight against negative and prejudiced attitudes?

10. Prejudice exists on both sides of a fence that divides any two groups. Talk about the prejudice against Jolie, and compare it to the prejudice Judd and Evette experienced personally when people realized that Jolie was a part of their family.

11. Read the following Scripture passages and talk about how they speak to the issue of racial unity: *Galatians* 3:26-28; *Philippians* 2:1-18; *1 Peter* 4:8-9.

12. The Scripture in the epigraph of this book is *Jeremiah* 17:9. How can a person's heart be deceitful and beyond cure? What is the answer to a deceitful heart? If the opposite of deceit is truth, where is truth to be found? Read *Jeremiah,* 17:5-10 and discuss the themes of *Above All Things* in light of this passage.

HEARTWARMING INSPIRATIONAL ROMANCE

Experience stories
centered on love and faith
with a variety of romances
just for you,
with 10 books every month!

Love Inspired®:
Enjoy four contemporary,
heartwarming romances every month.

Love Inspired® Historical:
Travel to a different time with two powerful
and engaging stories of romance, adventure
and faith every month.

Love Inspired® Suspense:
Enjoy four contemporary tales of intrigue
and romance every month.

**Steeple
Hill®**

*Available every month wherever books are
sold, including most bookstores, supermarkets,
drugstores and discount stores.*

LIINCREASE

REQUEST YOUR FREE BOOKS!

2 FREE INSPIRATIONAL NOVELS
PLUS 2
FREE
MYSTERY GIFTS

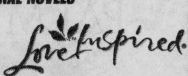

YES! Please send me 2 FREE Love Inspired® novels and my 2 FREE mystery gifts (gifts are worth about $10). After receiving them, if I don't wish to receive any more books, I can return the shipping statement marked "cancel". If I don't cancel, I will receive 4 brand-new novels every month and be billed just $4.24 per book in the U.S. or $4.74 per book in Canada. That's a savings of over 20% off the cover price. It's quite a bargain! Shipping and handling is just 50¢ per book.* I understand that accepting the 2 free books and gifts places me under no obligation to buy anything. I can always return a shipment and cancel at any time. Even if I never buy another book, the two free books and gifts are mine to keep forever.

113 IDN EYK2 313 IDN EYLE

Name _____ (PLEASE PRINT)

Address _____ Apt. #

City _____ State/Prov. _____ Zip/Postal Code

Signature (if under 18, a parent or guardian must sign)

Mail to Steeple Hill Reader Service:
IN U.S.A.: P.O. Box 1867, Buffalo, NY 14240-1867
IN CANADA: P.O. Box 609, Fort Erie, Ontario L2A 5X3

Not valid to current subscribers of Love Inspired books.

Want to try two free books from another series?
Call 1-800-873-8635 or visit www.morefreebooks.com

LIREG09